continued . . .

"Like a great fairytale, McKinlay transports readers into the world of cupcakes and all things sweet and frosted, minus the calories. Although . . . there are some pretty yummy recipes at the end." —AnnArbor.com

Buttercream Bump Off

"A charmingly entertaining story paired with a luscious assortment of cupcake recipes that, when combined, made for a deliciously thrilling mystery." —*Fresh Fiction*

"Another tasty entry, complete with cupcake recipes, into what is sure to grow into a perennial favorite series."
—*The Mystery Reader*

Sprinkle with Murder

"A tender cozy full of warm and likable characters and a refreshingly sympathetic murder victim. Readers will look forward to more of McKinlay's tasty concoctions."
—*Publishers Weekly* (starred review)

"McKinlay's debut mystery flows as smoothly as Melanie Cooper's buttercream frosting. Her characters are delicious, and the dash of romance is just the icing on the cake."
—Sheila Connolly, *New York Times* bestselling author of *Scandal in Skibbereen*

"Jenn McKinlay delivers all the ingredients for a winning read. Frost me another!"
—Cleo Coyle, *New York Times* bestselling author of the Coffeehouse Mysteries

"A delicious new series featuring a spirited heroine, luscious cupcakes, and a clever murder. Jenn McKinlay has baked a sweet read."

—Krista Davis, *New York Times* bestselling author of the Domestic Diva Mysteries

Praise for the Library Lover's Mysteries

Book, Line, and Sinker

"Entertaining . . . An outstanding cozy mystery . . . featuring engaging characters and an intriguing story."

—*Lesa's Book Critiques*

"A great read . . . in this delightfully charming series."

—*Dru's Book Musings*

Due or Die

"[A] terrific addition to an intelligent, fun, and lively series."

—Miranda James, *New York Times* bestselling author of the Cat in the Stacks Mysteries

"What a great read! . . . McKinlay has been a librarian, and her snappy story line, fun characters, and young library director with backbone make for a winning formula."

—*Library Journal*

Books Can Be Deceiving

"A sparkling setting, lovely characters, books, knitting, and chowder! What more could any reader ask?"

—Lorna Barrett, *New York Times* bestselling author of the Booktown Mysteries

"With a remote coastal setting as memorable as Manderley and a kindhearted, loyal librarian as the novel's heroine, *Books Can Be Deceiving* is sure to charm cozy readers everywhere."

> —Ellery Adams, *New York Times* bestselling author of
> the Books by the Bay Mysteries

"Fast-paced and fun, *Books Can Be Deceiving* is the first in Jenn McKinlay's appealing new mystery series featuring an endearing protagonist, delightful characters, a lovely New England setting, and a fascinating murder."

> —Kate Carlisle, *New York Times* bestselling author of
> the Bibliophile Mysteries

Praise for the Hat Shop Mysteries
Cloche and Dagger

"A delicious romp through my favorite part of London with a delightful new heroine."

> —Deborah Crombie, *New York Times* bestselling author

"Brimming with McKinlay's trademark wit and snappy one-liners, Anglophiles will love this thoroughly entertaining new murder mystery series. A hat trick of love, laughter, and suspense, and another feather in [Jenn McKinlay's] cap."

> —Hannah Dennison, author of the Vicky Hill
> Exclusive! Mysteries

"Fancy hats and British aristocrats make this my sort of delicious cozy read."

> —Rhys Bowen, *USA Today* bestselling author of
> the Royal Spyness Mysteries

Berkley Prime Crime titles by Jenn McKinlay

Cupcake Bakery Mysteries

SPRINKLE WITH MURDER
BUTTERCREAM BUMP OFF
DEATH BY THE DOZEN
RED VELVET REVENGE
GOING, GOING, GANACHE
SUGAR AND ICED

Library Lover's Mysteries

BOOKS CAN BE DECEIVING
DUE OR DIE
BOOK, LINE, AND SINKER
READ IT AND WEEP

Hat Shop Mysteries

CLOCHE AND DAGGER

Sugar and Iced

Jenn McKinlay

BERKLEY PRIME CRIME, NEW YORK

THE BERKLEY PUBLISHING GROUP
Published by the Penguin Group
Penguin Group (USA) LLC
375 Hudson Street, New York, New York 10014

USA • Canada • UK • Ireland • Australia • New Zealand • India • South Africa • China

penguin.com

A Penguin Random House Company

SUGAR AND ICED

A Berkley Prime Crime Book / published by arrangement with the author

Berkley Prime Crime Books are published by The Berkley Publishing Group.
BERKLEY® PRIME CRIME and the PRIME CRIME logo are registered trademarks of
Penguin Group (USA) LLC.

For information, address: The Berkley Publishing Group,
a division of Penguin Group (USA) LLC,
375 Hudson Street, New York, New York 10014.

ISBN: 978-0-425-25892-7

PUBLISHING HISTORY
Berkley Prime Crime mass-market edition / April 2014

PRINTED IN THE UNITED STATES OF AMERICA

10 9 8 7 6 5 4 3 2

Cover illustration by Jeff Fitz-Maurice.
Cover design by Lesley Worrell.
Interior text design by Laura K. Corless.

For my sister-in-law, Natalie Fontes. You are one of the most remarkable women I have ever known and have helped me to become a better mother, a better sister, and a better person by generously sharing your wisdom, your heart, and your creativity with me. I am so very glad my brother fell in love with you and had the smarts to make you his wife. Sister of my heart—I love you!

Acknowledgments

As always, I'd like to thank my terrific team, Kate Seaver, Katherine Pelz, and Jessica Faust. I am so very lucky to have you all keeping me on target. Special appreciation and hugs to my dudes, Chris, Beckett, and Wyatt: you three rock my world! Lastly, I want to give a special shout-out to my very talented author friend Coo Sweet, who shared with me the term "facially gifted," thus inspiring this book. You are amazing, girlfriend!

One

"We need to have a staff meeting," Angie DeLaura said. "Stat."

She was standing in front of the bakery's large picture window, which looked onto the street. Then she began making retching noises.

Melanie Cooper glanced up from the glass display counter that she was loading with the specialty item of the day at Fairy Tale Cupcakes: Salted Caramel Cupcakes. The moist caramel cake frosted with salted dulce de leche icing and drizzled with caramel had become a favorite among the Old Town Scottsdale tourists and regulars alike.

"Why?" Melanie asked. "What's going on?"

"Marty and Olivia," Angie said. She tossed her long brunet braid over her shoulder as she turned to face Mel. Her curled lip and wrinkled nose made it clear what she thought about the new couple.

"Oh," Mel said. "Give it time."

"Time?" Angie cried. "They've had months. I'm telling you we need to have an intervention."

"I thought you wanted a staff meeting," Mel said.

"Yes, a staff meeting, which are code words for an 'intervention,'" Angie said, making quotation marks in the air with her fingers.

Mel put the last cupcake in the display case and straightened up. She kept her blond hair short in the back but long on top, so she had to blow her bangs out of her eyes to meet Angie's gaze across the bakery.

"I'm pretty sure employers are not allowed to tell employees who to date," she said.

"But she's the competition!" Angie argued. "He could be giving her your recipes."

"He's not," Mel said.

"How do you know?" Angie insisted. "Maybe she's using sex to coerce them out of him."

"Ew," Mel said. "Thanks for that visual. Now how am I supposed to look Marty in the face?"

"I'm telling you, this is not good," Angie said. She jerked a thumb at the window.

Mel came from behind the counter and moved to stand beside Angie. She glanced out and saw Marty leaning on the open driver's window of Olivia's bright pink bakery truck with the word *Confections*, the name of her bakery, written on the side.

Marty was a scrawny, bald, old guy, which was a perfect counterpoint to Olivia's sturdier build. They had a Jack Sprat and Wife sort of thing going that Mel had to admit seemed to suit them.

While she watched, Olivia said something and then

Marty said something back. They glared at each other. Olivia said something else that appeared to make Marty even madder. Then he kissed her.

"I've never seen two people who enjoyed annoying each other more," Angie said. "This cannot be good for his heart. I'm telling you, we need an intervention."

Mel glanced back at Angie. "You're just sore because his love life is running more smoothly than ours are."

"No, I'm not," Angie argued. "Okay, maybe I am, but still . . . Olivia Puckett? Bleck!"

The front door to the bakery banged open and in strode Marty. He took one look at Mel and Angie standing in the window and frowned at them. Mel felt her face heat up as she realized he knew they'd been watching him.

"Sorry," she said.

"Sorry?" Angie looked at her as if she'd lost her nut. "We're not the ones who should be sorry. He should be sorry."

"Me?" Marty asked. He clapped a hand onto his bald head. "You two Nosey Parkers are watching me through the window and I should be sorry?"

"Yes!" Angie said. She marched across the room and jabbed him in the chest with her pointer finger. "You're fraternizing with the enemy!"

The door to the kitchen swung open and in walked Tate Harper, formerly the money behind the bakery but now just an employee.

"*Harry Potter and the Goblet of Fire*," he said.

They all turned to look at him.

"What?" he asked. "Wasn't that a movie quote? You know, when Ron is jealous because Hermione goes to the ball with what's his name."

3

"Viktor Krum and we're not playing that game right now," Mel said. Having grown up together watching movies and eating junk food, Mel, Tate, and Angie had a fondness for trying to trip one another up with movie quotes. "Angie was actually referring to Marty dating Olivia."

"We're not dating," Marty said. He rubbed his chest where Angie had poked him and gave her a reproachful look. "We're friends . . . no, that's not it. We're lovers . . . no, that's not it. We're enemies . . . no, that's not it, either. Oh, hell, I don't know what we are, but either way, it's none of your damn business."

With that, he strode past Angie, went around the counter, and pushed through the swinging door into the kitchen.

"He's right," Mel said. "Like it or not—"

"I don't," Angie interrupted.

Mel gave Tate a bug-eyed look. Since Tate and Angie were sort of dating—although not really because Tate had some sort of manly macho thing going on about making it on his own to prove his worth to Angie—Mel figured he'd have more luck trying to get her to see reason.

Tate gave Mel a small nod to let her know that her message was received. He ran a hand through his wavy brown hair and said, "Angie, it's Marty's life—"

"Exactly," Angie said, interrupting again. "And it's getting shorter with every minute he spends with her. He's too old to be under that sort of constant stress."

"Listen," Mel said. "At the first sign that his health is deteriorating, we'll have a staff meeting."

Tate gave her a questioning glance.

"Code words for an intervention," she explained.

"Ah," he said. "I think that is the best plan."

Glancing between them, Angie obviously realized that she was outnumbered. She did not look happy about it.

"Fine, but when he strokes out because of her, it's on your heads."

Tate and Mel exchanged a glance and they both shrugged. Mel suspected that if anything, Olivia was giving Marty a reason to get up every morning.

It had been a year since Marty had arrived at Fairy Tale Cupcakes, wearing a ratty old cardigan and a bad toupee and dishing out a surly attitude to match. A lonely widower, Marty Zelaznik had plopped himself down into one of their booths and had nearly eaten his way to a sugar coma in order to win a contest they were having for a free night out on the town for two.

Like a wrinkled-up fungus, Marty had grown on Mel and she had hired him to man the counter. Now she couldn't imagine the bakery without him.

"Can we talk business now?" Tate asked. "I have a new idea."

Mel stifled a groan. She'd known Tate even longer than she'd known Angie. They'd been best buddies since junior high school, when he'd make her laugh by doing what had to be the worst Groucho Marx impression ever, and in return she had shared with him her Hubba Bubba bubblegum from the secret stash in her locker.

There was nothing she wouldn't do for him. Since he had left his multimillion dollar investment business behind and come to work at the bakery, however, she had begun to think there could be too much of a good thing. Lately, she had been suffering from too much Tate.

The bakery had been Mel's dream. After an unfulfilling

career in business, she'd gone to cooking school and decided to open her own bakery. Angie had left teaching to join her, while Tate had been kind enough to bankroll the operation. Without him, Mel knew there would never have been a Fairy Tale Cupcakes bakery.

Since joining them, Tate had spent his days not merely baking and frosting and schmoozing customers, oh no. He had decided to take the bakery to the next level and hit Mel daily with one scheme after another to make the bakery not just the successful small business that it was but to turn it, oh horror, corporate.

"So, I'm thinking we need to get on this whole 'buy local' train," Tate said.

"I'm listening," Mel said. Which, of course, meant that she wasn't.

"Okay, how about we start carrying our cupcakes in local grocery stores?"

"Don't most of them have bakeries?" Angie asked. "Why would they want the competition in there?"

"Because we have the local-grown, organic thing going for us."

"We do?" Mel asked.

"We could," Tate said. "If we change a few of our suppliers. What do you think?"

Mel felt a heavy sigh welling up inside of her. She clamped it down. She didn't want to burst Tate's bubble, but what he wanted would require expansion and she just wasn't ready for that yet.

Mercifully, the front door opened, keeping her from having to answer. Saved by the customer. Mel turned toward the door with a welcoming smile.

When she saw who entered, her smile faded. In strode her

mother, Joyce, who hadn't spoken to her in three months, and her mother's bff, Ginny Lobo. Ginny was wearing a fur-lined leather coat over skinny jeans, and matching fur-lined leather boots. She looked like she was dressed for January in Minnesota, not central Arizona. Mel shook her head and looked at her mother, who was dressed more appropriately in jeans and a light turtleneck sweater.

"Hi, Ginny," Mel said. "Hi, Mom."

Joyce Cooper, with the same fair hair and hazel eyes as her daughter, turned to her friend and said, "Tell Melanie that I am still not speaking to her."

"Why?" Ginny asked. She paused to take a sip out of her pink water bottle. "I'm sure she heard you."

Mel rolled her eyes. Tate and Angie gave her commiserating looks and then the traitors both went over and gave her mother hugs. Backstabbers.

"Hi, Joyce," Angie said.

"You're looking lovely, Joyce," Tate said.

"Ahem," Ginny cleared her throat.

"You, too, Ginny," he said. "You really defy age."

Ginny gave him a beaming smile and Mel wondered if it was his compliment or the vodka in her water bottle that made her so happy. She suspected a combination of the two.

"Ginny, tell my mother that she has to speak to me eventually," Mel said.

Ginny glanced between them. Then she heaved a put-upon sigh. "She hasn't forgiven you for being engaged to 'dear Joe' and not telling her until after you broke it off, which is another thing she is not forgiving you for."

"I know," Mel said. "But it's been months. Really, Mom, come on."

Joyce glanced pointedly at her watch and then turned

away from Mel with a *humph* that somehow packed a wallop of guilt in it. Guilt was Joyce's weapon of choice and she had used it to mold and shape Mel and her brother, Charlie, into the responsible adults that they were. Of course, Mel was pretty sure it also contributed to her emotional eating habits. Was it too early to taste test a Salted Caramel Cupcake?

She shook her head. No. She was not going to feel guilty about keeping her personal life personal. That's why it was called a *personal life*. Besides, things were complicated with Joe. They may have called off the engagement, but it didn't mean she didn't love him. She just wasn't sure she could handle the "until death us do part" portion of the whole marriage thing. And then, complicating it even more, there was this certain homicide detective who kept fluttering around. Mel sighed. She wanted a vacation. In Tahiti. Now.

"She's not ready to forgive you yet," Ginny said.

Mel blew out a sigh. "Then why are you here?"

"I have a proposition for you," Ginny said.

Mel looked at her mother's friend. The alarm bells in her head were ringing so loudly that it was hard for Mel to hear what Ginny said next, but she was pretty sure she heard the words "beauty pageant" and "cupcakes."

"I'm sorry," Mel said. "Could you repeat that?"

"This year is the seventy-fifth annual Sweet Tiara Beauty Pageant," Ginny said. "I was Sweet Tiara Nineteen—well, it doesn't really matter. As a former Miss Sweet Tiara, I promised to help with the event. So, Joyce and I were talking about you, it's always about you," Ginny paused to give Mel a bored look. "But then, I thought that since it's called 'Sweet' Tiara, we should have a portion of the competition be devoted to having our contestants design cupcakes that you bake for them."

"Brilliant!" Tate said. "Think of the exposure for the bakery."

"Oh, hell, no!" Mel stated. "Absolutely not."

Two

"Mel, you have to think big picture," Tate said.

Mel growled at him. "Stop trying to go corporate on me."

"Mel," Tate said. He was using his most patient tone of voice, which to Mel just sounded patronizing. "What are our long-term objectives for the bakery?"

"To stay open," Mel said.

"Beyond that," Tate said.

"There is no beyond that," Mel said. "We are a small but popular bakery doing a solid business. I don't want to be any more than that."

"But we could be the next big national bakery," he said. "We could be known all over the world."

Mel jammed her fingers in her ears and sang, "La la la la la. I can't hear you. La la la la la."

"Mel!" Angie called her name, but Mel couldn't hear her, so Angie reached up and unplugged one of her ears. "Mel!"

"What?" Mel asked. She noticed that everyone was staring at her, but she refused to be embarrassed. She did not want her bakery to become a corporation. It was her sanctuary, her oasis, her baby.

"I think we should do the pageant," Angie said.

"Yay!" Ginny cheered, but when she saw Mel's frown, she quickly took a sip out of her pink bottle.

"You're joking," Mel said. "How can you say that?"

The front door opened and Oz Ruiz and his friend Lupe entered the bakery. Carrying skateboards and wearing matching all-black outfits, with multiple piercings and their bangs covering the upper half of their faces, the two teens looked like the last people you would find in a cupcake bakery. And probably that would be true, except Oz had come to Mel the year before as an intern and had proven so invaluable that she had hired him on as part-time help.

"Hear me out," Angie said. "I know you don't want to go corporate, but when we first opened we took big exposure gigs like this one all the time. Just because we've got a solid following, I don't think we should get lazy."

"But baking cupcakes for a beauty pageant? They're everything we're against. They debase women by making them sex objects whose worth is based solely on their outward appearance," Mel argued.

"Not true!" Ginny argued. "Sweet Tiara offers a full scholarship to the winner. We've paid the way for several prominent businesswomen, a judge, and two doctors."

"And what happened to the rest of them?" Mel asked. She gave Ginny a pointed look. "Got their MRS degrees, did they?"

Ginny sniffed. "There is nothing wrong with being a Mrs. Maybe if you gave it a try, you wouldn't be so cranky."

Jenn McKinlay

"Hear, hear," Joyce said and Mel glowered at the two of them.

"What's this about a scholarship?" Lupe asked. She tossed the dyed green fringe out of her eyes and looked at Ginny.

"The winner of the Sweet Tiara Pageant will have all four years of her college education paid for," Ginny said. "It's a pretty good deal given that you only have to wear the crown for one year. I would have worn it longer if they'd let me, but that's just me, the sex object, talking."

Mel rolled her eyes. "Why are you interested, Lupe?"

Lupe bit her lip but said nothing, so Oz spoke up for her, "Lupe wants to be a doctor. She's been accepted at Stanford, but there's no way her family can afford the tuition and she's only been offered a partial scholarship."

"If you won, the pageant would pick up the tab for all four years," Ginny said.

Lupe's eyes went wide, at least what Mel could see of them behind the green bangs.

"What do I need to do?" she asked.

"Well, you need to fill out the forms and there is an entrance fee of a hundred dollars," Ginny said. "Then, of course, you'll have to get an interview dress, a bathing suit, and a gown. Oh, and you have to have a talent and do some public speaking."

"Oh," Lupe sighed. "I don't think I can afford the entrance fee or clothes. My dad passed away a few years ago, and my mom works as a secretary at the high school. Not great pay but she can keep an eye on my three sisters. My paycheck from my job at the bookstore has to go to the family."

Oz stared at his friend. "I'll pay your entrance fee."

"What?" Lupe shook her head. "I can't let you do that."

"You're not letting me," he grumbled. "You're going to pay me back."

"But what if I don't win?" she asked.

"You'll win," he said. "You're the smartest person I've ever met. They'd be crazy not to pick you."

"Beauty pageants aren't generally based on smarts," Mel said. She knew she sounded sour, but she couldn't help it.

"It doesn't matter," Lupe sighed. "Even if you pay the entrance fee, Oz, I can't afford the clothes and I don't think my current hairdo is going to cut it."

"I'll help with your hair," Joyce said. "And we'll figure out the clothes."

Mel whipped her head in her mother's direction. She and Ginny began circling Lupe. They pushed her green hair away from her face and scrutinized the body she was hiding under several layers of black denim.

"I think the raw material is all there," Ginny said. "I'll help, too, as much as I can. We don't want my assistance to be considered a conflict of interest."

"Oh, good grief!" Mel said. "Mom, you can't honestly be encouraging this."

Joyce cupped Lupe's face as she studied her bone structure. "I'm sorry, was someone speaking?"

Lupe glanced from Mel to her mother with wide eyes. Then she looked at Mel and said, "If you were me and the scholarship meant culinary school and opening your bakery, would you do it?"

Mel opened her mouth to argue that it was different, but she couldn't. The truth was, she'd had Tate to bankroll the bakery, which was essentially what her mother and Ginny were going to do for Lupe.

"Fine, but you'd better get straight A's when you get your full ride to Stanford," Mel said. "I will be checking on you."

Lupe grinned and Mel was momentarily stunned. The girl beneath the shaggy green-and-black fringe was a knockout.

"Does this mean we're taking the pageant as a cupcake gig?" Oz asked. "After all, I have to keep an eye on my investment."

Lupe slugged him in the shoulder with a laugh and Oz winced and rubbed his arm.

"Okay, lesson one," Joyce said as she looped an arm through Lupe's. "No punching."

"That should be lesson two," Ginny interrupted. "Lesson one should be a study in split ends."

"Christine's Salon?" Joyce asked.

"ASAP," Ginny replied.

"It's so nice to have a daughter again," Joyce said as they walked out the door with Lupe wedged between them like a hostage.

"Better her than me," Mel griped as the door swung closed behind them.

"Don't fret," Tate said. "Your mom will come around. Maybe working on the pageant together will bridge the gap between you two."

"Yeah, your mom isn't one to hold a grudge," Angie said. "This will give you a common purpose."

"Don't bet on it," Mel said. "The only thing that is going to get her to forgive me is a walk down the aisle with 'dear Joe' waiting at the end of it."

"Would that be so bad?" a voice asked from the front door.

Mel glanced up and saw the man in the doorway and a grin parted her lips. Without hesitation, she jogged across the room and threw herself into his arms.

Three

"Charlie!" Mel cried as she wrapped her brother in a hug that strangled. "What are you doing here? Why didn't you call? You just missed Mom."

Charlie lifted her up off her feet and squeezed her tight before setting her back down. "I didn't know until this morning that I was coming into town. It's just a quick business trip, but I'll probably take Mom out to dinner and crash at her place before heading back to Flagstaff tomorrow. Care to join us?"

"I think that would make it infinitely less fun," Mel said. "She's still not speaking to me."

"Really?" he asked. "But it's been months."

"Really," Angie confirmed as she gave Charlie a hug.

Tate stepped forward and shook Charlie's hand and confirmed, "It's bad."

"Really bad," Oz agreed as he stepped forward and shook Charlie's hand, too.

"Maybe you should just marry the guy," Charlie said to Mel. He pushed his glasses up on his nose and Mel could see their late father, Charlie Senior, who had gone on to the eternally open bar ten years before, in the gesture. It made her heart hurt.

An awkward silence filled the room.

"Or not," Charlie added.

"Can you guys run the show for a bit?" Mel asked Tate, Oz, and Angie. "I want to visit with Charlie for a while."

"Of course."

"Absolutely."

"On it."

Mel gestured for Charlie to follow her into the kitchen. There they ran into Marty, who was sitting at the big steel table in the center of the room fortifying himself with one of the Salted Caramels.

"What? A man can't even eat a cupcake without people spying on him?"

"I am not spying on you, Marty," Mel protested.

"Oh, please, I know you and Angie want me to break up with Olivia, but I'm not going to, so you can just save all your hot air for arguing with Tate about the business. Hi, Charlie."

"Hi, Marty," Charlie answered as Marty crammed the last bite of his cupcake into his mouth and pushed through the door back into the bakery.

"Funny, I never think of a bakery as being a hotbed of drama until I come and visit you," Charlie said.

"We're special like that," Mel said. She loaded up a tray

with a variety of cupcakes and led the way out the back door and up the stairs to her apartment.

When she pushed the door open, Captain Jack, her adopted white cat with a black patch of fur over his right eye, launched himself at Charlie. Thankfully, Charlie had been by enough that he knew to brace himself for the incoming fur ball and he bent down and caught the cat around the middle, hoisting him up into his arms.

"Hey, Jackster," Charlie said. "How you doing?"

"Mad at me," Mel said. "Like Mom."

"Misses Joe, does he?" As if in answer to Charlie's question, Jack went limp and hung over Charlie's arm, as if the feline were dying of a broken heart.

"Oh, quit it, you big faker," Mel said. She put the tray down on her coffee table and reached over to scratch Captain Jack's chin. "You just saw him the other day. It's not like Joe is out of your life."

"But he doesn't spend the night anymore, does he?" Charlie asked.

Mel and Charlie were super close, but she wasn't sure she wanted to have a candid convo about her love life with her brother. Besides, it was way more complicated than she could explain at this juncture.

"I'm not having this talk," she said.

"Oh, come on," he said. "Nancy will kill me if I don't come home with details. Us married-with-children types are living vicariously through you now. You have to give me something."

"Watch cable television," Mel said. "It'll be more entertaining, I'm sure."

"What about the detective?" Charlie asked. "Is he still in the picture?"

Mel felt her face get warm and she cursed her fair skin.

"Oh, he is, is he?" Charlie asked. His eyebrows shot up behind his glasses. "How does Joe feel about that?"

"Why don't you ask him?" Mel asked.

"You're not going to play, are you?" He sighed and reached for a cupcake.

"Nope," she said. "You'll have to get your thrills elsewhere."

"Listen, Sis, when you called me a few months ago and asked me to dinner, you told me that you didn't know what you wanted. You said you were going to break the engagement with Joe and ask for more time. Now it's been months and you seem to be in a holding pattern." Charlie paused to take a bite out of his cupcake. Mel waited while he looked momentarily blissed out and then swallowed.

"Yeah, I'm in a stall, for sure," she agreed.

"Well, if you won't give me any particulars, tell me this, are you happy?" Charlie asked.

Mel picked up a Salted Caramel. She wondered if this was going to replace the chocolate with coconut as her current favorite cupcake. Then she thought if she combined them she might have the mother of all cupcakes: salted caramel icing with coconut filling and chocolate cake. Her vision went fuzzy while she tried to picture it and she had to shake her head to get her focus back.

"I'm baking some of the best cupcakes of my life," she said. "I'm inspired like never before."

"Yes, but you always do that when your love life is a mess. The question remains, are you happy?" Charlie persisted.

Mel took a bite and chewed. Everything was better with the rush of cake and frosting, at least for the moment. Then she swallowed.

"Happiness is overrated," she said.

Charlie gave her a concerned look.

"All right, fine," she said. "My personal life is in the toilet. Joe and I are, well, it's complicated. And Manny? Ugh, he's made it very clear that he's interested, and I'm tempted but I don't want to ruin what I have with Joe, but if Joe keeps insisting on marriage . . . see? It's a mess. There. Feel better now?"

"Not really, no," Charlie said. "Well, you've got nothing but time."

"Not according to Mom," Mel said. "Since she's not speaking to me, I don't have to hear it, but I know she's convinced my biological clock is ticking like a time bomb."

"If she's not speaking to you, how do you know that?" Charlie asked.

"Because every time she sees me, she glances pointedly at her watch," Mel said. "And she's not trying to tell me I'm late for dinner."

"She does not," Charlie said through a mouthful of cupcake.

"She does," Mel said. "Ask Angie she noticed it, too."

"She just wants what's best for you," Charlie said. Unfortunately, he didn't sound as if he believed it, either.

"Well, marriage is not it," Mel said. "At least, not right now."

"Why not?" Charlie asked. "You've loved Joe since you were twelve years old. Why is getting married to him a bad thing?"

"I don't want to get married," Mel said. "It requires a lot of paperwork and I think there's even a blood test involved."

"Seriously?" Charlie asked. "That's your objection? Paperwork and a blood test?"

Sugar and Iced

"I don't like needles," she said.

"Lame!" Charlie roared. "Do you even listen to yourself when you speak? Why can't you be like most girls and have the wedding of your dreams already completely planned out and all you have to do is insert the approved male?"

"Because I was always the chubette," Mel said. "Day-dreaming about weddings when the only time boys ever noticed me was to mock and deride me was never as satis-fying as eating an entire bag of potato chips."

"Your issues have issues, you know that, right?" he asked.

"I know," Mel said. She was quiet for a moment and then she sighed. "Here's the thing, what if Joe and I do get mar-ried, how long until I start packing on the pounds and he leaves me for some skinny young thing?"

"You won't and he won't and even if you did, he wouldn't," Charlie said.

"Okay, so we're happily married for fifty years," Mel said. "We have kids and grandkids and great-grandkids and then he up and dies on me."

"Most people would feel lucky to have had all that," Charlie said.

"Losing Dad was so hard," Mel said. She felt her throat get tight and her eyes were burning but she refused to cry.

"Aw, I know." Charlie held out one arm and Mel scooted under it and he hugged her close. "There isn't a day that goes by that I don't miss Dad."

"I just don't think I can go through that," Mel said. "I know it's wimpy and pathetic, but if I let myself love Joe as deeply as I want to, well, if he was taken away from me, Charlie, I'd die. I'd just die."

"So, you'd rather keep him at a distance and never know what it's like to be one with your true love?"

21

Mel pulled back and looked at him. He gave her a dark look and said, "If you ever tell anyone I said anything that sappy, I'll join ranks with Mom and never speak to you again."

Mel smiled and then teased, "I won't, but gosh, that was sweet."

The tips of Charlie's ears turned pink, which Mel knew meant he was embarrassed. He cleared his throat and frowned.

"Do you think that all of this may be because you've had an unusual preponderance of dead bodies popping up in your life over the past two years?" Charlie asked. "I mean it's just not normal."

"Oh, 'preponderance'—big word," Mel teased.

"From my word-of-the-day calendar," Charlie confirmed with a superior look. "But seriously, do you?"

"Maybe, but it's not like I go looking for them," she said.

"No, but they certainly know how to find you."

She watched as Captain Jack hooked an empty cupcake liner off of the tray and then flicked it. As it fluttered to the ground like a butterfly, he wiggled his haunches and launched. He overshot and the breeze he created made the cupcake liner skitter across the floor. He skidded to a stop and turned around, giving the paper chase.

"So what should I do about Mom?" she asked. "I've tried talking to her, but she won't listen."

"I don't know," Charlie said. "She loves dear Joe."

Mel rolled her eyes. Her mother always called Joe "dear Joe," making it very clear how she felt about having an assistant district attorney dating her daughter.

"She's sponsoring a girl in the Sweet Tiara Beauty Pageant, which her friend Ginny wants us to make cupcakes for. Do you think I should do the pageant to force us together?" Mel asked. "Maybe if she has to be around me all the time, she won't be able to stay mad."

"Mom is a lousy grudge holder," Charlie said. "Frankly, I'm amazed she's lasted this long. I say do the pageant. You'll wear her down."

"Even though it goes against everything I believe in?" Mel asked.

"It's a bunch of girls in poufy dresses competing for a sparkly crown and some scholarship money," Charlie said. "How bad can it really be?"

Four

Mel spent the afternoon and the next morning brooding about what her brother had said. Was he right? Was it silly of her to refuse to do the pageant, especially now that her mother was going to be helping Lupe?

There was no doubt this would make it pretty impossible for Joyce to keep ignoring her. Ugh, the things she did for her family.

"Mel, we have to go!" Angie called from the front of the bakery.

"I'm almost ready," Mel called back. She had just finished frosting a batch of Classic Chocolate Cupcakes with vanilla frosting. Yes, it was an old-school cupcake, but judging by her sales numbers, it was also the most popular cupcake, beating out every other exotic flavor hands down.

She hefted the tray onto her shoulder and carried it to the walk-in cooler. She was dreading today's meeting with Cici

Hastings, the Sweet Tiara Pageant coordinator. She could not imagine what she would have to say to the woman. Even though she knew this was an opportunity to mend the rift with her mother, she really struggled with the whole pageanty thing.

"Come on!" Angie barked from the door. "We've got to go or we're going to be late."

"I'm coming," Mel said. She stood in the chiller for a moment to assess the array of cupcakes. Maybe she should stay and bake more and let Angie take the meeting.

"I've seen desert tortoises that move faster than you," Angie said, appearing in the doorway to the walk-in. She reached out and grabbed Mel's hand and yanked her out of the chiller. "Now come on."

"Fine," Mel said. She took off her apron and grabbed her purse from her office.

Together, she and Angie left the kitchen through the bakery. Tate and Marty were manning the counter. Three of the bakery's regulars, Wendy Resnik, Darenna Rainsdon, and Diana Welsch, were standing in front of the counter, debating flavors.

"What's the flavor of the day?" Darenna asked. She tossed her long blond hair over her shoulder as she leaned close to the display case, pressing her lips together in concentration as if willing a cupcake to call out to her.

"The Salted Caramel," Marty said. "It's to die for."

"I'll take a dozen," Wendy said.

Darenna and Diana gave her matching raised-eyebrow looks of concern. This was particularly intimidating coming from Diana, with her rectangular-framed glasses and close-cropped hair.

"What? I'm bringing them back to the library," Wendy

said. The other two continued to stare at her and Wendy shook her auburn bob in exasperation and added, "To share with everyone."

"Uh-huh," Diana said.

Mel laughed. All three ladies worked at the Phoenix Public Library and she always looked forward to their book input.

"Hello, ladies," she said. "So, fire away, what's on your current recommended reading list?"

Angie glanced at her watch. "We are officially late. Stop stalling."

"I am not stalling," Mel protested as Angie pushed her toward the door. "Besides, it isn't like the beauty pageant needs our cupcakes *today*."

"Beauty pageant? You're doing a beauty pageant? In that case, read the Sweet Potato Queens," Darenna said, raising her voice as the door began to shut. "They'll get you in the right frame of—"

On the sidewalk, Mel frowned at Angie. "That was rude."

"So is being late for a business meeting," she said. "Now move it."

Mel drove her Mini Cooper to the upscale resort where the pageant was taking place. She parked in the small visitor's lot and she and Angie crossed the circular drive in front of the main doors to enter the lobby.

The resort was an older one, converted from the shell of a ranch house. It was all whitewashed stucco and thick wooden beams. A fire was roaring in the huge stone fireplace and the furniture was the sort of thick pine log and leather stuff you'd expect to find on a ranch in the middle of the high country.

A smartly dressed Native American woman with long black hair and pretty features greeted them.

"Welcome to the Lazy J resort," she said. "My name is Lydia. What can I do for you?"

"We're here to meet with Cici Hastings," Mel said. "About the pageant."

Lydia nodded. "I believe she is in our main ballroom. If you'll follow me?"

She came around the counter and Mel and Angie fell into step beside her. She walked in long, loping strides that were easy for Mel to match but left Angie doing double time, as she was much shorter than the other two.

They crossed through an opulent lounge that featured a cozy bar, which opened up to an expansive poolside patio, and through a set of large French doors into a cavernous ballroom. Several of the hotel staff were scurrying around the room setting up tables and chairs while a camera and sound crew rigged their equipment. At the far end of the ballroom was the stage, where several men in work attire were erecting a spectacularly glittered backdrop that featured a tiara the size of a Cadillac floating in the air.

In front of the stage, a slight woman stood with her back to them. Mel noted that her platinum hair was done up in a fancy cascade of curls. She was dressed in an aqua chemise with a black jacket that had matching aqua piping along its hem. Her shoes were black platforms that made Mel's feet hurt just to look at them.

"Mrs. Hastings," Lydia said. "I have some young women here to see you."

The woman turned to face them and Mel heard Angie gasp beside her. She was not surprised. From behind, she had expected Cici Hastings to be somewhere in her thirties or forties, but when she turned to face them, Mel saw that Cici had the well-preserved good looks of a woman who knew how to apply makeup after about eighty-odd years of living.

Instead of the thick spackle that a lot of older women used, Cici seemed to have a light hand with the foundation and her eye makeup was soft, making her pretty blue eyes sparkle. But there was no denying the wrinkles that creased the corners of her eyes and around her lips.

"Thank you, Lydia," Mrs. Hastings said and Lydia departed with a nod.

"How can I help, y'all?" Cici asked. Mel noted there was a southern flare to Cici's speech and she wondered where she came from originally.

"I'm Melanie Cooper and this is my partner, Angie DeLaura," Mel said. "We own Fairy Tale Cupcakes, the bakery."

"Oh, yes, Ginny told me about your little shop," Cici said. Mel decided that Cici wasn't trying to insult them by using the word *little*. It was just the way she talked, making everything sound cute and lovely. Mel had met her type before.

"I'm not sure how we'd work it," Mel said. "Having us bake cupcakes that the contestants come up with. We generally just provide cupcakes for venues."

Cici gave Mel a sharp look and Mel had the feeling that Cici could hear the disdain in her voice for the pageant even though she was quite certain she had buried it way down deep.

"You could do both," Cici said. "If we could have a tower of cupcakes on each day of the pageant, well, that would certainly be special, and with live television coverage, it would give your little shop quite a surge of publicity."

Mel frowned. Now she was pretty sure the *little* comment was intended as an insult. She glanced at Angie, expecting her fiery friend to jump into the fray with her hot temper, but no. Angie was staring at the huge floating tiara with something akin to wonder.

"Is that where Miss Sweet Tiara is crowned?" Angie asked.

Cici turned back to the stage. "Yes, indeed. Come and check it out."

"No, thank you, we're really pressed for time," Mel said.

"No, we're not," Angie said. "Tate and Marty have everything under control."

Cici turned and walked around the front of the stage to the side. She stepped over a pile of cables and a toolbox, leaving Mel and Angie no choice but to follow.

They stood in the center of the stage, with the catwalk that Miss Sweet Tiara would walk looming in front of them like a fashion show runway.

"Picture this room full of people with their eyes on you, and you have an idea what our contestants are facing," Cici said. "They need to comport themselves with the utmost poise, grace, and decorum."

"And a big pair of ta-tas wouldn't hurt, either," Mel whispered to Angie.

To Mel's surprise, Angie didn't laugh. Instead, she gave Mel an annoyed look and said, "Shh."

"Oh, no, you are not buying into this," Mel said. "Angie, this is ridiculous. It's a beauty pageant."

Cici strode over to a black velvet box on the table. Beside it was a deep pink satin sash. She popped the latch and pulled out a sparkling tiara. She said nothing but moved to stand behind Angie and put the tiara on her head.

She started humming some sappy tune and gave Angie a gentle push toward the catwalk. "Don't forget to wave," she sang.

To Mel's shock, Angie straightened her back and walked down the catwalk, waving at the imaginary audience. Everyone in the room paused in what they were doing and began to clap and cheer. Angie spun around at the end of the catwalk and began to stride back to the stage. She looked radiant, with a beaming smile parting her lips and a sparkle in her eyes.

"Mel, seriously, you have got to try this," Angie said.

"No."

"Come on," Angie said, jumping up and down. "For me."

Mel felt her usually dormant stubborn streak kick in. She wasn't sure why she was being so difficult about it, but she didn't like the knowing gleam in Cici's eyes and she definitely didn't want the hotel staff and stage builders watching as she sashayed down the catwalk. She'd probably trip and make a complete ass of herself.

"I don't—" she began to protest but it was too late.

Cici put the tiara on her head and gave her a much less gentle shove toward the catwalk.

"This is stupid!" she hissed at Angie as she walked by her.

But Angie wasn't listening. She had moved to stand beside Cici and the two of them were humming some ridiculous theme.

"I'm not doing this," Mel said. She could feel the fine combs of the tiara biting into her scalp. "I feel ridiculous."

One of the set builders came over with an armful of

plastic tulips and held them out to her with a bow, giving Mel no choice but to accept them or look churlish.

Getting into the spirit of things, a woman who'd been fussing with the draping on the platform came over and dropped a cloth swag around Mel's shoulders as if it were a long gown.

"This will give you the swish effect," the woman said. She gave Mel a hard nudge while Angie and Cici kept humming through their noses.

"Fine," Mel said. She began to stomp down the catwalk that divided the room, hoping to get this over with as quickly as possible.

About halfway down the platform, she noticed that some of the hotel staff people were waving at her. With a sigh she shifted her flowers and waved back. They broke into enthusiastic applause, and Mel couldn't stop the smile that parted her lips. At the end she turned around and the stage crew clapped and cheered her return. She cradled the plastic flowers in one arm while giving a dainty wave with her right hand.

Okay, Mel had to admit there was something pretty sweet about having a tiara planted on your head while you strolled down a catwalk to raucous cries and enthusiastic applause.

When she reached Cici and Angie, she grinned and said, "Okay, there's something about sparkly headgear that makes your brain turn to goo, isn't there?"

"Now you're getting it," Cici said with a wink. "I think we can talk particulars now."

"What is this?" a woman stepped out onto the stage, looking irritated. "Why isn't this stage set done yet? We are on a tight schedule, people."

Mel felt the drapery get yanked off of her shoulders and the man who had handed her the faux tulips snatched them back and hurried away.

A woman with long dark hair strode across the floor toward them. She wore a satin lavender tank top over a black pencil skirt and spiky heels. There was a sheen of sweat on her skin and she looked supremely cranky.

She fanned her face and asked, "Do they not have air conditioning in here?"

"No one else is hot," Cici said. "Just you." In a stage whisper she added, "The change will do that to a gal."

The woman with the dark hair gave her an unpleasant look and then said, "Oh, that's right, you went through it ages ago, didn't you, Cici?"

Angie gave Mel a look that said "Ouch!" and Mel raised her eyebrows.

"Mariel Mars, may I introduce Melanie Cooper and Angie DeLaura," Cici said. She turned to Mel and Angie and said, "Mariel is our head judge and a former winner of the Sweet Tiara Beauty Pageant."

"Who are you and why are you here?" Mariel asked. She looked them up and down, obviously finding their casual attire wanting.

"Cupcake bakers," Angie said. "We'll be baking what the contestants invent and we'll be providing a cupcake tower for each day's events."

"Oh." Mariel looked unimpressed. She glanced at Mel and her look turned mean. "I didn't realize that being cupcake bakers was a crown-worthy occupation. Obviously I'm in the wrong profession."

Mel felt her face get hot with mortification and she reached up and lifted the tiara off of her and handed it to Cici.

"I was just giving the girls a demonstration of the pageant winner's perspective," Cici said to Mariel with a frown. "There is certainly no need for you to be nasty."

"There is every need," Mariel said. "You know how much I have riding on this pageant, and I am not going to let you or some ridiculous cupcake bakers muck it up."

With that, she spun on her spiky heel and stormed toward the stage. She had a few choice words for the man working on the set and then she stomped away, fanning herself with one hand as she went.

"Sorry about that. She always was a bit high-strung," Cici said. "She thought she would walk into an instant career in showbiz after the pageant, but she failed as a model and a singer and an actress and she squandered her scholarship, dropping out before graduation. She was not one of our better picks."

"But she's judging now," Angie said. "She must be happy about that."

"Did that look happy to you?" Cici asked as she put the tiara back into its box. "She's trying to launch her own nail polish line, but honestly, the competition is fierce and she never really had the star power one needs to launch a brand of one's own."

"So, she's counting on the pageant to give her business a boost?" Mel asked. The irony that she was here doing the same thing was not lost on her.

"Exactly," Cici said. "In her favor, she's hired some real talent. Ji Lily, who is the beauty consultant for the pageant, is designing the nail polish. Ji is an amazingly talented young woman. She is just getting her own cosmetics company off the ground and is hoping that the pageant and working with Mariel will give her business some buzz. I worry that Mariel will be too much of a diva for her to handle."

Given that Mariel had just performed a hostile diva showcase all her own, Mel had a feeling Cici was right to be worried. She made a mental note to avoid all contact with Mariel Mars if at all possible.

Angie and Mel spent the next half hour talking about Cici's expectation of their participation in the pageant. It was a three-day event that would culminate in a splashy pageant finale. Mel tried to picture Lupe of the green bangs competing against girls who had probably been racking up pageant trophies since they were toddlers. She did not feel good about it.

When they arrived back at the bakery, Tate had the juke-box cranking AC/DC as the after-school crowd drifted in, ordered their cupcakes, and then headed back out into the sunny day while Marty swept the floor up after them.

"How did it go?" Tate asked. He glanced between them as if trying to get a read on the situation.

"It was amazing," Angie gushed. "Cici let us try on the tiara. It was totally cool."

Tate raised his eyebrows and glanced at Mel. "You wore the tiara?"

She refused to answer, which didn't stop Angie from oversharing. "And we walked the catwalk."

"You didn't!" Marty said in a feigned girly voice.

"Did, too," Angie said, and she struck a pose and began to walk across the bakery while humming the Miss America theme.

"'I haven't seen a walk like that since *Jurassic Park*,'" Marty teased.

"*Miss Congeniality*," Mel said, and she slapped Marty on the back.

Angie stuck her tongue out at them. Then she grinned and said, "I don't care what you say, Melanie Cooper, it was fun and you can't deny it."

"I will admit that I can see the appeal," Mel conceded. "But that's it."

Marty made clucking sounds and Tate grinned as if he knew what Mel wasn't saying. That it was way more fun than she had anticipated and she wasn't about to admit it.

The front door swung open and Oz came hurrying in, looking panicked.

"Is she here yet?" he asked.

Five

"Who?" Marty asked. "Miss America? Yeah, we're full up." Then he wheezed at his own joke.

Mel and Angie both gave him sour looks, which only made him laugh more, and Tate looked hard-pressed to hide his smile as well.

"No, I'm looking for Lupe," Oz said. "She texted me from the salon and said she was on her way over here. She sounded freaked out."

"How does a text sound freaked out?" Tate asked.

"It was all in caps," Oz said.

"But that could be good, right?" Angie asked.

"I suppose, if Lupe were the type to gush about stuff, but she's not," he said.

"Yeah, I really can't see her doing the girly-girl 'squeee,'" Angie said. "She's too cool for that."

Just then the door burst open and in strode Joyce and

Ginny. They were both looking newly coifed, waxed, and buffed, so Mel figured they'd taken some time at the salon for themselves as well.

"Drumroll, please," Joyce announced.

They all stood and stared until Joyce stamped her foot, and Marty and Tate began to lightly drum their fingers on the top of the glass display counter.

"Ladies and gentlemen." Joyce addressed the room. "I am pleased to present the darling—"

"The delightful—" Ginny added.

"The debutante—" Joyce said.

"Guadalupe Guzman," Joyce and Ginny said together. They held out their hands and a beautiful young woman walked through the open door of the bakery.

Mel gaped at her. Gone were the green bangs, the voluminous black T-shirts, and baggie black jeans. In their place was a head of shiny black hair that hung like silk, framing a delicate face with just a hint of makeup on it. The young woman stood uncertainly on stylish black pumps, wearing a knee-length pewter chemise with a narrow black belt.

"Lupe?" Oz asked. He came around the counter and stood staring openmouthed at his former skateboard buddy. "What happened to you?"

Lupe smiled at him and asked, "'Why? Claire did it . . . What's wrong?'"

"What?" Joyce asked. "What is she talking about? Who is Claire? We did this to her, not some Claire. Well, I suppose Christine did help."

Tate moved to stand between Angie and Mel, and he draped an arm around each of them. They all watched Oz.

"'Nothing's wrong . . . it's just so different, you know? I can see your face.'" Oz said.

Oz and Lupe stared at each other for a heartbeat and then Lupe punched him in the shoulder—hard.

"*The Breakfast Club*," she said. She pointed both index fingers at Oz and they laughed.

Tate made a sniffing noise and then pretended to wipe tears from his eyes. "I'm so proud of our second string."

Mel laughed. It was good to see Oz and Lupe teasing each other with movie quotes. It reminded her of her, Tate, and Angie when they were the same age.

"What the hell are they talking about?" Ginny asked. She took a swig off of her water bottle and stared at everyone as if they were lunatics who'd escaped their rubber rooms in the asylum.

"Movie quotes," Joyce said. "We're going to have to deprogram her before the pageant."

"Good grief, yes," Ginny agreed. "It starts in a couple of days. Should we take her to my doctor for some electroshock therapy?"

"Not necessary," Oz said. Looking alarmed, he stepped between Lupe and Ginny. "She only jokes like that with me. I promise."

Lupe gave him a surprised glance and Mel wondered if it was the first time Oz had made such a chivalrous gesture for her. She glanced between the two teens. She doubted Oz had ever seen Lupe looking so feminine. This could get really interesting.

The door to the bakery opened again, and Mel put on her "greet the customer" smile. It wobbled only for a moment when Joe DeLaura strode into the room.

Six

Mel's heart did the same ridiculous flip-flop thing it always did when Joe DeLaura entered her orbit. He was tall with dark wavy hair, warm chocolate brown eyes, a square jaw, and a lean but solid build. Mel had been crushing on him since she was twelve and he was sixteen.

It took him twenty years to notice her *that* way, but to her delight he had finally asked her out and they'd spent most of the past year and a half dating. Then he had asked her to marry him and Mel had gotten a severe case of the wiggins.

Although she loved Joe, she wasn't sure she was ready for marriage. He tried to understand but it had caused a rift between them. Of course, her mother, who adored Joe, had taken his side.

"Dear Joe," Joyce cried. She crossed the room and hugged him hard. "How are you? You look thin. Have you been eating?"

Mel rolled her eyes. No wonder she'd been such a chunk as a kid. Her mother had never met a problem that she didn't try to cure with a snack. Not that she blamed her mother for her childhood largess, but still.

Joe returned Joyce's hug. He took in the crowded room over her shoulder and raised his eyebrows at Mel.

She shrugged. Joe gave her a small nod before he released Joyce.

"Hey, big brother," Angie said as she hugged him next. "What brings you here?"

Angie looked from him to Mel as if she expected it was Mel that had lured Joe here and she was hoping for confirmation.

"Rough day at the office," he said as he shook hands with Tate, Marty, and Oz and nodded at Lupe and Ginny. "I felt the need for a Death by Chocolate."

"Oh." Mel glanced at the display. Their spot in the case was empty. "I think I have some in back."

"I don't want to put you to any trouble," he said.

"It's no trouble," she said. Sheesh. Could it be any more awkward between them?

She noted that everyone was staring at them. It was almost as excruciating as the time she fell backwards in her chair in the fourth grade and her skirt had flipped up over her head, showing the entire class her Rugrats underwear. She had feigned a head injury and quickly run to the nurse, where she cried her eyes out. Sadly, that was not an option right now.

"If you'll excuse us," she said pointedly to the room, and everyone immediately glanced away, even Joyce, although Mel saw her trying to watch them out of the corner of her eye.

Mel looked back at Joe and said, "Follow me."

"Anywhere," he whispered so that only she could hear. His gaze met hers and the look in his eyes made Mel's entire body kick into the red zone.

"Oh, my," Ginny said as they walked past her through the swinging doors into the kitchen.

Mel could hear the room break into whispers of speculation as soon as the door shut behind them. Oh, if they only knew.

"I think I have some Death by Chocolate in the walk-in cooler," Mel said. She glanced at Joe over her shoulder and noted he had a decidedly predatory gleam in his eye. She swallowed hard.

She yanked open the door and stepped inside, aware that Joe was right behind her. She reached the shelf where a tray full of the popular chocolate cupcakes sat. She never got the chance to plate one for him.

In a deft move, Joe circled her waist with his large square hands, spun her around, and, before she could get her bearings, kissed her.

Mel didn't hesitate. She wrapped her arms around his neck and kissed him back. Despite the chill of the cooler, the kiss was a scorcher, and Mel was pretty sure they were going to melt the frosting on her cupcakes.

Joe pulled back and rested his forehead against hers. He was breathing hard and Mel knew exactly how he felt.

"Marry me," he said.

"No," she said.

He leaned back and studied her in the dim light. A small smile lifted the corner of his lips. "You know, every time you say no I just get more determined."

"So I've noticed," she said, returning his smile. "You're stubborn like that."

Joe brushed the bangs off of her forehead. "I'm a DeLaura. Bullheaded tenacity is sort of the family trait."

Mel nodded. It was indeed. A few months ago she had thought that she and Joe were through. But then, Olivia Puckett of all people had cautioned Mel against making her business her whole life.

It had been a decisive moment for Mel. Though she knew she wasn't ready to marry Joe, she also knew she wasn't ready to let him go, either. They had hammered out an understanding and downshifted their relationship to just friends with limited benefits while they tried to figure out how to manage Joe's desire to get married and Mel's resistance to it.

"If you quit on me, I'll understand," Mel said.

It was a total lie. She wouldn't understand and it would hurt very badly, but she knew she was the lame duck in this relationship and it wasn't fair to put Joe on hold while she tried to sort out her head.

Joe hugged her close. "Nah, you're worth the wait. Besides, this covert friends with benefits thing we've got going is pretty hot."

He glanced at the open cooler door and, seeing no one, he kissed her again. This time Mel was sure the damage to her baked goods would be significant. When she came up for air, she was surprised to see that everything in the chiller was fine, but she and Joe both looked as if they'd been hit by lightning.

"If you could figure out how to bake that into a cupcake, you'd make a fortune," Joe said, and he wiggled his eyebrows at her.

Mel laughed and reluctantly pushed him away. "Good thing I have you for research purposes."

"It's a dirty job," Joe sighed and shoved a hand through his hair. When he looked at her, Mel could see how much he was trying to keep the mood between them light, and she felt a pang of guilt.

"We'd better . . . before they get suspicious," she said. She reached around him and grabbed two Death by Chocolates. Once they were out of the cooler, she put the cupcakes on a plate and set them down on the table.

Joe took a seat and Mel could feel him watching her as she poured a glass of ice-cold milk for him. When she set it down at the table, he caught her hand and gave it a quick squeeze. He didn't let go.

"Just for the record, I'm not," he said. Mel felt her breath catch as he explained. "Seeing anyone else."

"We agreed we wouldn't talk about that," she said. "It's none of my business since—"

"We broke up," he said. "I know."

There was an awkward pause and Mel knew he was trying very hard to be patient. She knew if the situation were reversed, she'd be miserable.

"I'm not, either," she said.

Joe flashed his patent-worthy grin at her and she realized he'd just been looking for confirmation of her status.

"So, marry me," he said.

"No," she said, softening her answer by squeezing his fingers before letting go. He was still smiling, but she saw his chin jut out and she knew the trademark DeLaura tenacity had just been fully engaged.

Seven

"Big Brother sure looked happy when he left," Angie said as she and Tate joined Mel in the kitchen.

Mel was channeling all of her relationship angst into her baking and was creating a new version of her popular Chocolate Peanut Butter Cupcake. Angie and Tate sat in seats across from her at the steel table and watched her work.

"Death by Chocolate will do that for you," Mel said.

"Uh-huh," Angie said. "Anything you care to share?"

"Nope."

"We're not going to have another incident where you are engaged and not telling us, are we?" Tate asked. "Because that wouldn't go over well a second time."

He reached for some of Mel's chopped peanut butter cups and she smacked his hand away with the back of her wooden spoon.

"No!" Mel said. "I promise the next time I get engaged, I'll be comfortable enough with it to tell everyone, even my mother."

"You'd better," Angie agreed. "I didn't think Joyce had it in her to hold a grudge this long."

"I'm hoping that working the pageant will give me a chance to mend the rift," Mel said.

"Have you thought of having Joe talk to her?" Tate asked. "I mean, since he's okay with the change in status, maybe he could talk her into it, too."

"Or she'll just remember why she loves him so much and get even madder at me," Mel said.

"Um, I don't think she could get any madder at you," Angie said.

Mel sighed.

"So, what's the itinerary for the pageant?" Tate asked. "Angie says you've agreed to install a cupcake display every day of the pageant in addition to baking the cupcakes that the girls design themselves. Correct?"

"Cici seemed to think it would tie the whole thing together," Mel said. "They're paying us and the publicity should be, pardon the pun, sweet."

"What do you need me to do?" he asked.

"I'll need you and Marty to mind the store," Mel said. "And no making any deals to go local while I'm gone. We need to discuss that more before we make any changes."

"Fine," Tate said.

Mel paused as she was scooping her chocolate batter into her cupcake pan and stared at him.

"What?" he asked. He didn't meet her eyes.

"Tate, what have you done?" she asked.

Angie snapped her head between Tate and Mel.

Jenn McKinlay

"It's no big deal," he began. "I just set up some meetings."

"Tate," Mel's voice was a low growl.

"Just let me work up a proposal," he said. "I know you like the size of your operation, but Mel, the expansion possibilities are endless."

"But I don't want to expand," she protested. She knew she sounded petulant but she couldn't help it. "I like my operation exactly as it is."

"I do, too," Angie said.

Given that Angie and Tate were now a thing, sort of, she really appreciated the backup, and if she could have reached Angie to hug her, she would have.

"Look, we all know that it was my start-up capital that got the business off the ground," Tate said.

"Agreed," Mel said. "I can never thank you enough."

"I don't want thanks," Tate said. "It was the best investment of my life."

They smiled at each other and Mel knew he meant it.

"But—" Tate began, and both Mel and Angie groaned. "Hear me out. Without access to big bucks, you're going to have to expand, Mel, or you're going to have to trim back on staffing."

"What?"

Tate shrugged. "Sorry, but you're not going to be able to maintain a staff of five if you don't grow the biz a bit."

"So, I'm supposed to let go of Marty or Oz?" Mel asked. "Aren't we making enough to keep everyone on?"

"Barely," Tate said. "A big chunk of money went into the cupcake van and we haven't been utilizing it as much as we should."

"Well, maybe that's what you could be doing," Mel said. "We could load you up and you could drive down to central

46

Phoenix and work the heart of the city. Who wouldn't want a cupcake for lunch?"

Tate frowned at her.

"That's a pretty good idea," Angie said. "I always felt like we should have the van out every day. The advertising alone would surely help boost our sales."

"So it's agreed," Mel said. "I'll do some extra baking tonight and tomorrow you can roll out, Tate."

"This wasn't really what I had in mind—" Tate began to protest.

"You wanted expansion," Mel said. "Here it is."

She gave him her best brick-wall face, as in nothing he said was going to change her mind because she was as intractable as a wall.

Tate rose from his seat and went back into the bakery, frowning as if he'd lost an argument he didn't even know he was in.

Mel glanced at Angie. She had been surprised by Angie's full support on the decision to outsource Tate into the van. She gave her a questioning look and Angie gave her a small smile.

"Tate needs a kick in the pants," she said in explanation. "I'm hoping if he logs some time in the cupcake van, he'll have a chance to figure out his life a bit."

"It's possible," Mel said. "So, any progress between the two of you?"

Angie frowned. "Some. We're officially dating, but he says he still needs to prove that he can be a provider before he can commit to more. Mel, I am running out of patience."

"Well, maybe a week or two in the cupcake van will get him motivated to seek his fortune."

Angie made a grumbling sound that Mel took as assent.

The swinging door to the kitchen opened and Mel glanced up, expecting to see Tate coming back ready to debate his tenure in the cupcake van now that he'd had a chance to think it over.

Instead, it was Oz. He was dressed in his usual black clothing with his blue Fairy Tale Cupcakes apron on. His bangs hung down past his nose, which always made Mel regard him as the bakery's own personal Muppet.

"'Sup, Oz?" she asked. She did love to talk in teenspeak with him.

"Lupe," he said. "I'm concerned."

"About the pageant?" Mel asked. "See? Doesn't it bother you to have your friend evaluated on her looks like she's just a hollowed-out shell?"

Angie rolled her eyes and murmured, "Scholarship."

"No, actually, I'm worried that she has no talent," he said. "I mean, really, other than study, that girl can't do a thing. What is she going to do?"

"You seem awfully twitchy, Oz." Angie narrowed her eyes as she looked at him. "Uh-oh, you've got it bad, don't you?"

"Got what?" he asked.

"You've got feelings for Lupe, don't you?" Angie asked.

Oz shook his head and said, "Just friends."

At least that's what Mel thought he said. It was hard to tell since he was growling.

"Please," Angie said. "Would you care this much if she was just a friend?"

"Yeah," Oz said. Sarcasm enriched the word with a sprinkling of attitude and more syllables than necessary. "I put up one hundred dollars. That's one hundred reasons to care right there."

Mel raised her hands before Angie could poke holes in his defense. "Oz, between my mother and Ginny, they'll have a talent for Lupe. Don't worry."

Oz stared at her for a long moment, then nodded and went back to the bakery.

"Really?" Angie asked. "You think they'll be able to figure that out in a couple of days?"

"Oh, heck no," Mel said. "But there's no need for Oz to make himself crazy over it."

"Interesting," Angie said. She narrowed her gaze at Mel.

"What?" Mel asked, not enjoying the scrutiny.

"I just have to wonder," Angie said. "Since you've obviously gone pro in the fibbing department, what else are you hiding?"

"Nothing," Mel insisted. She hoped Angie didn't notice that she didn't meet her eyes.

Eight

They used the van to deliver the cupcake tier on the first day of the pageant. After helping them to set up, Tate took off to hit the downtown lunchtime crowd while Marty held down the bakery until Oz joined him after school.

The resort had given Mel and Angie a nice piece of lobby real estate. They were nestled in an alcove between the bar that led to the pool patio and the hallway that led to the pageant events. Today was the interview day. This was the day when the candidates met individually with the three judges so that the judges could get a feel for their personalities.

Cici dragged Mel and Angie into the interview room to meet the judges before the interviews began. Mariel had been too busy barking at someone on her cell phone to do more than wave at them, quite dismissively, but the other two were personable enough. Lexi Armstrong, a willowy brunette, stood and shook their hands.

"I've heard an awful lot about you two," she said.

Mel and Angie exchanged a look. Was this good or bad?

"Lexi is the features director at *Southwest Style* magazine," Cici said.

"Oh!" Mel clapped her hands together. She and Angie had become friends with the staff of the magazine after they did a spread on the bakery for one of their issues. "How is everyone at SWS?"

"They're doing fine," Lexi said. She glanced at the phone in her hand. "Oh, but Justin Freehold wanted me to give you a message. Hang on. It's in my phone. He said to say, "'I like a woman who can take it on the chin.'"

She glanced up at them and frowned. "I hope you know what that means because I haven't a clue."

Mel and Angie exchanged a grin and said together, *"Miss Firecracker."*

"Huh?" grunted the other judge. He was tall and thin, dressed all in black from his cowboy boots to his dark sunglasses. Mel recognized him immediately.

"It's a movie quote," Angie explained. The man made a sour face.

"Jay Driscoll," Cici introduced him. "Fashion photographer."

"Angie DeLaura," Angie said and held out her hand, which he ignored.

"You're too short," Jay said. "Great hair, though."

"We've met before," Mel said before he could give her his assessment.

"Oh, well, if that's all, I'm off to the bar," he said.

Angie looked at Mel as if checking to see that Mel thought Jay was as rude as she did.

Mel nodded. "Yes, he is. I've met him before. He's the

photographer who was so charming to me after Christy died."

Angie frowned. "The one who told you that you were too heavy and too old to be a model."

"Same one," Mel said.

"Gee, thanks for the intro, Cici."

"He's not that bad, okay, yes, he is, but he's still connected to the New York fashion industry," Cici said. "And so we tolerate him. See you girls later."

As they made their way back to their cupcake tower, Angie fretted. "Sheesh, I hope he's nicer to the girls when they interview. He could do some serious damage to a young girl's self-esteem."

"Which is why I don't like pageants to begin with," Mel said.

"Let it go," Angie chided her. "Remember, this is business."

"Fine," Mel said. But she couldn't help but worry that Jay Driscoll would be mean to Lupe and she'd want to stomp him. Even more worrisome, if he was mean, Oz would probably do it for real. She could only hope that Lupe shined, for all their sakes.

Joyce and Ginny had spent the day before at the bakery, quizzing Lupe on her answers while Oz watched in growing alarm. When Ginny had asked Lupe what her favorite feature on a man was, Oz had looked at Mel in horror.

"They're not going to ask her stuff like that, are they?" he'd asked.

"No, Ginny probably just mixed up her practice questions with a quiz out of *Cosmopolitan*," Mel had assured him.

He'd blown out a breath in relief. However, she'd noted that he had leaned close to hear Lupe's answer, which had been a man's smile. Joyce had beamed at her while Ginny scoffed. Oz had looked relieved but then Mel saw him checking his smile in the reflection of a silver napkin holder. Poor guy.

As Mel relaxed behind the tower of cupcakes, she watched while Angie worked the lobby, carrying a tray full of their most popular flavors. She noticed that even the sourest looking oldster paused to take a cupcake and left with a smile. It reminded her that this was why she'd picked cupcakes as the signature item in her bakery. Only a real curmudgeon could remain unmoved by a cupcake.

"When will we find out how we did?" a voice asked.

Mel glanced up to see a sharp-looking, redheaded teen walk by. The young woman was shredding a tissue with her fingers while an older-looking version of her walked beside her, making soothing noises and rubbing the girl's arm.

"Stop touching me, Mom," the girl snapped. "It's just creepy."

"I'm sorry, Sarah." The mother withdrew her hand as if she'd been bitten.

The angry energy pouring off of the young woman made Mel long for a cupcake, or at least to offer one to the mother. What a brat!

Were the interviews really that scary? Maybe public speaking wasn't the redhead's forte. Mel tried to picture Lupe in an interview situation. Given that she'd known her since Oz had come to work at the bakery and that she always hid behind colorful bangs, Mel didn't really have a feel for how Lupe would do. She had always been pleasant and polite, but this was a high-pressure situation where the charm factor was critical.

The thought made her edgy, as she'd promised to text Oz as soon as she heard anything. What if it was bad news? What would she say?

Mel fretted, rearranging the cupcakes on the large tower in an effort to combat her anxiety with action.

A leggy, blond young woman dressed in a becoming blue print dress strolled by with a woman who looked to be an older, plasticized version of the young woman. Mel was noticing a theme now.

This pair caught Mel's attention because she could see from the daughter's natural glow the beauty that the mother must have been at one time—like, before her lips had been plumped up beyond repair and her skin had been poisoned into the sort of immobility found only on a mannequin.

Mel had noted that the pageant positively swarmed with mothers and daughters, and for the first time ever Mel was grateful that she had been a Large Marge and the pageant scene had never even been an option when she was a teen.

As they paused beside the cupcake tower, the teen glanced from the tower to Mel as if uncertain of whether she was allowed to touch them or not.

"Help yourself," Mel encouraged with a smile. "We're Fairy Tale Cupcakes and we'll be baking the cupcakes you design as part of your competition."

The young woman reached out to take a cupcake with a pretty pink flower on top, but her mother snatched it out of her hand. The mother, Mel noted, was dressed in tight leather pants, wedge heels, and an animal-print blouse. She was also draped in enough gold jewelry and diamonds to make a pirate giddy.

Mel found it interesting that the daughter was light on jewelry and makeup, and her print dress was demure, as if they were going for sweet and innocent for her interview. Mel had another spasm of worry about Lupe. She had no idea what she had worn to her interview.

"No, Destiny!" the woman scolded. "You may not stuff yourself with cupcakes. Need I remind you that you're in competition and have to watch your figure?"

"No," Destiny's voice came out in a sad sigh that made Mel want to give her a box of cupcakes of her own.

"I'll eat this one," the mother said. "Just to make sure this baker is up to creating your vision. Oh, and maybe that one and that one, too."

Mel watched as the woman grabbed two more cupcakes.

"What about your diet, Mom?" the teen asked with a definite note of annoyance in her voice.

"No problem," the mother said, taking a bite out of the first one. "I'll throw them up later."

Without so much as a thank-you, the woman continued eating as she walked away. Mel watched her lecture her daughter through her mouthful of cupcake.

She stared after them in wonder. Throw them up? That was sacrilege! She had to force herself not to race after the woman and smack the cupcakes out of her hand.

"She's a horror show, isn't she?" a voice asked.

Mel whirled around to find Ginny standing behind her. Today's water bottle was purple and Ginny had a tight grip on it, but she'd abandoned her fur-lined coat for a pale blue cashmere sweater that accentuated her eyes and blond hair.

Mel realized that Destiny and Ginny had the same sort of fragile, porcelain-doll look and she wondered if that was a requirement for success in the pageant circuit. She hoped for Lupe's sake it wasn't.

Mel nodded toward the girl and her mother. "Who are they?"

"Destiny Richards is a contestant," Ginny said. "Her mother, Brittany, is a pain in the a—"

"Aside from that," Mel clarified. "What I meant was, did Brittany ever win the Miss Sweet Tiara title?"

"Oh, hell, no," Ginny said. "What you have there is a case of a loser mother using her child's youth and beauty to make up for the lack of her own. Sort of like a tick on a deer."

"You're calling Brittany a bloodsucker?"

"Metaphorically, yes," Ginny said. "She's one of the worst stage mothers I've ever seen and believe me, I've seen my share."

Ginny glanced around the lobby to make sure no one was in earshot and then wiggled a finger at Mel indicating that she should come closer.

"For Destiny's sixteenth birthday, her mother gave her bolt-ons," Ginny whispered in a voice that still managed to carry across the lobby.

"What?" Mel asked. "What does that even mean?"

Ginny held her free hand in front of her chest and made a gesture like screwing on the lid of a jar. "You know, bolt-ons."

"A boob job?" Mel asked. "At sixteen? Is that legal?"

"Oh, please. Don't even get me started on her nose," Ginny said. "Did you see the snot locker on Brittany? That thing has been modified at least three times. There is no way that little button is Destiny's real nose."

Ginny took a swig from her water bottle while Mel processed the horror of it all.

"You're not making me feel good about being here," Mel said. "I already witnessed one case of nasty daughter and cowed mother."

"Let me guess," Ginny said. "Redheaded girl with more attitude than looks?"

"That's the one," Mel said.

"Sarah Hendricks," Ginny said. "Pageant crybaby who also happens to have a vicious mean streak and a serious lack of people-pleasing skills. She's the current bane of the pageant circuit."

"Lovely," Mel said. "Why do I feel like we've put Lupe in a viper pit?"

"Nah, there are some genuinely nice girls here, too. It's just that the nasties are more memorable." Ginny shrugged. "Our girl Lupe is going to kill, don't worry. She's the real deal."

Mel raised her eyebrows. She vowed to have a chat with Lupe at the earliest possible moment about the dangers of elective surgery and why beauty was really something beyond measure on the inside of a person and had nothing to do with her bra size, or her schnoz size for that matter.

"Ready for another walkabout?" Angie asked as she returned to the tower with an empty tray. "They are scarfing these babies up. Great idea to put the bakery name on the paper cupcake liners."

"Thanks," Mel said.

She started putting cupcakes on Angie's tray while Angie took a sip of the iced tea she'd left behind the tower. Mel was halfway done when the sound of a door slamming boomed down the hallway.

She glanced around with the rest of the people in the lobby and saw Mariel Mars stomping toward them as if she wished someone's head was beneath the spiky points of her heels.

"Ms. Mars!" a voice called after her. "Wait!"

Mel and Ginny exchanged a glance before they both leaned forward. They knew that voice. It was Joyce and she was running after Mariel.

As if aware of the lobby watching her, Mariel came to an abrupt stop and appeared to force her lips into a smile that came out more like a grimace.

"I'm sorry, Ms.—" Mariel shrugged as if Joyce's name was of no importance and continued. "I really have nothing more to say."

Joyce was breathing hard as she stopped in front of the judge.

"But these scores," Joyce said, holding a sheet of paper out to her. "They're so incredibly low. They could knock Lupe out of the first round of the competition."

"So?" Mariel asked, tossing her long black hair over her shoulder.

And that's when Mel saw it. The hellfire that was normally banked in her mother's hazel-blue eyes crackled to life. The only other time Mel had seen her mother ignite like this was when someone went after Mel or her brother, Charlie.

"So?" Joyce repeated as if talking to a half wit. "None of the other judges scored her anywhere near as low as you did."

"I have higher standards," Mariel said. She examined her manicure as if it were infinitely more interesting than the conversation she was having.

"Perhaps," Joyce said. "Or maybe you're cheating."

Nine

"How dare you!" Mariel gasped as if she'd been struck.

"That was a bad move," Ginny said to Mel. "Now Mariel's going to have a hissy fit and her hissy fits are the stuff of legend."

"Should we call someone?" Mel asked.

"Let's wait until we see bloodshed," Ginny said. Then she smiled. "I always love to watch your mother when she gets her back up. She's just as cute as a hedgehog until she bites."

Mel moved to step forward but Angie held her back with a hand on her elbow. "I'm with Ginny on this one. 'Let us see what Squirt does flying solo.'"

"You're quoting *Finding Nemo* now?" Mel asked.

Angie tipped her head in the direction of the altercation and made a shushing noise.

"I will not stand for this!" Mariel sputtered. She lashed out and kicked over a nearby chair.

"Fine," Joyce said. "I'm just as happy to sit. Oh, well, I would have until you started kicking over the furniture. For goodness sake, act your age!"

"Ah!" Mariel gasped and Mel suspected she thought that was an age slam when really it was just a mom thing to say.

"I will not tolerate being called a cheater." Mariel leaned forward until her face was inches from Joyce's.

"Then make it right," Joyce said through gritted teeth. She didn't back up but rather leaned forward until the two women were nose-to-nose.

"Mrs. Cooper, Joyce," Lupe implored. "Please don't go to any trouble for me."

Mel glanced at Lupe, who had joined the ladies, and again she was struck by how lovely the young woman beneath the dyed fringe and baggy black clothes was. Today she was in a delicate floral lace sheath dress in a pretty shade of turquoise with beige open-toed pumps. She looked as if she should be strutting down the runway at a fashion show.

"Wow," Angie said, echoing Mel's thoughts exactly.

"If Oz were here right now, he'd stroke out," Mel said, and Angie nodded.

"It's no trouble, Lupe," Joyce said. She stepped back from Mariel and yanked on the lapels of her plum-colored jacket. "I have already called Cici Hastings and plan to have her go over these scores. Maybe she can shed some light on why Mariel's scores are thirty points lower than all of the other judges."

"You dare to question me?" Mariel's nostrils flared.

"When your scores are so out of whack?" Joyce asked.

"You bet I do. Oh, and we'll be checking to see if you did this to every contestant or just Lupe."

Mariel stepped around Joyce. She looked Lupe over with a sneer that lifted the corner of her upper lip, making her look as vicious as a wild dog about to attack.

"You don't belong here," Mariel hissed. "Just because you combed your hair and they shoved you in a nice dress does not make you worthy of the title of Miss Sweet Tiara and you know it."

Lupe ducked her head and her curtain of thick black hair swept forward, covering her face. Shame poured off of her in waves, and Mel felt her stomach clench in sympathy. She wanted to smack the smirk right off of Mariel's face.

Angie stiffened beside her, and Mel was afraid that Angie would launch herself at Mariel. Ginny and Mel each put a hand on Angie's arms, holding her back. Much as Mel wanted to jump in as well, she knew this wasn't their fight and if it turned ugly, it would put an end to Lupe's dreams of a scholarship, which would do her no good at all.

Joyce reached out and cupped Lupe's chin. She raised the girl's head until Lupe met her gaze.

"Do not listen to her. She doesn't know what she's talking about," Joyce said. Mariel squawked in protest, but Joyce kept going, drowning her out. "They would be lucky to have a young woman like you wearing their crown. Now show me the beauty that I know is in there."

Lupe nodded and straightened her back. She blinked as if to keep back her tears and she tipped her chin up. Her smile was brave and all the more beautiful because Mel knew it was costing her on a soul level.

Mariel made a derisive snort and muttered, "Trash."

Joyce whipped around and leveled Mariel with a glare.

"Do not speak to her. You don't even deserve to be in the same room with her. And mark my words, I'm going to have you removed from the panel of judges."

"You don't have that kind of power," Mariel sniped.

"She doesn't," Ginny said as she stepped forward. "But I do."

Mariel glared. "Oh, please. Now I have two dried-up old prunes coming after me? You have no power, Ginny Lobo. You're just a drunk and she's your silly sidekick. The two of you are pathetic and the only reason you're even allowed to be here is because your husband is loaded."

"Don't talk to them like that," Lupe snapped. "They're ladies while you—you're just a bitter, nasty has-been."

Mariel's eyes narrowed and she stepped forward, but Ginny and Joyce pushed Lupe behind them, blocking Mariel's path.

"You just made a powerful enemy, young lady," Mariel sneered.

"I'm not afraid of you," Lupe said. "And if you go after my friends, I'll make you pay. I swear I will."

There was the skateboarding daredevil Mel knew and loved. She and Angie went to stand with the others. Mariel now had a group of five to contend with and no one running to her side.

"You? Make me pay? Ha!" Mariel said. "I'd like to see you try it."

Lupe glared. She pushed past Ginny and Joyce.

"Make no mistake," Lupe said. "Hurt them and I'll hurt you—more."

"Are you threatening me?" Mariel asked. She spun away from them and yelled across the lobby. "Witnesses! I need witnesses! This contestant just threatened to hurt me because she didn't like her scores!"

"She did not." Joyce protested.

"I heard it, too," a voice said from across the lobby. The vomiting mom, Brittany Richards, and her daughter Destiny were at the far end of the lobby. Brittany scurried forward, giving Mariel an ingratiating smile.

"Oh, for Pete's sake!" Ginny snapped. "You couldn't have heard a word she said from all the way over there."

"I have exceptional hearing," Brittany said.

Her daughter followed her, and while Brittany fussed over Mariel as if she'd been the victim of a mugging, Destiny looked as if she'd rather be anywhere but here. Mel thought the idea had distinct possibilities.

"Are you all right?" Brittany asked Mariel, loud enough for everyone within a one-hundred-yard radius to hear. "You look a bit faint."

"I'll be fine," Mariel said. Then she leaned close to their group and hissed, "This isn't over. You'll be tossed from this competition if it's the last thing I do."

Ginny stepped forward. "Try it. I double dare you."

Maybe it was the alcohol on her breath or the crazy light in her eyes, but Mariel spun away from Ginny. Brittany fell in behind her like a good little sycophantic minion, yanking Destiny behind her as she went.

"Well, shoot. I'd better find Cici first, so I can remind her of how much money I'm kicking into this shindig," Ginny said. "Come on, Lupe, Joyce, we've got some damage control to do."

"Can you control it?" Joyce asked worriedly.

"I may have Cici remind Mariel that she can be replaced.

Oh, and I know just the woman, too. Anka Holland wanted very much to be a judge in the pageant. That would really chap Mariel's uppity behind."

"Who is Anka Holland?" Lupe asked.

"The bane of Mariel's existence," Ginny said. "Anka was always one step behind Mariel, always breathing down her neck on the pageant circuit. Anka managed to beat Mariel a few times, but Mariel always won the big titles. Anka is the only one who gave Mariel any competition and Mariel still hates her for it.

"Of course, Anka is no fan of Mariel's, either. I remember when Mariel took the title of Miss Glitz from Anka back in their heyday. It was not pretty. There had been some sabotage in the dressing room. Someone smeared Anka's evening gown with lipstick while Mariel's bathing suit was found to have itching powder in it. They each blamed the other but no one could prove it."

Ginny led the others away, and Mel and Angie watched them go.

"I don't know about you, but I have a really bad feeling about this," Mel said.

Angie looked thoughtful. "Agreed. There was something off about that whole scene. I mean, I got the feeling Mariel wanted Lupe to come after her."

"I did, too," Mel said. "The question is *why*."

Ten

The next day, Mel was back at her cupcake tower while the judging of the swimsuit competition went on poolside. They had a pretty good vantage point from their corner of the lobby. She saw Lupe with Joyce. Lupe was wearing a robe and looked distinctly uncomfortable. Mel understood completely. This would have ranked right up there in her top worst nightmares as a teen, coming in second only to showing up naked to class.

Angie was again working the crowd in the lobby. She seemed to have made a few friends and Mel saw her chatting up people as she passed out the cupcakes. Today's specialty was the Pretty in Pink, a strawberry cupcake with a dollop of vanilla buttercream rolled in bright pink sprinkles around the edges.

Cici Hastings was working her way through the lobby.

She looked amazing in an emerald silk blouse and black capri pants with her hair and makeup done to perfection.

Mel knew that the minimum amount of personal maintenance required to stay as well preserved as Cici meant that she would never look anywhere near that good at any age, but still, Mel hoped she had a little of the pizzazz Cici had when she was in her advanced years.

"Looking good, Cici," she called as the older lady went by her.

"Thanks," Cici paused. "Have you seen Mariel? We were supposed to start the swimsuit competition fifteen minutes ago, but she hasn't shown up yet."

"No, come to think of it, I haven't seen her all morning," Mel said. She had been surprised, too, because after yesterday's kerfuffle in the lobby, she had fully expected Mariel to make another scene today.

"She's probably sulking." Cici sighed. "A total diva, that one."

"Why would she be sulking?" Mel asked.

"Because in reviewing her scores from yesterday, it became apparent that she *is* playing favorites. She low-balled anyone who might provide competition for her chosen one, especially Lupe Guzman, who was scoring very high with the other two judges," Cici said. "So I made the decision to throw out every contestant's lowest score and I let her know I'd do it again, too. That should keep the voting honest."

"Nicely done," Mel said.

"I thought so, except now I have a big poutypants for a head judge and I really don't have the time or patience for it," Cici said. "Honestly, I should have brought Anka Holland in as the judge, but given that she was always number two to Mariel's number one spot on the pageant circuit, Mariel seemed to be the better choice. Ugh, live and learn."

"Can I help you look for her?" Mel asked. "I can check the prep rooms."

"Oh, would you?" Cici asked. "Then I could cover the same ground twice as fast."

"No problem," Mel said. She turned and signaled to Angie that she was going to leave the tower. Angie nodded in understanding. Mel knew that Angie would come and keep an eye on the goods for her.

Mel and Cici split up in the main lobby, with Mel taking one side and Cici the other. Mel entered the large room that was used for a dressing room. Several harried-looking mothers and their daughters were in there prepping their bathing suits for showtime.

One exasperated-looking woman was using double-stick tape on her daughter's bottom to keep the young woman's swimsuit from riding up. The girl didn't seem fazed as she stood texting on her smartphone, and Mel looked away, feeling embarrassed for the both of them.

She glanced around the room, got pushed aside by another mother and daughter bolting out the door, leaned against the wall, and looked for a head of dark hair and a frowning face. She simply could not envision Mariel with a smile.

She checked the next two rooms, but still no Mariel. Mel crossed the hall and continued checking, opening every door on her way back to the lobby. Some rooms were empty and some were full of people, but there was no one who resembled the missing judge.

She hoped Cici had better luck. She was closing the door to the last room when an ear-piercing shriek sounded from the lobby. Mel knew that shriek. She had heard it every time she, Angie, and Tate had ridden the Zipper at the Arizona State Fair. It wasn't Tate and it wasn't her, so that left—Angie!

Mel ran to the lobby. Her heart was pounding, her hands were sweating, and she could feel the icy clutch of dread grabbing at her as she came around the corner.

What could have happened to make Angie scream like that? Had someone knocked over the cupcake tower? Did Angie get into a fight? Had Tate broken up with her?

When Mel reached the lobby a crowd was forming around the cupcake table. She saw Lupe and her mother on the fringe and yelled, "What happened?"

Joyce gave her a scared look and for the first time in months she spoke directly to Mel, "I don't know, honey. We can't get in there."

Mel glanced at the crowd that was five deep ahead of her. There were shrieks and gasps but no one was moving. She used her elbows and began to force her way through the crowd.

When she reached the front, she stopped in her tracks. Angie was kneeling on the floor, holding up the navy blue tablecloth that covered their circular table.

A head of dark hair was sticking out from under the cloth. It was Mariel Mars, and Mel knew with the unwelcome knowledge that comes from seeing too many bodies up close and personal that she was dead.

Eleven

"Finding the body is not *my* job," Angie said. "That's supposed to be you."

Mel put an arm around her friend's shoulders. She knew it was shock making Angie babble.

"I wouldn't say it was my job exactly," Mel said. "Did you call the police?"

"Lydia is on it," Angie said. She gestured to the far side of the table and Mel saw Lydia, the pretty woman from the front desk, on her cell phone. She looked stressed as she paced back and forth in the narrow area.

"Are you sure she's dead?" Mel asked.

Angie gestured for Mel to look closer. Mel took a deep breath and leaned over Mariel's still form.

There was no rise and fall to her chest. No warmth coming off of her body. Her bloodshot eyes were unseeing. A wide pink satin sash was wrapped around her neck and Mel could see scratch marks along her throat, as if she'd been clawed by something or someone.

"The police are on their way," Lydia said as she crouched beside them. "I've had security paged to move the crowd out of the lobby."

As she spoke, a big burly man in a navy blue uniform with a radio on his hip arrived and began pushing the crowd back. Lydia rose to go and speak with him.

"How did you find her?" Mel asked.

"I dropped a cupcake," Angie said. "When I couldn't find it, I thought it rolled under the table. When I lifted the cloth, there she was."

"That was quite a scream you let out," Mel said. "I'm pretty sure they heard you all the way out to the main road."

"And I'm pretty sure I'm going to have nightmares tonight and for many nights after," Angie said. She shuddered and lowered the cloth, letting it fall carefully around Mariel's middle.

"Melanie, Angela, what's happening?" Joyce Cooper hissed. She ignored the arm of the security guard as he tried to keep her back.

They looked from Joyce to the body. Mel wasn't comfortable leaving but she didn't really want to keep watch, either.

"It's all right," Lydia said, rejoining them beside the body. "Go talk to her. I'll stay with—her. I can't get any more freaked out than I already am."

Mel and Angie studied Lydia. She looked as if she was fighting to keep it together. Mel was pretty sure they didn't have a course for this in hospitality school. Angie met her gaze and Mel knew she was thinking the same thing.

"Call us if you need us," Mel said.

Lydia nodded with a grateful glance.

"Ma'am, I'm sorry but you've got to keep back with everyone else until the police arrive," the security guard said to Joyce.

"That is my daughter," Joyce argued, pointing at Mel. "And I will not back up until I know what is happening."

The security guard glanced behind him just as Mel and Angie joined them. The look he gave Mel was one of relief, and she nodded. Having been the one to hold her mother back a few times, she commiserated with the poor guy who was obviously out of his depth.

"I'm here, Mom," Mel said. "It's okay."

Lupe was standing behind Joyce and the two of them followed Mel and Angie off to the far side of the lobby. Lupe's eyes were huge and she was biting her lower lip as if to keep herself from crying. She was knotting the belt of her robe in her hands and Mel wondered if she should send her to go and change. Surely, they wouldn't be going ahead with the pageant now.

"I'm sorry this happened, Lupe," Mel said. They each sat down on the edge of a large planter with precisely arranged bromeliads in it.

"What happened exactly?" Joyce asked. "All we heard was that a woman was found underneath the cupcake table. Is that true? Who is it?"

"It's Mariel Mars," Angie said.

"What? But how? Why?" Joyce stammered, looking stunned.

"From what I saw, I'm guessing she was strangled with a sash," Mel said. "No idea why, though."

She reached out and took her mother's hand. Joyce's skin felt cold, and Mel squeezed her fingers tight as if she

71

could transfer some warmth. Joyce squeezed back letting Mel know that it was appreciated. Joyce reached out and hugged Mel.

"I'm sorry, honey," she said. "That must have been awful."

Mel heaved a huge sigh. It felt so good to have her mother speaking to her again. Joyce squeezed her tight and then let her go so that she could do the same with Angie. Mel sat back and watched as her mother comforted her best friend.

She felt movement beside her and glanced over to see Lupe rise to her feet. She started backing away with a fearful look in her eyes.

"Lupe, where are you going?" Joyce asked.

"I have to get out of here," Lupe said.

"I don't think anyone will be allowed to leave until the police have talked to us," Mel said.

"Oh, that's not happening," Lupe said with a shake of her head.

"I don't think you have any choice," Angie said.

"That's why I need to leave now before the cops get here," Lupe said.

"Lupe, honey, what are you afraid of?" Joyce asked.

Lupe looked at Mel. "She really doesn't get it, does she?"

"And neither do I," Mel said. "What's got you so worried?"

"Look at me," Lupe said. She pointed to herself. "I'm a Latina in a room full of white blondies. Who do you think the cops are going to suspect first?"

"No," Joyce said with a shake of her head. "My brother-in-law Stan is a longtime detective with the Scottsdale PD, and he's not like that."

Lupe shook her head. Her long dark hair hid her face, and Mel wondered if she missed the colored bangs that used to hide her from the world.

"And if you don't believe that," Mel said, "Uncle Stan's partner is Hispanic and he isn't like that, either."

"It doesn't matter," Lupe said. Her voice quavered and she sounded on the verge of crying.

"Why not?" Angie asked.

"Because even if the color of my skin doesn't make them suspect me, what happened yesterday will. We had a fight with Mariel Mars in a room full of witnesses. I threatened her! How long do you think it will take them to look at me after they find out about that?"

"Find out about what?" a voice asked from behind Lupe. Mel glanced up to see Detective Manny Martinez standing there. He did not look happy to see them.

Twelve

"Manny!" Mel greeted the tall, dark, and annoyingly handsome detective. "What are you doing here?"

"I'm not checking the flower arrangements," he said, giving her a look that made her feel flustered and not just because she had evaded his question.

"Oh, right," Mel said. She stepped forward and gave him an awkward half hug. He looked amused, as if he knew she was uncertain how to behave around him. "Homicide detective. Body. It all adds up now."

"The hotel manager said you were the one to find the victim," he said. His black eyes looked concerned and Mel gave him a rueful smile.

"It wasn't me this time," she said. "It was Angie."

"Hi." Angie rose from her seat on the planter and gave him a small wave.

Manny and Angie had an uneasy relationship. Mel knew

74

it was mostly her fault. With Joe being Angie's older brother, Angie felt a certain loyalty to him to not like any man who showed an interest in the woman Joe wanted to marry, which would be Mel. On the other hand, Angie was Mel's best friend and wanted her to be happy, so she tried to be extra nice to Manny on the off—very off—chance that Mel and Manny ended up together.

"How are you doing?" he asked. He gave Angie the same concerned look he'd given Mel.

"Not great," Angie said.

"Understandable," Manny said. "Can you talk about it? We can wait for Stan if you want. He's coming here from another call."

"No, it's fine," Angie said. "I can do this."

It sounded to Mel like she was talking herself into it.

"Are you sure?" she asked.

"Yeah." Angie gave her a stiff nod.

"If you could just walk me through what happened." Manny said. He gestured to the crime scene.

The uniformed police who had responded had already cordoned off the area with plastic yellow tape, and gawkers were being dispersed by the resort's security staff. While Mel watched, she noted that the crime scene investigators had arrived and were surveying the surrounding scene.

Manny and Angie walked closer to the perimeter of the tape and Mel saw Angie explaining how she'd found the body. Even from across the room, she could see that Angie's hands were shaking. She wished she could go over and hug her friend.

"She'll be okay," Joyce said, and she hugged Mel to her side.

Mel turned to look at her. "Thanks, Mom. Does this mean you've forgiven me?"

"It seems silly now to have been so annoyed with you." Joyce let go of her and reached up to brush the blond bangs out of Mel's eyes. "My feelings were hurt that you left me out of your big news and then you broke up with dear Joe."

Joyce let out a sigh that sounded like it came from her feet. "An assistant district attorney." She sighed again. "I'm sure I'll be able to let it go, eventually."

Mel smiled at her. "That's my girl."

Joyce gave her a rueful look.

Mel glanced at Lupe and noticed she was scanning the room as if looking for the nearest exit.

"Trust me," she said to the teen. "You're going to be okay. Mariel must have been under the table before Angie and I set up today's cupcake tower. Whoever harmed her had to have done it earlier today when you were prepping for the bathing suit event, so you have Mom as an alibi."

Lupe and Joyce exchanged a glance. It was the bottom-heavy look of two people who were sharing a secret.

"Oh, no, spill it," Mel said.

Joyce put a protective arm around Lupe. "No one is accountable for every second of their day."

"Are you trying to tell me that you weren't with Lupe all morning?" Mel asked.

Lupe looked down and away as if afraid to meet Mel's gaze directly. Mel could feel her stomach knot up with anxiety. This wasn't good. Much as she hated to admit it, Lupe had been right. Her spat with Mariel yesterday didn't bode well for her. She would be the one that Manny and Uncle Stan looked at first. She had to have an alibi.

"Where were you this morning?" Mel asked.

"Studying," Lupe said. She looked miserable.

"Did anyone see you?" Mel asked. "Please tell me some-one saw you."

"You're being overly dramatic. She doesn't need an alibi," Joyce insisted. "She's an eighteen-year-old girl, not a killer."

"Who's not a killer?" Uncle Stan asked as he joined them.

Joyce and Mel exchanged alarmed glances. When did he get here and how much had he heard?

A love of Mel's cupcakes and every other sweet he could lay his chubby fingers on had given Uncle Stan a physique that took up more than its fair share of real estate, so it wasn't often that he got the drop on anyone.

"They're talking about me," Lupe said. Mel and Joyce began to protest, but Lupe held up her hand. "Let's just get it out there. Mariel Mars tried to have me booted from the pageant yesterday. She was pretty mean, but I didn't kill her."

Uncle Stan blinked as he took in the young woman before him. "Hey, aren't you the girl who hangs out with Oz?"

Lupe nodded.

"I almost didn't recognize you without the . . ." Uncle Stan paused and wiggled his fingers over his bare forehead.

Lupe cracked a smile. "Green bangs?"

"I think they were pink the last time I saw you," he said.

"I liked the pink," Lupe said. Her voice was wistful, as if she were longing for more than her old hairdo—like, maybe her old life.

Stan glanced at the three of them. "So, what happened?"

"Well, Mariel Mars is a hideous, vile, nasty woman," Joyce began.

"This is the victim?" Stan asked.

"Yes," Joyce confirmed.

"And still you're describing her to me in such derogatory terms, knowing that I am a homicide detective?" he asked.

"You're my brother-in-law," Joyce said. "I am giving you the unvarnished truth."

Mel met Uncle Stan's gaze and rolled her eyes. He tucked his lips in, trying to hide his smile.

"Anyway, Mariel scored Lupe thirty points lower than any other judge on her interview yesterday," Joyce said. "So I challenged Mariel about it and, oh, did she ever throw a fit."

Stan's smile disappeared. "You challenged her?"

"I was just looking for some accountability," Joyce said.

"Did anyone else see this quest for accountability?" Stan asked.

"Well, Lupe was with me," Joyce said. Mel could tell she was trying to avoid answering the question. Probably she was afraid she was going to give Stan a heart attack. Mel figured they'd best just get it over with.

"The entire lobby area, which was full, heard Mom and Mariel disagree."

"They also might have heard me threaten her," Lupe said.

"Threaten her how?" Stan asked.

"I may have said something like 'hurt my friends and I'll make you pay,'" Lupe said.

"Oh, and you told her if she hurt us, you'd hurt her bad," Joyce said. Lupe gave her a wide-eyed stare. "Or something like that," Joyce muttered.

Uncle Stan started patting his shirtfront pocket and Mel knew he was searching for his antacid pills. When that yielded no results, he patted his front pants pockets. Then he looked around as if a pack of Tums might appear on the floor.

"Here you go." Manny held out an unopened roll of the chalky tablets to Stan. He looked at Mel and said, "I started carrying them when we partnered up."

Stan glowered but took the pack. "What have we got?"

"At a quick glance, we have a middle-aged female vic, strangled with a beauty pageant sash. Given the claw marks on her throat, she put up a fight," Manny said. "You ready to have a look?"

Uncle Stan nodded. Mel studied him, wondering if he was going to tell Manny what they had told him.

"Stick around," Uncle Stan said to Joyce. "I'm going to look over the scene. I'll be back shortly."

Joyce nodded. Mel wondered if she had finally caught on that they were not in the best possible situation here.

"Oh, man, I'm dead," Lupe moaned.

"Don't panic," Angie said. "Think about it this way—if Mariel was as nasty to the others as she was to you, and that seems likely, than you're hardly the only one with a motive to kill her."

"But how are we going to find out who she was mean to?" Lupe asked. "I was already an outsider before this happened. I think it's safe to say none of the other pageant girls are ever going to talk to me."

"We can ask Cici," Mel said.

"She does seem to like us," Angie said. "And I don't think she was terribly fond of Mariel, either."

"Mom, since Ginny is connected in the pageant world, can you ask her to dig up what she can?"

"Good idea," Joyce said. "I'm sure Mariel left a trail of unhappy behind her and all we need to do is follow it." She turned to Lupe. "Don't you worry, honey, your pageant dream is alive and well."

"Scholarship dream," Lupe said.

"Yes, of course," Joyce agreed. "That's what I meant."

Mel looked at the glint in her mother's eye. She wondered if this was what her mother had hoped for when she was a teenage girl, to be the champion of a beauty pageant daughter. To Joyce's credit, if she had felt that way, Mel had never known. Still, she felt a little bad that she might have let her mother down by being the chunk she'd been all those years ago. The thought didn't sit well.

"Mel, can I have a word?" Manny approached their group and Mel felt her face get warm.

Joyce looked perturbed, but said nothing. Angie glanced away as if she hadn't heard.

"Sure," she said.

They walked across the room toward the French doors that led out to the pool. Several of the contestants were sitting on the padded lounge chairs with their knees drawn up to their chests, as if they could tuck and roll away from the tragedy inside.

Mel saw the blunt-featured redhead called Sarah, who she remembered was particularly nasty to her mother the day before, after her interview. When she'd asked Ginny about her, Ginny had told her that Sarah Hendricks was the scourge of the pageant circuit, known for weeping when she lost, which she usually did due to her serious lack of people skills. Presently, Sarah was pacing in the corner, with her mother pacing beside her.

Mel also spotted Destiny Richards with her mother, Brittany. Destiny was watching a hummingbird working its way around a potted plant of petunias while her mother talked animatedly on her cell phone.

Manny moved to the side of the doors and Mel followed him, turning away from the view of the stressed contestants. He was quiet for a moment and she got a bad feeling down deep.

She had met Manny when he was investigating the murder of Baxter Malloy, a man her mother had been dating. Since he had been murdered on their very first date, Joyce had not been dating Baxter for very long. Still, she had been a suspect and Mel and Manny had not hit it off, not until a few months ago when Manny transferred to the Scottsdale PD and became her uncle's partner. Murder had brought them together again, but that time, Manny had saved her life, forever altering their relationship.

Mel glanced at the handsome detective out of the corner of her eye. He was good-looking in a raw-boned, rugged, "not afraid to punch a guy in the face if it was needed" sort of way. Frankly, Mel found it very attractive, which only served to make her feel even more awkward around the man, since she was quite sure that her heart belonged to Joe. She cleared her throat and forced her mind back to the situation at hand.

"So, is this where you break it to me gently that you're arresting my mother or Lupe for the murder of Mariel Mars?" she asked.

Manny met her gaze with a grim one of his own before he said, "Yes."

Thirteen

"What?" Mel snapped. Any attraction she felt for the big Neanderthal vanished, and she stepped closer to him, as if she could intimidate him with her ire. "You can't! They're innocent! Does Uncle Stan know about this? He cannot be going along with this!"

"Um, yeah, I was just kidding," he said. He gave her a sheepish look. "You gave me the perfect set up. Sorry."

"Ugh!" Mel swatted his arm with her hand. "For future reference, normal people do not joke about arresting other people's loved ones."

"Noted," Manny said. He caught her hand in his and held on to her fingers. Mel tried to tug free but he didn't let go.

"Still not available," she said.

He let go of her hand with a sigh. "Are you still hung up on that pesky attorney?"

"Now is that a nice way to talk about a guy behind his back?" a voice asked.

Mel glanced over her shoulder to see a dapper man in a shiny suit join their little group.

"Steve? Steve Wolfmeier," she said. She gave him a quick hug. "How are you?"

"Better now that I'm talking to you," he said. He returned her hug and gave her a smile that rivaled a shark's in whiteness and points.

"Did you call him?" Manny asked in disgust, as if Mel had just confessed to enjoying deep fried sandwiches of peanut butter and bologna.

"No," Mel said. "In fact, I haven't seen him since—"

"You held her in your office to interrogate her about her mother, and I gracefully removed her from the situation," Steve said to Manny.

"Oh, yeah," Manny frowned. "As I remember it, DeLaura was the one who got her out."

"I'm her attorney," Steve said. "Once my client, always my client."

"But you turned down my case," Mel said.

"Details. You're still my client," Steve retorted. "Always."

The two men glared at each other. Well, Manny glared and Steve looked bored, which Mel suspected he was doing just to bug Manny.

"Let me guess," she said. "You two have a history."

"Everyone has a history with 'the weasel,'" Manny said with a glower.

"Now, now, let's not start name-calling just because I freed a man that you wrongly arrested," Steve said. He ran a hand over his slick suit, as if to be sure Manny's barbed words had left no tears in the fabric. "And it's 'the wolf,' get your mammal right."

"That dirtbag was not wrongly arrested, and I didn't lose the case, since I'm not an attorney," Manny said. "But let's be honest, he only got off because you found a legal loophole and *weaseled* him out of the charges."

"Don't hate me because I'm good at my job," Steve said. His silver hair was trimmed perfectly and Mel suspected that he spent five times as much on personal upkeep than she did. As if sensing her scrutiny, Steve turned to her and asked, "So, Melanie, are you still dating DeLaura?"

"Yes, she is," Manny answered for her. "And if she's not dating him, she's dating me. You'll have to take a number."

"Fine by me," Steve said. "Three has always been my lucky number."

"Excuse me. What am I, deli meat?" Mel asked.

She gave them her most severe frown. Steve grinned while Manny continued to glower.

"Sorry, it's just that—" Steve began but was interrupted.

"Steve!" Joyce cried and came running across the room to join them. "How did you know? Did Mel call you? Do you think you can help Lupe?"

"What? Mom, no," Mel said. "He just happens to be here. I didn't call him. Lupe is innocent. We don't need a law—"

It was too late. Joyce had wrapped her hand around Steve's elbow and was dragging him toward Lupe and Angie.

Mel watched them go. When Joyce made up her mind, she was like a force of nature. There was no stopping her.

"I'd better go," Mel said to Manny.

He nodded, then he leaned close and gave her a look that smoldered. "Just remember. I'm your number two."

Mel smiled. The detective certainly had charm. Not

many men would be content to play second-string. It made her wonder.

"How come you're so willing to wait and see what happens between me and Joe?" she said. "A good-looking guy like you could have any girl he wants."

"But I don't want any girl," he said. "I've got my heart set on a sassy cupcake baker."

Mel felt her face get warm. She met his dark gaze and wondered what might have happened between them if she had met him before Joe had come back into her life. Could she have fallen for the handsome detective? With a shake of her head, she decided it was probably better not to think about it.

"Flirt," she accused.

"Only with you," he said.

"Manny!" Stan called from across the lobby. He was chomping on what looked like another antacid pill and waving Martinez over with a hand.

Manny waved to indicate he was on his way. Then he turned to Mel and said, "All bantering aside, did you see anything suspicious this morning when you set up? Anything at all?"

Mel thought about the mad scramble they had been in to get the cupcake tower loaded that morning.

"No, we were running late because Tate was taking the van into downtown Phoenix today to work the lunch crowd, so Angie and I barely had time to unload before we were handing out cupcakes."

"We're going to have to take all of those cupcakes in," he said. "I think it's a given that the body was under the table well before you set up, but who knows, maybe the perp came by later to admire their handiwork and left a fingerprint."

Mel felt her gag reflex kick in. "I'll talk to Angie and see if we can remember who came by this morning."

"Thanks. If you or Angie remember anything that seems weird or unusual, give me a call."

"We will," she said.

He paused, looking as if he wanted to say something else, but instead he just nodded and walked back over to the crime scene. Mel watched him go with mixed emotions. A part of her was curious about what it would be like to date the detective and another part of her felt that until she had things figured out with Joe, she really should not be speculating about anyone else.

She turned and went to join the others as they stood in a group at the far end of the room. Steve glanced over Joyce's head at her and winked.

"Oh, for Pete's sake," Angie whispered. "Don't tell me you've got another one."

"Another what?" Mel asked.

"Admirer," Angie said.

"No," Mel said. "Absolutely not."

"Really?" Angie asked. "Because he's looking at you like you'd make a lovely snack."

"That's just the lawyer in him," Mel said.

"The lawyer in who?" a voice asked from behind them.

Mel and Angie spun around to find Ginny Lobo standing there. She was in her usual skintight outfit—today's was a leopard-print skirt and black hose with a gold blouse. Her blond hair was twisted up onto her head, and per usual, she had her water bottle at the ready.

She wore her usual unperturbed look, and Mel wondered if she even knew what was happening.

"Ginny!" Joyce cried. "What did Cici say? Does she have any idea who might have done this?"

"Done what?" Ginny asked.

"Murdered Mariel Mars," Joyce said.

"What?" Ginny blinked. "I just got here. I had a slow start this morning. Monty had to literally push me out of bed. Huh. So, that's what all of the police are doing here?"

"Yes, Ginny, we are now in the middle of a murder investigation," Joyce said with a dab of exasperation in her voice.

Mel studied her mother's best friend. Ginny was a former beauty queen who had married Monty Lobo, a billionaire who thought Ginny was the prettiest thing he'd ever seen. He indulged her every crazy whim, and Mel knew Ginny had spent a considerable amount of Monty's billions trying to prove she was the illegitimate love child of Elvis Presley and Marilyn Monroe. So far she'd had no luck. Despite all of the crazy, however, Mel suspected that deep down Ginny was one sharp cookie.

"Well, I'll be damned. Does Lupe have an alibi?" Ginny asked.

"Why does everyone keep asking that?" Joyce asked.

"Because she's not a pageant regular, because she threatened Mariel yesterday, and because the cops are going to find out those two things and look at her first," Ginny said.

"But she's innocent," Joyce protested.

"You know that and I know that," Ginny said. "But I can pretty much guarantee you that the other contestants are going to do everything in their power to finger her for the murder, thus removing some competition for themselves."

Mel looked at her mother as if to say *I told you so*, but Joyce was ignoring her.

"Well, none of that matters because we have Steve," Joyce said.

"Steve who?"

"Wolfmeier." Steve stepped forward with his card. Ginny took it and glanced from it to him as if she were carding him for buying booze.

"I've heard of you," she said. "What's your Martindale-Hubbell rating?"

"AV all the way," he said.

Ginny looked somewhat mollified, but before she could say anything else, Brittany and Destiny entered the lobby from the pool patio outside. Destiny was wearing her terrycloth robe tied tightly over her middle, while Brittany was wearing a black-lace coverall over what looked like a micro mini-bikini. Mel refused to look too closely at her, mostly because she suspected that was what Brittany wanted.

Brittany gave Destiny a hearty shove into the center of the lobby. Destiny cast her mother an irritated look, but Brittany crossed her arms over her chest, making it clear that she was expecting something from her daughter. Destiny stood and slowly shook her head. Brittany let out a huff and then strode to the center of the lobby to stand beside Destiny. Brittany let out a dramatic shriek and put her hand to her forehead as if she might faint.

"Ma'am, are you all right?" One of the uniformed security guards went to help her, but she shoved off of him and then pointed at Lupe.

"There! There she is!" Brittany yelled. Her voice was brittle and stiff, as if she were reading the words off a cue card. "She killed poor Mariel! You have to arrest her!"

Fourteen

Joyce, Mel, and Angie reflexively stepped in front of Lupe. Steve frowned at Brittany and her daughter, who stood looking at her mother in disgust.

"Told you she was a pain in the a—" Ginny said but Joyce interrupted.

"So, Steve, will you take the case?" Joyce asked. She shot Ginny a look, but she just shrugged and took a sip off of her water bottle.

Steve glanced at Lupe and then at Brittany. Mel noticed that his lips compressed into a firm line and his gray eyes narrowed. For the first time since she'd met him, he looked serious. In fact, he looked seriously annoyed.

"Absolutely, I'll take the case," he said. He glanced down at Lupe and said, "Don't you worry. I'm not going to let anyone bully you and I'm definitely not going to let them railroad you for a crime you didn't commit."

Angie leaned close to Mel and said, "Okay, I like him."

"Me, too," Mel agreed. When she turned and grinned at Steve, he blinked in surprise.

"Good plan," Ginny said as she moved to stand in between Mel and Angie.

"What's a good plan?"

"Having a pair and a spare," she said. She looked at Angie. "You could learn a thing or two from her."

"What are you talking about?" Mel asked.

Ginny counted on her fingers. "District attorney and homicide detective, the pair you're dating, and now the defense attorney, your spare."

Mel heard Angie snort and felt her face get hot with embarrassment. "I do *not* have a pair and a spare."

"Mel, can I talk to you for a sec?" Steve asked.

Ginny smirked at her.

"Don't even think it," she said.

She stepped away from the group and followed Steve into the corner.

"What is it?" she asked.

"Do you know who that woman and her daughter are?" he asked. His face was set in harsh lines and she could tell he was in full lawyer mode.

"Destiny and Brittany Richards. According to Ginny, a real pageant princess and her stage mother," she said.

"Yeah, no," he said. "They are the wife and daughter of Brandon Richards."

Mel looked at him. Brandon Richards? Was this a name she was supposed to know?

"Scanning, scanning, scanning," she said in a robotic voice. "Sorry, I'm getting nothing."

Steve's lips twitched. "Of course you're not. He's a noted

plastic surgeon. Most of my richy-rich clients have standing appointments with him."

"Ah, not surprising that I haven't heard of him, given that elective surgery—an oxymoron if you ask me—is not really in my budget," Mel said.

"Well, that and the fact that you don't need it," he said.

His voice was so matter-of-fact that Mel smiled. It was definitely one of the better compliments she'd ever gotten.

"Thanks," she began but Steve interrupted.

"Listen," he said. He glanced over his shoulder at their group, all of which were pretending not to watch them. "The reason I'm mentioning this is because Brandon Richards has a lot of connections and power in this town. He can make or break people with just a well-placed phone call."

Mel paused. There was something she had to ask, but she wasn't sure how to say it without sounding ungrateful and a little mean.

"Yes?" he asked.

"Um, why are you offering to represent Lupe when the Richards seem to be the sort you'd normally represent?" she asked. Then she covered her face with her hands and peered at him through her fingers. "Ugh, I tried but that still didn't come out nice, did it?"

Steve smiled at her. This time he was clearly amused.

"It's personal," he said. "Let's leave it at I don't like bullies."

Mel let out a pent-up breath. She knew Steve was one of the best defense attorneys in the valley. She was relieved he was willing to help them even if he wouldn't share the full whys with her.

"I can respect that," she said. "Thanks."

"No problem, but now I have to warn you. If the Richards go after Lupe in some misguided attempt to get her bounced from the pageant, they will throw everything they have at her."

Mel glanced over to where the teen stood with Joyce. They were covertly watching Mel and Steve, and she could tell they were wondering what he was saying. She forced a reassuring smile. Instead of looking relieved, her mother looked even more concerned and Mel knew that her mother knew her too well to be fooled.

"Do you think you can beat them?" she asked Steve.

The grin he gave her was pure predator and Mel realized that he loved this. With his client's back against the wall, Steve would have to be very, very good to get Lupe off and he relished the challenge.

"Oh, yeah," he said. "This is going to be fun."

"We have very different ideas of what constitutes fun," Mel said.

Steve met her gaze and his grin deepened. "Oh, I don't know. I think there might be some common ground between us."

His words were as innuendo-laden as a direct proposition. Mel gave him her best quelling look. She was not going to become what Ginny described as "a girl with a pair and a spare." The idea was too mortifying for words.

"No, just no," she said. He grinned and she realized that issuing a challenge was the worst way to handle him. She'd do better to get down on one knee and propose. Then, she was quite certain, the guy would leave skid marks.

"No," she said again. Mel turned away from him and crossed back over to her mother and the rest of their group.

"Steve will represent Lupe, right?" her mother asked.

"If she needs it, yes," Mel said. "I'm really hoping she doesn't."

"Me, too," Joyce said. "I'm going to check with Stan and if he says it's okay, I'm going to get her out of here. I'm not sure if there's even going to be a pageant now."

"Oh, there'll be a pageant," Ginny said. "There's too much money with sponsors and prizes for them to cancel it."

Mel glanced over toward the crime scene. Mariel Mars was dead. Like her or not, it seemed wrong that the pageant would just carry on as if her role as a judge was insignificant and her life replaceable.

Fifteen

"Mel, I had the most amazing epiphany in the van today!" Tate said as he pushed through her office door and stepped into her inner sanctum.

Mel glanced up from the computer on her desk. She was trying to combine a triple word and triple letter tile in Words with Friends to beat her friend Erika Ona Sanborn, a Canadian cupcake baker who was also an elementary school teacher, bless her heart. Erika had dusted her in their last match and Mel was looking to even the score.

"Can you make a word out of three L's, two P's, a Z, and a Q?" she asked.

"Qlzlplp?" he offered.

Mel growled and slammed the lid on her laptop.

"Back to me now?" Tate asked.

"Yes, you had an epiphany," Mel said just to prove she had sort of been listening.

"So, I was parked down by Patriots Square Park in Phoenix and what did I notice but tons of delivery trucks," he said. "And it hit me—all of those trucks are delivering packages."

"Hence the name *delivery truck*," Mel said.

He ignored her and took the seat across from her. He looked positively giddy, which was Mel's first clue that she probably wouldn't like what was coming.

"Just think," he said. "What if all those trucks were delivering our cupcakes? Come on, say it with me, *Cha-ching*."

"Did you hit your head on the service window in the van?" Mel asked.

"No, why?"

"Tate, I appreciate your enthusiasm, but cupcakes are an extremely perishable food item, not to mention they get mushed pretty easily," she said. "Even if there were enough people who wanted us to send cupcakes for them, it would be prohibitively expensive. We'd be better served opening a franchise in downtown Phoenix."

"Hey, now you're talking," he said.

"No."

"I could study up on franchises and do a cost analysis."

"No."

"Aw, come on, Mel, you're killing me," he said.

Tate looked so crestfallen that Mel felt herself weaken. Darn it.

"If I say yes to you writing up a business proposal, will you go away?" she asked.

"I will be nothing but a memory," he promised.

"'Memories are meant to fade. They're designed that way for a reason,'" Mel said.

"Ha!" Tate grinned at her. "From the movie *Strange Days*."

"Correct," Mel said returning his grin. "Now go away."

Tate raised his hands in surrender and backed out of her office and into the kitchen.

Mel knew that taking the bakery to the next level had become Tate's personal mission. The trouble with that was if they expanded she feared their product—*Ack!* That was the problem right there. When she started thinking of her cupcakes as product instead of yummies from her own kitchen, well, she was going corporate and she really didn't want to venture down that path.

She rose from her desk and went into the kitchen. The telltale whoosh of the kitchen door clued her in that Tate had gone into the front part of the bakery.

Mel thought about going out front to see what was happening, but she knew she had to finish up tomorrow's cupcakes for the pageant. Ginny had been right. They didn't cancel the pageant or postpone it; they just rolled it back one day. Tomorrow they would finish the swimsuit contest and the girls would submit their cupcake recipes, the day after that would be the talent show and finally the last day would be cupcake tasting and evening gowns and the winner would be crowned. It made Mel tired just to think about it.

She went to the walk-in cooler and pulled out a large tray of butter-flavored cupcakes. She planned to decorate them with vanilla buttercream and then put on the finishing touch. She used her standing mixer to whip up a fresh batch of buttercream. Using a pastry bag with an open tip, she piped a fat dollop of frosting onto the cupcake.

The door swung open and she was about to give Tate a

hairy eyeball for interrupting her again. Instead it was Angie who joined her.

"The bakery is closed for the night. The boys have all been booted," she said. "I figured you could use some help prepping the goods for tomorrow's cupcake tower."

"Thanks," Mel said. She gestured to the other side of the table and said, "Grab a seat."

"What are we making?" Angie asked.

Mel put down her pastry bag and opened one of her tubs of yellow and orange fondant butterflies.

"I cut out and molded the fondant butterflies last night," Mel said. "We just need to brush them with luster dust to make them sparkly and plant them in the vanilla buttercream."

Mel opened one of the three containers of luster dust and, using a paintbrush, she swept an edible coating of glitter onto a butterfly's wings.

"Oh, wow, these are too pretty to eat," Angie said as she examined the tub of butterflies.

Mel gave her a look and Angie laughed. "Okay, yeah, I could totally bite the wings off of these buggers."

Mel laughed. "I wish we could bite the wings off of Tate."

Angie frowned. "What do you mean?"

"He's just so into taking the business to the next level," Mel said. "He's driving me bananas."

"He's just an overachiever," Angie said. "Since he left the world of high finance, he's struggling to find a place to put his financial prowess."

"Well, he needs to find something other than *my* bakery," Mel said.

"It's not *your* bakery," Angie corrected her.

Mel frowned. She did not appreciate the tone Angie was taking with her.

"Well, excuse me," Mel said.

"No, I won't," Angie said.

There was a fire in Angie's eyes, which should have warned Mel off. But she'd had a rough day, too, and wasn't really in the mood for attitude, even from her best friend.

"It belongs to all of us and frankly your fear of commitment is holding us back," Angie said.

"Hey, what happened to liking our operation as it is and 'Tate needs a kick in the pants'?" Mel asked.

Angie blew out a breath. "Tate and I have been talking, and I've reconsidered. Also, I think my words might have come out more harshly than I intended."

"You think? How can you say *I* have a fear of commitment?" Mel asked. She slammed her little paintbrush with the luster dust on it onto the steel table. "That's rich, coming from you."

"What's that supposed to mean?" Angie asked.

"You gave up a career in teaching to work in a bakery," Mel said.

"I wanted to help you," Angie said.

"Oh, please," Mel shook her head. "You were just avoiding a commitment to a career. Just like pining after Tate keeps you from having a real relationship."

"What?" Angie snapped.

"You heard me," Mel retorted. "Look at you, you dumped a rock star who was in love with you for a childhood friend who is still holding you at arm's length. And you say I have a fear of commitment? Look in the mirror, sweetie."

Mel knew she had gone too far when Angie's face turned

a mottled shade of red and she started breathing through her nose like a bull about to charge.

"I don't have to," Angie growled. "I'm looking at the poster child for commitment phobia and low self-esteem right now. You're terrified of making a commitment because you don't believe in your own self-worth and you're afraid you might get hurt. That's why you broke up with my brother and broke his heart, because you're a big chicken."

"That is not—You are so off base—So you *are* mad at me!" Mel shouted. "I knew it!"

"Of course I'm mad at you!" Angie shouted in return. "Joe is my brother and you're my best friend. Did you even stop to think about how your breakup would tear me up? No!"

"You got one part of that sentence right. It was my breakup, not yours! It has nothing to do with you!"

"It has everything to do with me! You're two of the people I love the most!"

"It's still none of your business. Just like when you and Tate were doing your ridiculous little dance around each other, it was none of my business and I butted out. Do you think that was easy for me?"

"Oh, yeah, you butted out," Angie scoffed. "You told him he'd had everything handed to him all of his life and that he didn't know how to go after what he wanted. So he up and quit his investment job, you know, where he was making oodles of money, so he could come and work here. If it's anyone's fault that he's keeping me at arm's length, it's yours! Well played, Mel."

"How was I supposed to know the numb-nut was going to quit his job?" Mel asked. "You can't blame me because he's an idiot."

They stared at each other over the steel worktable. Both were red-faced and breathing heavy.

"This is ridiculous! I don't know how talking about the business turned into a fight over our personal lives," Angie said. She looked as if she was visibly trying to calm herself with deep breathing exercises. Mel wasn't there yet.

"It's your fault," Mel said, still peeved. "You brought commitment issues and low self-esteem into it."

"Well, it was overdue," Angie snapped. Obviously, the breathing hadn't worked. "You're *not* the fat girl anymore. You're a beautiful, brilliant small businesswoman and shoving away the guy you love to flirt with someone else just because you're a scaredy-cat is just stupid."

"Oh, so now I'm stupid?" Mel asked.

Angie growled. "Fine, don't listen to the important stuff I'm saying, just hear the insults you're looking for."

"Hard not to hear them when you're shouting them at me, Miss Temper Tantrum," Mel snapped.

"Fine! I'll stop talking to you altogether," Angie snapped. "In fact, I'll just go work in the other room."

"Good!" Mel said as Angie packed up a tray full of butterflies and luster dust.

"Great!" Angie agreed.

"Fantastic!"

"Terrific!"

Angie banged through the swinging kitchen door to the front of the bakery. Mel watched until the door swung to a stop.

"Damn," she said.

Sixteen

"Am I interrupting something?" a voice asked from the back door.

Mel turned around and there was Joe. Her shoulders, which had ratcheted up around her ears while tiffing with Angie, sank back down.

"Can I have a hug?" she asked.

Joe opened his arms and Mel scooted across the kitchen, and into his embrace.

"Uncle Stan called me at the office," he said. His hand ran up and down her back. "You okay?"

"Yes," she said. She stepped back and studied him. "Angie is the one who found the body. She could probably use a hug, too."

Joe glanced around the kitchen. "Where is she?"

"She's in the front of the bakery," Mel said. She glanced

down at her hands, which were clenched together. "We're fighting."

Joe nodded. As the middle brother of Angie's seven older brothers, he was the one who negotiated the peace treaties within the family. Mel was pretty sure that was how he'd ended up going into law. With six hotheaded Italian brothers, Joe's skills at hammering out a compromise were unparalleled.

He threw an arm around her shoulders and led her toward the door. "Come on. Let's go work this out."

In the front of the bakery, Angie had taken over a booth. She was brushing luster dust onto fondant butterflies and muttering under her breath. Her legendary temper looked ready to erupt.

"Maybe I'll just let you talk to her on your own," Mel said and began to back out of the doorway.

Joe glanced from Mel to Angie and back. "That might be best."

Mel slipped behind Joe and back through the door as he strode forward. Mel heard him say, "Ange! How's my favorite baby sister?"

"I'm your only baby sis—" Angie's voice was cut off as the door closed.

Mel hoped that Joe could work his magic. She really hated fighting with Angie. She opened up another tub of butterflies and picked out an orange one. She brushed it with the pearly dust and the butterfly's wings sparkled and shimmered. Well, at least something in her life was going right.

The back door opened and in walked Tate and Oz. Mel frowned at them.

"I thought everyone went home for the night," she said.

"I did," Tate said. "But I hate my apartment."

He was renting a duplex in the old section of Scottsdale. It was small and cramped and the other half of the duplex was currently being rented by a young couple who made a lot of noise, mostly because they seemed to spend their time together either really, really happy or fighting.

"I did, too, but my family is driving me crazy," Oz said. "My cousins are visiting from Hermosillo and I have to share my room with two of them. Can I sleep here?"

"No."

"Why not?" Oz persisted. "I'll just sleep in the cupcake truck if you won't let me crash in a booth."

"I've got dibs on the cupcake truck," Tate argued.

"No one is sleeping in the truck," Mel said. "Tate was only allowed to do that because he refused to crash with any of us when he gave up his luxury penthouse apartment."

She gave him a dark look, which he returned in full.

"Why did you give it up, T?" Oz asked. "We both could have slept there tonight."

"I gave it up so I could prove to myself that I could make it on my own," Tate said.

Mel and Oz both looked at him as if he were deranged.

"Honestly, I didn't think it was going to take this long," he said. "Of course, it wouldn't be so hard if I could just get some support for my expansion ideas."

"You have support," Mel said. "I just don't want to change the bakery. I like it exactly the way it is. I don't want to go corporate or figure out how to franchise."

Oz looked from one to the other. "So, he wants to expand and you don't."

"Basically," Mel said.

"So, you don't," Oz said to Mel and then he turned to Tate and said, "And you do."

"Yes, Oz, that is the drift," Tate said. He sounded annoyed.

They both frowned at the teen. With his black fringe hanging over his face, Mel couldn't tell if he was mocking them or not.

"T-man, what's our customer base made up of?" Oz asked.

"Sixty percent walk-in tourists, forty percent locals," Tate said. "Although, near holidays our local traffic is much higher."

"What's the one thing our customers always ask?"

"Do we have any other locations," Tate said without hesitation.

"Correct," Oz said. "What is your standard answer, Mel?"

"No, because opening a second location is complicated," she said. "And quality would suffer."

"But it's not and it won't," Tate protested. "I've been doing research and there are several cupcake bakeries that are opening franchises for their product."

"Stop calling it 'product,'" Mel said. Tate rolled his eyes.

"Listen, I know you think you birthed each and every cupcake," Tate said. "But they are 'product' and you're in 'business' and you need to stop acting so artsy-fartsy about the whole thing."

"Ah!" Mel gasped. She turned to Oz and he nodded.

"Sorry, boss," Oz said. "As a student of the culinary arts myself, I totally get how you feel, but T-man is right. It's a business."

"Well, I—" Mel stammered. "I'm not ready to—"

The kitchen door swung open and Joe and Angie walked into the room. Joe was carrying Angie's tray and she looked distinctly less pissed than she had a few minutes ago.

"What's going on?" Angie asked, glancing at the three

of them as if she thought they'd decided to hold a meeting and had not invited her.

"Why don't we call Marty?" Mel asked. "Surely, he'll want to weigh in on this decision."

"Texting him now," Oz said. Sure enough, his thumbs were flying across the front of his phone.

"Marty texts?" Tate asked.

"Olivia's been getting him up to speed," Oz said. "I think they text each other some pretty kinky stuff."

Everyone blanched.

"Really?" Tate asked. "You had to share that?"

Oz raised his hands, including the one still holding the phone, in a sign of surrender. "Why should I suffer alone?"

"Point taken," Mel said. "Why do you think it's suggestive stuff?"

"Because his head lights up like a stop light," Oz laughed. "The other day I was afraid he was going to stroke out on me."

"See?" Angie cried. "This is why we need an intervention."

"You can't break them up," Joe protested. "The heart wants what the heart wants. No intervention is going to stop it."

"Agreed," Mel said. She and Joe met each other's eyes and he smiled.

"Oh, good grief," Angie muttered. "Are they having a moment?"

"I think so," Tate said. Then he grinned at her. "Here, let's try it." He took her hand in his and gazed at her and said, "The heart wants what the heart wants."

Mel glanced over at them to see Angie look all melty at Tate.

"Did I look at you like that?" she asked Joe.

"Yes," he said. Then he grinned.

Oz started texting furiously into his phone.

"Are you texting this to Marty?" Tate asked.

"No, I'm putting it in my notepad for future reference," Oz said. "A guy can use all the chick advice he can get when he's just starting out."

His phone beeped and he checked the screen. "Incoming from Marty. It says, 'Why are you bugging me? You people need lives. Tell Tate to get off his keister and make it happen and for Mel to butt out of his business plan and it'll work just fine.'"

"Wow, it's like he's right here with us," Angie said.

"Classic Marty," Mel agreed.

"So, do we have a deal?" Tate asked.

"My reputation is to be scrupulously maintained," Mel said. "If you do this franchise thingy the name of Fairy Tale Cupcakes must never be sullied by dry cupcakes, sloppy cupcakes, or, heaven forbid"—she paused to clutch her chest and take a steadying breath—"a bad frosting-to-cake ratio."

Tate put his hand over his heart. "I promise. It is going to be epic."

Angie clapped her hands in front of her and stood up on her toes. "So, it's a go?"

Mel held out her hand to Tate and he grabbed it, shook it hard twice, and then pulled her in for a hug. Mel squeezed him back and then opened her arms for Angie, Oz, and then Joe to join in.

Oz texted furiously from the huddle before he squeezed everyone back. When they broke apart and stepped back, Oz glanced at his phone and burst out laughing.

"What?" Mel asked.

"I told Marty we were having a group hug and he said he's glad he isn't here because he would have vomited."

Mel started laughing, and then she looked at Angie. "So we ambush him tomorrow?"

"And hug the stuffing out of him? Hell, yeah!" They high-fived each other and then Angie pulled her aside and said, "Sorry about before. Joe talked some sense into me and I was going to apologize even before you agreed to let Tate try his new idea. I want you to know that."

"I'm sorry, too," Mel said. "I know I'm working through some stuff. And I know it hasn't been easy for you, but I'm trying to figure it out. I really am. And maybe this expansion plan will work out for us."

Angie gazed at Tate with her heart in her eyes, "I hope so."

"Let's celebrate," Tate said. "Cupcakes all around!"

He and Angie headed to the walk-in cooler while Mel, Joe, and Oz took seats at the table.

"Now that the business is all settled," Oz said. "I was hoping to talk to you about Lupe."

"What about her?" Mel asked.

"Um, well, that is to say—" Oz glanced through his fringe at Joe.

"Earmuffs?" Mel asked.

Oz nodded.

Mel looked at Joe. "Earmuffs, Joe."

"What?" he asked.

Mel demonstrated putting her hands over her ears.

"Seriously?" he asked.

Mel nodded and Oz seconded the motion. "You're the assistant district attorney. It's just for a sec."

"Fine," Joe said. He clapped his hands over his ears and started to hum.

Mel leaned closer to Oz. "What is it?"

"I was just wondering how things will go for Lupe with this investigation if she has a record."

Seventeen

Mel stared at him with her mouth hanging open as she tried to process his words. She shook her head. She must have heard him wrong.

"What are you saying, Oz?" she asked.

"I'm just wondering, that's all," he said.

"Does she have a record? A criminal record?" Mel asked. "Isn't that against the pageant rules and regs?"

"She was only eleven," Oz said. "She got caught shoplifting a Snickers."

"Did she go to court?" Joe asked.

Mel glanced at him and he lowered his hands with a shrug. "Hands are not soundproof earmuffs."

"No, no court date." Oz shook his head. "But the cops came to her house and I think they filled out a report. They said they were going to put it in her file."

"You mean like her 'permanent record'?" Mel asked. "That's the oldest scare tactic in the world."

"Yeah, well, she's freaked out that if Stan and Manny dig into her background, they'll see that she got picked up for shoplifting and they'll be convinced she murdered Mariel Mars," Oz said.

Tate and Angie returned to the table bearing a tray full of cupcakes. Mel wondered how many she could shove into her mouth at once. She was beginning to think there was not enough buttercream in the world to make her feel better about this day.

"It's a pretty big leap from shoplifting a Snickers to homicide," Joe said. "I think Mel is right and the cops who picked her up when she was a kid were just trying to scare her by telling her it was going on her record."

"She returned the candy bar and apologized," Oz said.

"Who are we talking about?" Angie asked.

"Lupe," Mel said.

As Oz explained his concerns to Tate and Angie, Joe leaned close to Mel and said, "So Stan *and* Martinez are on the homicide investigation?"

She noted that he did not call Manny by his first name. "Yes, they are," she said.

"Well, I wouldn't worry about it," Tate said. "From what Angie told me, that Steve Wolfmeier guy seems like he knows what he's doing."

Mel felt Joe stiffen beside her. "Wolfmeier?"

She blew out a breath. "He just happened to be at the resort when the body was found and Mom saw him and asked him to represent Lupe should the need arise."

"I thought your mother liked *me*?" Joe asked.

"She does, she adores you," Mel assured him. "She doesn't know that you and Steve have a history."

"You do?" Oz asked.

The look Joe gave him made Oz halt his line of questioning and shove a Cherry Bomb Cupcake into his mouth.

"It's no big deal," Joe said. "We went to law school together."

"No big deal?" Angie asked. "You hate him! You called him a plea-peddling, ambulance-chasing, justice-joyriding judgment jockey."

Joe ignored his sister and examined the cupcakes on the tray as if looking for the perfect one.

"Wow, I don't think I can even wrap my tongue around that many syllables," Tate said.

"Yup, that's hatin' words," Oz said.

"We've had some issues," Joe said. He chose a Carrot Cupcake with cream cheese frosting. "So, is he going to be around, too?"

"I doubt it," Mel said. "Unless Lupe gets arrested for the murder of Mariel Mars."

"She's not!" Oz protested. "She didn't!"

"Easy, big guy, no one is accusing your girlfriend of murder," Tate said.

"She's *not* my girlfriend," Oz protested. "We're just friends."

"That can change," Tate said. He and Angie exchanged a look that was so steamy it made everyone else look away.

Angie glanced at the clock on the wall and then yawned. A yawn that looked suspiciously forced to Mel.

"Look at the time. I'd better go," Angie said.

"Uh, yeah, me, too," Tate agreed. He crammed the last

of his cupcake into his mouth and followed Angie out the back door.

"Something I said?" Oz asked. He scratched his head while he stared at the door.

Mel and Joe shared a grin.

"No, I think it's safe to say it had nothing to do with you," Mel said.

Oz turned back around and faced Mel. "Are you still going to be doing a cupcake tower at the pageant tomorrow?"

"Apparently," she said. "Cici called earlier and confirmed what Ginny said about the pageant going forward."

"I want to work it," Oz said.

Mel considered him. She was trying to picture how the hulking goth figure of Oz would fit into the beauty pageant.

"Hair has to be out of the eyes," Mel said. "I don't care if you use a sparkly flower hair clip, people will need to see your peepers."

"Okay," Oz said. He tossed his hair as if reassuring himself that it would be okay to pull it back.

"And no spiked leather jewelry," Mel said.

Oz heaved a put-upon sigh.

"What about the nose stud and the lip rings?" Joe asked. His eyes twinkled and Mel knew he was teasing, but he made a good point. "Probably, he should lose those, too."

"Ah! Why don't you just make me go naked?" Oz asked.

Mel and Joe burst out laughing and Oz pushed aside his black bangs to glare at them.

"Really funny," he said. "Hilarious, in fact."

"Sorry, Oz, I couldn't resist," Joe said. He clapped Oz on the shoulder and the teen looked somewhat mollified.

"You can come with me to the pageant," Mel said.

"Angie can stay here and listen to Tate's plans for franchising the business."

Mel tried to keep the disdain out of her voice, but judging by the raised-eyebrow looks she got from both Joe and Oz, her delivery needed some work.

"Cool," Oz said. "I'm going to bounce, then."

He and Joe banged knuckles. He was about to do the same with Mel, but she pushed his hand away and gave him a solid hug instead. She figured he needed one.

"Don't worry about Lupe," she said. She kept her hands on his shoulders and stepped back to glance through his fringe and meet his gaze. "She's one of ours and we'll make sure she's protected."

"Thanks, Mel," Oz said.

She felt the tension in his shoulders release and she knew she'd been right to hug him. She handed him another cupcake and shooed him out the door.

As the door shut behind him, Joe turned to Mel and asked, "Why did you lie to him?"

Eighteen

"I didn't lie," Mel protested.

"Oh, please," Joe said. "I've watched you tell your mother that you've taken your vitamins, when I know for a fact you don't even own any, and you always get that little crinkle at the top of your nose. It's a tell."

Mel rubbed the skin at the top of her nose between her eyes. She had a tell? She'd had no idea.

"That's not lying, that's fibbing to give her reassurance, so at best I was fibbing to Oz," she said.

"Fine, so why were you fibbing?" he asked.

"I wasn't," she said. "Not completely. I do think of Lupe as one of ours and we will protect her."

Mel rose from her seat and started putting away the cupcakes and fondant, while Joe began shutting down the bakery. She was dead-dog tired and even though she wasn't a morning person, she'd just have to get up early to finish the butterflies.

"What if she did it?" Joe asked.

"She didn't do it," Mel said.

"How do you know?" he asked. He was clearing up the mess left behind by the others, and Mel remembered that back when they were engaged it had always been like this. Joe's off-the-chart sweet tooth usually found him in the bakery at the end of the day helping her close. She realized she liked having him here and had really missed this.

"What?" he asked.

"Huh?"

"You're staring at me," he said. He put the dishes in the sink. "What are you thinking?"

Mel felt her face get warm. She really didn't want to tell him that she'd been missing them. It would give him an opening to zing her about calling off their engagement. Then again, she had never lied to him and she didn't want to start now, even to save face.

"I miss us," she said.

Joe hit her with his bone-wilter of a grin. It was charming and seductive and she felt its impact all the way down to her toes.

"Then marry me," he said.

She shook her head.

"I'm just going to keep asking," he said.

"I know," she said. "I'm sorry I can't give you the answer you want."

"It's okay," he said. His warm brown eyes looked hurt but then he shook his head and said, "It has to be the answer you want to give. I know you're working through some stuff. I'll wait."

Mel felt her throat get tight. She could not love Joe DeLaura any more than she did at this moment. She wondered if she should just say yes, but then, the what-ifs swamped her and she couldn't bear it. She knew it was stupid to think that keeping their relationship less than it could be would make losing him any easier, but the thought of throwing herself into marriage, a lifetime commitment, made her positively queasy.

"Come on," he said. "I'll walk you up."

He took her hand in his and led her out the back door, which she paused to lock, and up to her apartment. He waited while she opened the door. Captain Jack, the cat they had co-parented since Mel found him abandoned in a Dumpster, leapt at Joe as if he were his long-lost love.

"Somebody has missed his kitty daddy," Mel said.

Joe scooped up Captain Jack and held him so they were face-to-face, then they both leaned forward and butted heads. Mel looked at her two boys and felt her insides get squishy all over again.

"Do you want to come in?" she offered.

Joe snuggled with Captain Jack for a moment before he handed him over. "It's late. I'd better not."

"Oh, okay," she said.

Joe kissed her on the forehead. "Sleep well."

"You, too," she said. Mel watched him walk down the stairs. He waved at the bottom and she returned it, feeling a bit forlorn.

As Joe turned the corner around the building, she wondered if he was going to be able to wait as long as it took for her to get her head together. She couldn't really blame him if he didn't.

"I'm messed up, aren't I?" she asked Captain Jack as she went into her apartment and locked the door.

He gave a long and pitiful meow and then pressed his head under her chin as if he understood. It made her feel slightly better. Maybe her brother was right. Maybe it wasn't just her soul-deep grief over her father's death that made her think she couldn't handle losing Joe after a lifetime together.

Maybe it was all of the freaking dead bodies that kept cropping up in her life. Honestly, how often was a girl supposed to stare death in the face, literally, before she started thinking that everyone she loved could die at any moment? It just wasn't normal.

The cupcake tower was located in a different part of the lobby and there was no cloth draping the table. Mel wondered if the hotel staff were afraid another body might get stuffed under it and were avoiding the possibility by leaving it bare. She couldn't blame them.

The white cupcakes covered in shimmering butterflies were a huge hit and even though she'd had to get up well before the sun, the effort was worth it.

"Now that's perfect," Cici Hastings said as she approached the table. "That will drive away thoughts of murder."

"You think?" Mel asked.

"Definitely," Ginny said as she joined them. "Hey there, handsome."

Mel looked over her shoulder at Oz, who was arranging the last of the cupcakes. He was looking pretty spiffy with his hair slicked back and his piercings toned down. He'd even removed the big silver skull rings he usually wore on his middle fingers.

Oz looked at Ginny in horror and Mel could tell he desperately wanted to shake loose his slicked-back hair and hide under his black fringe. She gave him a small shake of her head and he sighed.

Mel glanced around the lobby. Despite what Cici and Ginny said, there was a somber air that seemed to pervade the place and no amount of cute-shaped fondant was going to get rid of it.

"It is unfortunate about Mariel, but I'm sure the police will figure out who did it. If you think about it, this is actually a marvelous test for our contestants to see how they handle pressure." Cici patted her curls into place and tugged on the lapels of her bright pink jacket.

Mel stared at her. She thought Cici might be joking, but no. The woman was as serious as a heart attack.

"I guess you could look at it that way," Mel said. "You know, if you were completely coldhearted and compartmentalized about it."

"Exactly," Cici said. "Some of the things Miss Sweet Tiara will have to do, like visiting the poor, the sick, the elderly, well, it can be pretty brutal and she will have to smile through it all."

Mel nodded. Cici's heartlessness made a little more sense now.

"I used to cry," Ginny said.

Cici and Mel both turned to look at her. Cici looked disapproving.

"Oh, not in front of them," Ginny said. "But sometimes it was just hard, you know? I remember I was visiting a daycare center on the west side and I was reading to the children. The place was small and dirty, the playground was rusty and had razor wire running along the top of the chain-link fence. I felt like I was visiting a prison, but there I was in my poufy pink dress and tiara. When it was time to go, a little girl, no more than two, with the biggest blue eyes I've ever seen, hugged me and wouldn't let go."

Mel saw the faraway look in Ginny's eyes and knew she was reliving the memory.

"She kept crying and saying, 'You no leave me,'" Ginny said. "It was so sad. Finally, the day-care worker had to pry her off of me. I sat in the car and cried for an hour."

Cici reached out and patted Ginny's arm, which seemed to snap her out of her trance.

"Just think, for a brief shining moment, you gave that little girl a glimpse into a world bigger than the one she lived in," Cici said.

Mel would have pointed out that Ginny also left the girl in the midst of horrific poverty, teaching her at a very young age that some people just lived better lives than others, but she didn't want to be mean.

"Now, we're finishing up the bathing suit competition today," Cici said. "Also, the contestants will be submitting their recipes to you—"

"We most certainly will not!"

Mel turned to see Brittany Richards approaching with Destiny in tow. Brittany was once again wearing a see-through cover-up—a fashion oxymoron—over a string bikini. Today, the cover-up was white while the bikini beneath was neon green, which matched her stiletto sandals. Destiny trailed behind her, looking miserable, in a pink robe that covered her from knee to neck. Both of them wore an excessive amount of makeup and had the really big hair thing going.

Jenn McKinlay

"Excuse me?" Cici raised her finely plucked eyebrows.

"This person," Brittany said as she pointed a boney finger at Mel, "is supporting that Loopy girl."

"Lupe," Oz growled. "Her name in Guadalupe Guzman."

Brittany glared at him. "I'm sorry, did it look like I was talking to you?" Oz opened his mouth to answer but Brittany cut him off. "Because I was not."

"Rude!" Ginny snapped.

Brittany glared at her. "Drunk!"

Ginny gasped and looked like she was going to take a swing at Brittany. Mel snatched a cupcake off of the table and shoved it under Ginny's nose.

"See how the wings sparkle?" she asked.

"Oh, shiny," Ginny said.

If there was one thing Mel liked about her mother's best friend, it was her ability to be distracted like a toddler by anything that sparkled.

"Why don't you go find Mom?" Mel suggested and she gave Ginny a gentle push in the opposite direction.

As Ginny toodled off, Brittany made a derisive snort. "If that one wasn't as rich as a small oil-loaded nation, she'd be utterly worthless."

Mel clenched her teeth. Ginny might be a little drunk and a little crazy but she was also the person who had kept Joyce from collapsing completely into her grief when her husband, Mel's father, had died. For that, Mel would forever be indebted to Ginny, and she certainly wasn't going to stand here and listen to some rotten cow belittle her.

"At least she knows what it's like to wear a tiara," Mel said. The acid in her voice could have left burn marks. "You don't, do you?"

Oz let out a low whistle like a grenade being deployed, and then he made a blowing-up noise. If looks could do that, Mel was sure Brittany's glare would have left her picking shrapnel out of her eyebrows.

Nineteen

"You will not be baking my daughter's cupcakes!" Brittany hissed, and Mel knew her words had been a direct hit.

She tried not to smile. A glance over Brittany's shoulder and she saw Destiny looking as if she wished the floor would open up and swallow her whole. As much as Mel disliked Brittany, she would never do anything to sabotage Destiny's chance of winning.

"You're being ridiculous," Cici said. "Mel is a professional."

"Ha!" Brittany scoffed. "Either hire someone else or I'll file a complaint that might go as far as a lawsuit."

"Confections might be a good option," Oz said. He looked at Cici and explained, "The owner hates Mel."

Mel gave him an outraged look. He was sending work Olivia's way?

"Excellent!" Brittany said. "We'll take her as our baker."

"Fine," Cici snapped. "Anka Holland has taken over the position of lead judge in Mariel's place. I will apprise her of the situation. If this Confections person agrees, we'll divide the competitors amongst the two of you and make sure the recipes are anonymous, assuring that there is no advantage given."

"That will do," Brittany said. Without another word, she turned on her heel and strode away. Destiny followed her mother like a submissive shadow. Mel had never been more grateful for her own mother than she was at that moment.

"You know, it's actually a good idea," Mel said.

Honestly, she was relieved, mostly because now she wouldn't have to bake a million lousy-tasting cupcakes. She could only imagine what a teen girl would put in a cupcake. Artificial sweetener? Bleck. Mountain Dew? Gross. Pixy Stix? Gag. The possibilities were endlessly horrifying.

"Who is Anka Holland?" Oz asked.

"Second runner-up to Mariel Mars her entire pageant career," Cici said. "I was lucky that she happened to be in town and available to take Mariel's place."

"She just happened to be in town?" Mel asked.

"Well, she was hoping to be involved in the Miss Sweet Tiara seventy-fifth anniversary event, but as a runner-up, we really didn't need her until—well, until now," Cici said. "She lives in Los Angeles, but was in Scottsdale to attend the Barrett Jackson car auction with her husband and do some charity work for underprivileged children."

Oz and Mel exchanged a look and Mel knew he was thinking the same thing she was—that it was awfully convenient for this Anka person to be here just when they needed her most. It felt almost as if it had been planned.

Mel wanted to ask Cici about it, but she was unclear as

to how to go about that without it sounding as if she were accusing Anka the runner-up of being a murderess.

"Well, I'd better go contact this Confections person," Cici said. She glanced sourly after Brittany and Destiny. "Are you sure she'll be willing to do it?"

"Oh, mention my name and you can bet your sparkly tiara on it," Mel said.

"Huh." Cici gave an unladylike snort before she strode off in the direction of the pageant headquarters.

"Why do I get the feeling Cici isn't telling us everything?" Mel asked Oz.

"'That's why her hair is so big, it's full of secrets,'" he replied.

Mel glanced at him and frowned. "Oh, I know it, don't help me."

Oz watched her as Mel tried to pull the movie he had just quoted from her memory banks. Mel pressed her fingertips to her temples and concentrated. She could see it, but it was just out of reach.

"What's wrong with her?" a male voice asked Oz. "She looks like she's trying to blow things up with her mind."

"Movie quote," Oz muttered out of the corner of his mouth. "I think I've stumped her. A first."

"Shhh," Mel hushed them. "I almost have it."

"What was it?" the male voice whispered, and Mel realized it was Manny, which made her even more flustered, although she told herself that was ridiculous.

Oz repeated his big hair with secrets line.

"Oh, that's easy," Manny said. Mel held up her hand to stop him but it was too late. "*Mean Girls.*"

Mel opened her eyes and glared at them. "I knew that!"

Manny and Oz were watching her with matching doleful expressions.

"Sure you did," Manny said. He winked at her and Mel felt her cheeks grow warm.

How did he do that? The man had magnetism coming out his ears, but she would not succumb to it. She was barely managing her whatever with Joe. She was not going to add the handsome detective into the mix.

A group of pageant attendees approached the cupcake tower and Oz nodded at Mel, letting her know he was on it.

"I did too know it," Mel said as they moved aside, giving Oz more room to work.

"Uh-huh," he said.

"So, what's going on with the investigation?" she asked. "Any leads?"

"None that you want to hear about," he said.

Mel stiffened. She heard the cautionary tone of his voice and she knew that it meant Lupe was far from being off the suspect list.

"She didn't do it," Mel said.

"Who?" Manny returned. His dark eyes were watching her intently.

"Oh, don't go all detective on me," she chided him. "You know who I'm talking about."

"Mel, she had motive and opportunity," he said. "You may not like it, but there it is."

"She's not the only one," Mel said. "What about this new judge, Anka Holland? Awfully convenient that she just happens to be in town and ready to fill in when her lifetime rival Mariel is murdered, don't you think?"

Mel didn't realize that she had her hands on her hips and

was walking forward, forcing Manny to put it in reverse until they'd crossed the room and she had him trapped against the wall.

"You're gorgeous when you're mad, you know that, right?" he asked. Now his gaze positively crackled with heat and Mel stepped back as if she might get hit by an errant blast of electricity.

"I . . . uh . . . that's not . . ." She stammered to a stop. She shook her head to regroup, cleared her throat, and glowered at him. "My point is that Lupe is not the only one with a motive, not that I even admit that she has one, and you need to be looking at others and not her."

Manny tipped his head to the side and studied her. "I make you nervous, don't I?"

"Off topic," Mel declared. She put her hand over her throat as if she could calm her erratic heartbeat.

Manny smiled. "So, what's going on with you and DeLaura?"

"Way off topic!" Mel said. Her voice was shrill, as if she were calling a foul.

"That's a non-answer," he said. "If I'm going to be your number two, I think I should be kept apprised of my status."

"You're not my number two," Mel said.

"Oh, am I getting moved up to the number one spot?" he asked. Manny wiggled his eyebrows and Mel shook her head.

"I'm not discussing this with you," she said.

"Fine. So long as "the weasel" doesn't jump the line," he said.

Mel slapped her forehead with her palm. "You're impossible."

Manny nodded as if this was a fair assessment. "Sort of comes with the job."

"Does Uncle Stan think Lupe is the most likely suspect?" Mel asked.

"He's pretty resistant to the idea," Manny said. "I think it's because he knows her as Oz's skateboard buddy. It's clouding his judgment."

"Is it?" Mel asked. "Or are his instincts correct?"

"Mel, a woman was murdered," Manny said. "All personal stuff aside, I take that very seriously and I will see that justice is served."

He set his jaw. All flirtatiousness was gone and in its place was the very determined-looking detective she had first met on the scene of a murder. He looked as immovable as a pile of granite.

"I still say Anka is suspicious, and I'm going to find out who else might have had a motive to murder Mariel. She wasn't a nice person, as I'm sure your investigation has shown."

"Just because you lack social skills doesn't mean you deserve to be strangled with a sash," Manny said.

"Well, of course not," Mel said. "I'm just saying that mean people acquire lots of enemies and before you accuse anyone of the crime, you need to make sure you have the right person."

Manny crossed his arms over his chest and stared at her. "Really? Stan and I were unclear on that."

"Sarcasm does not become you," Mel said, meeting his stony gaze with one of her own. She mimicked his stance and crossed her arms in front of her.

"Mel!" Someone called her from across the lobby. She turned to see Joyce running toward her. "Mel, we have a situation!"

Twenty

"Mom, what do you mean?" Mel asked. She could feel Manny stiffen beside her, as if waiting for the announcement of another body.

"It's Lupe," Joyce said. "We have a major problem with Lupe."

"What sort of problem?" Manny asked.

Joyce glanced at him and then shook her head. "Really, detective, unless you know how to teach a girl to carry a tune or bust out the hip-hop moves in twenty-four hours, this is of no interest to you."

Manny and Mel exchanged bewildered looks.

"In English, Mom," Mel said. "What's the problem?"

"Lupe has no talent," Joyce wailed. "None!"

Manny looked at Joyce in disbelief and Mel knew he had been expecting a confession of Lupe's involvement in the murder.

"And that's just the beginning," Joyce said. "I've been checking out the dresses and gowns of some of the competition. Oh, my, we are in way over our heads. Did you know that horrible Richards woman paid over three thousand dollars for Destiny's gown?"

"Mom, you didn't, did you?"

"No! Not only do I not have that kind of money but there is no time!"

"Maybe I can contact Alma Rodriguez," Mel said. "She's a designer, maybe she has some rejects she can loan us."

"But what about Lupe's talent?" Joyce cried.

"Hey, is that Stan calling me?" Manny glanced across the lobby. There was no sign of Uncle Stan. "Why, yes, I think it is. Excuse me."

Mel watched him go, noting that only the speed of sound moved faster.

"Where is Lupe now?" Mel asked.

"She's talking to Oz. I think she is feeling utterly defeated," Joyce said. "This is all my fault."

"No, it isn't," Mel said. "She wanted to enter the pageant for the scholarship and you're helping her. That was very kind of you, and this competition is far from over."

Together they walked back to the cupcake tower, where they found Lupe standing beside Oz. Lupe was wearing a short robe over her bathing suit. It was pale blue, the same shade as her suit and high-heeled sandals. Her hair was long and loose and her makeup was light. She looked like she should be on the cover of *Sports Illustrated*. Mel was once again shocked that such a young beauty had been hidden beneath the colorfully dyed bangs and baggy black clothes all this time.

She was about to say as much to Oz, but he had the most

peculiar look on his face. She realized that with his hair slick backed he couldn't hide his face, or the fact that his gaze kept straying to Lupe's very long legs as if he, too, couldn't believe such a pretty girl had been his skateboard sidekick all this time. Mel almost felt bad for him.

"Oz, are you listening to me?" Lupe implored.

"Of course, I'm listening," he said as he fussed with the cupcake tower. Mel noticed he kept moving the same cupcakes up and down, as if he couldn't decide where to put them. She suspected it was so he could stay busy and not stare at his friend.

"Well, what do you think I should do?" Lupe asked. "The scholarship is riding on this. I can't blow it."

Her voice wobbled and Mel could tell she was on the brink of tears. Oz must have heard it, too, because he finally turned to face her and his voice was kind when he said, "It'll be okay. You'll come up with a talent. Don't worry."

"But what if I can't?" Lupe cried. "And then there's the whole murder investigation. Everyone here thinks I did it and they stare and whisper about me whenever I come into the room."

"Hey, hey," Oz said as he opened his arms and pulled her into a hug. "The only reason they stare and whisper is because you're the most beautiful girl in the room and they can't believe their eyes when they look at you."

Lupe snorted, but Oz was undeterred.

"Now, I don't want to see any tears or hear any more negative talk," he said. "I'll take care of your talent. Don't you worry. You just get out to the pool area and sashay your little butt off. Don't forget I have a stake in you winning this thing."

Lupe stepped back and smiled at Oz. Then she quickly

stepped forward and kissed his cheek. He looked temporarily blinded.

"Thanks, Oz, I knew you'd have my back," Lupe said.

An announcer's voice on the intercom announced that the swimsuit portion of the pageant was about to begin poolside.

"Okay, we're on." Joyce stepped forward and grabbed Lupe's hand. Together they hurried toward the patio where the judges, guests, and contestants were gathering.

Mel watched them go before she turned back to Oz.

"That was really nice of you," she said.

He shrugged. "I need my hundred dollars back."

"Sure you do," Mel said. "And I'm sure it has nothing to do with the fact that you have just noticed that Lupe is in fact a girl."

Oz's mouth dropped open. He looked shocked by the accusation but Mel knew better.

"I always knew she was a girl," he protested.

"Pfff," Mel scoffed.

"I did," he said. "Okay, I didn't know she was a hot girl, but I knew she was a girl."

Mel grinned. "So still just friends?"

Oz groaned, as if his mortification were physically painful. "Please stop talking now."

Mel pressed her lips together to keep from laughing. "I'll try but it's just so cute."

"Oh, god." Oz closed his eyes and looked as if he were praying to be removed from the situation by any means available.

"Settle down, big guy, I'll quit teasing," Mel said. "Can you hold the fort by yourself for a while?"

"Why? Where are you going?" Oz looked alarmed.

"To tell everyone I've ever met about your crush on Lupe," Mel said. Oz visibly paled and Mel slapped him on the shoulder. "Gotcha!"

"You're trying to kill me, aren't you?" he asked.

"Nah, I'd miss you too much," she said.

"Please don't say anything to anyone. I'm having a hard enough time in my own head," he said.

Mel immediately softened. She remembered how painful it had been to love Joe from afar when she was Oz's age.

"I won't say a word," she said. "I promise."

Oz slumped with relief.

"I am, however, going to see what we can do about Lupe's dress, and if I can find out anything about Mariel from the other contestants," Mel said.

"Do you think another contestant did her in?" Oz asked.

Mel shrugged. "No idea. But I want to throw any and every name that might have even the tiniest motive at Uncle Stan and Manny to, you know, help them out."

Oz grinned. "In case I haven't told you often enough, I'm really glad you're on my team."

"Likewise, Oz," Mel said. "Back in a bit."

With the bathing suit competition underway, Mel figured now was as good a time as any to try and chat up the legion of stage mothers who seemed to be flooding the resort.

Given that she was one of the bakers for the cupcake portion of the competition, she figured she could use that role as leverage to get the mothers to talk to her.

She glanced over her shoulder to check on Oz one last time and noted that he stood with his phone to his ear. Any embarrassment he felt had obviously been left behind. She envied the resiliency of youth. If it had been her, she would have snarfed down four cupcakes by now, be considering her fifth, and still be mortified.

Since the bathing suit competition had been divided into three groups, Lupe being in the first group, Mel went to the large changing room/green room reserved for the contestants to dress and practice their talents and interviews.

Mel passed a girl in her bathing suit working on a spunky dance routine, another holding a hairbrush up to her mouth pretending to answer interview questions, and a third berating her mother about her makeup.

"I wanted the sparkly blue eye shadow, Mom," the girl said with a whine that Mel suspected could cause ears to bleed. "Green is so last year and it doesn't bring out the color of my eyes or match my bathing suit. Sheesh, can't you get anything right?"

The mother apologized as she fumbled through the makeup bag, presumably looking for the blue eye shadow. Mel wasn't sure who she wanted to slap more: the daughter for behaving so badly or the mother for taking it.

She scanned the room until she saw Lupe's familiar purple tote bag sitting beside a vanity table in the corner. Next to the bag on a clothing rack hung Lupe's very plain ivory gown.

Mel took out her phone. She figured she could take a picture of the gown and send it to Alma. Maybe the designer would have a quick fix for making it more of an eye popper.

As Mel fussed with getting the dress out of its clear plastic covering, she noted the other women in the room seemed to be keeping their distance. Mel wasn't sure if it was because she was an outsider in the pageant world or because Lupe was the prime suspect in Mariel Mars's murder.

"Hi," she greeted the woman at the next makeup table.

The woman gave her an alarmed look and muttered something that sounded like "hello" but Mel wasn't quite sure. The woman turned her back to Mel as if to discourage any further conversation.

Mel snapped a couple of pics and carefully rewrapped the dress. She wandered out of the room and into the hallway, where she quickly composed a text with the picture attached and sent it to Alma.

A man in a pale yellow polo shirt, khaki shorts, and brown loafers stopped beside her. He looked her up and down and then made a puckered expression of concern with his lips.

"Here's my card," he said. He handed Mel a card in the shape of a woman's silhouette—a very well-endowed woman. "I notice you don't have a rock on that finger, so I'm assuming you're single or having a problem sealing the deal?"

Mel opened her mouth to speak, but he didn't give her the chance.

"You're not bad looking, but if you really want to nail down a guy, you might want to consider enhancing the package."

He made an hourglass gesture with his hands and if shock hadn't rooted Mel to the spot, she was pretty sure she would have kicked him in the privates on principle alone.

"And don't worry. We can work out a payment plan," the man said. Then he gave her a wink and a flash of his incandescent veneers and he was off.

Mel stood looking at the card in her hand as if it were printed in a foreign language that she couldn't decipher. When she realized it was outrage making it hard to focus, she closed her eyes for a second and pictured punching the jerk in the face. That helped.

When she opened her eyes, she could read the card. And, oh shocker, it belonged to Dr. Brandon Richards. She might have known. For a moment, she wondered if Brittany had sent him just to insult her. Then she glanced down at her figure. Yeah, no. Probably, he had seen her lack of endowments and decided to hold his own personal intervention.

Mel was just settling into her funk when she heard a shout from the lobby. It sounded like a deep male voice and the last time she'd looked out there, Oz was the only male capable of that sort of bark.

Mel started toward the lobby, but she only got a few steps down the hall when she spotted Oz coming at her with a dripping wet Lupe being carried in his arms.

Joyce was racing behind them, looking equal parts worried and furious.

"What happened?" Mel asked as she followed them.

"Karma," a petite little blonde said from behind Mel. Mel turned to see the girl toss her hair with a look of disdain.

"What's that supposed to mean?" Mel snapped. She stopped following the others to face down the little brat.

The delicate blonde looked at her in surprise and then slunk behind a sturdier version of herself—presumably, her mother.

The mother gave Mel a sharp look. "It means a murderer has no business competing in this pageant. She needs to go and if she doesn't, well, it looks like karma is going to catch up to her."

"Shut up," Destiny Richards snapped as she strode into the room. "If karma was involved, you two meanies would

135

have been bounced a long time ago." Destiny was carrying Lupe's robe and she handed it to Mel. "She left this behind."

"Thanks," Mel said.

"Sure." Destiny turned and left the room before Mel had a chance to say any more.

Mel quickly crossed the room to where Joyce and Oz stood hovering over Lupe, who had one leg propped up. Her face was pale and her expression tight. Mel guessed she was holding back some tears.

"Destiny Richards brought your robe," she said. She held it out so that Lupe could shrug into it. "Pretty nice of her, huh?"

"Huh," Joyce said. "That's the least she could do."

"What do you mean?" Mel asked. "What happened out there?"

"Lupe was making her final walk back to her spot on the dais, after passing the judges, when suddenly there was a puddle of water on the concrete. Lupe's shoes slipped right out from under her and she fell into the pool. Brittany Richards was standing right by the puddle with an empty glass in her hand."

Twenty-one

"She didn't even care if anyone saw her! If Lupe hadn't used her momentum to fall into the pool, she could have broken her leg!" Oz shouted.

Mel had known Oz for a long time and she'd never seen him lose his temper. Right now, he looked as if he'd happily strangle someone, preferably Brittany Richards.

"I'm okay," Lupe said. "I've taken worse falls off of my board. Remember that time my right butt cheek hit the curb so hard it looked like a Rand McNally road atlas? I swear I could have charted a course to San Diego."

Mel knew she was trying to make light of the situation. Oz was having none of it.

"This is different," he said. "Someone tried to hurt you."

The two teens stared at each other. Lupe reached out and took Oz's hand.

"Thanks," she said. "But I'm okay. Seriously, I don't think you're supposed to be in here."

Oz looked away from her and glanced around the room. Sure enough, it was filled with women, contestants and mothers, and all of them were staring at him.

A hot red suffused Oz's face, but he didn't run out of the room. Instead, he looked at Lupe and said, "You call me if anyone so much as gives you a dirty look. Am I clear?"

He said it loud enough for even the women in the back of the room to hear him, then he strode through the room shooting ferocious looks at anyone brave enough to meet his gaze.

Joyce watched him go and then gave Lupe a small smile. "You've got quite a champion there, don't you?"

A small smile parted Lupe's lips and her pallor gave way to a faint blush of pink. Joyce and Mel exchanged a glance. Mel felt a surge of relief that Lupe seemed to have the same feelings for Oz that he was having for her. It would have crushed her to see Oz get his heart stomped on.

"Now that you don't have to keep up the brave face for Oz, how are you really feeling?" she asked Lupe.

Lupe met Mel's gaze in the mirror. She cringed.

"Like a loser, actually," she said.

"Now, Lupe, we talked about that," Joyce said in her most bolstering voice. "You are not a loser. We just have to upgrade your wardrobe a bit and nail down your talent and you'll be fine."

Lupe's eyes got damp and she glanced down at her hands. "I don't have a talent. It doesn't matter anyway because I'm probably going to be arrested for murder."

"No, you're not," Mel said. She picked up a hairbrush from the table and began to brush the tangles out of Lupe's wet hair. Mel remembered when she had been little and had long hair; it had always soothed her when her mother brushed it out at night. She worked the brush from the crown of Lupe's head down to the tips of her hair in gentle strokes.

A girl across the room was strumming a guitar and singing. It was a pretty folk song and Mel had to admit the girl had a beautiful voice.

Lupe met her gaze in the mirror and heaved a sigh. Mel kept brushing while Joyce took a seat next to Lupe and patted her hands.

"Now, listen to me," Mel said. "You know how I feel about these pageants."

"You think they're stupid," Lupe said.

"Mostly, yes," Mel admitted. "But you went into this to win a scholarship. Now you have the cupcake competition, the formal wear, and the talent portions left. You have hung around the bakery enough to be able to submit an idea for a cupcake that will be amazing, yes?"

Lupe nodded.

"And you are beautiful enough that even if your gown doesn't cost a fortune and isn't covered in ruffles and sparkles, you will outshine all of the others," Joyce said.

Lupe gave a long, shuddering sigh. She closed her eyes for a moment and Mel kept brushing her hair. When Lupe opened her eyes, they weren't watery with a sheen of tears anymore.

"You're right," she said. She straightened in her chair and looked at her reflection in the mirror. "I can do this."

Mel and Joyce exchanged a smile. So long as Lupe was in, they were in.

A murmur began in the room, drawing Mel's attention

away from their group. She glanced over her shoulder and saw Uncle Stan and Cici standing in the doorway. Cici glanced in their direction, gave Uncle Stan a nod, and hurried toward them.

"This can't be good," Mel said. Joyce rose and stood beside her as if they could make a human shield and block Uncle Stan's view of Lupe.

Joyce frowned. Mel glanced at her and noted that she had her "scary mother" face on. Mel hoped Uncle Stan was wearing flame-retardant underwear because if he thought he was coming after Lupe without Joyce going volcanic on him, he was seriously mistaken.

"Detective Cooper says he needs to speak with Miss Guzman," Cici said. "I would appreciate it if you would go quietly so as not to upset any of the other contestants."

The entire room was staring at them. Mel was not overly concerned with upsetting them and she could tell her mother couldn't give two hoots, either.

"Sorry, Cici," Joyce said. "'Quietly' is not in my vocabulary."

She then marched across the room, looking ready for battle.

"Stan!" she yelled in a voice that made everyone jump, including Stan. "I want a word with you."

"I'm doomed, aren't I?" Lupe asked.

"Let's give Mom a minute to handle it," Mel said, and she put a reassuring hand on Lupe's shoulder. She glanced at Cici and asked, "Did Stan say anything else?"

"No, just if I would let Miss Guzman know that they would like to ask her some questions."

"See?" Mel said to Lupe. "That's not so bad. Come on, let's go see what this is all about. You'll feel better if you know."

Lupe gave her a dubious look. As they crossed through the room, the whispers that followed them made Mel roll her eyes. This is exactly how she'd felt in her chunky youth when the whispers started every time she was called up to the front of the class to read or work a problem out on the board. She had always felt as if everyone was just waiting for the fat kid to trip or fall. The ghost of the memory made her clench her teeth in slow-burning anger.

Sarah Hendricks, the sharp-featured, underfed redhead she'd seen before, the one who was so nasty to her mother, was whispering frantically to a petite blonde as they passed.

"See? I told you she did it," Sarah hissed. "Look at how manly her walk is. She is so not Miss Sweet Tiara material. I bet they only let her in to make the pageant more ethnically diverse. She probably works in farm fields when she's not here. I mean, look at her hands. They're huge. And did you see her gown? It was totally off the rack. She is *so* not one of us."

Mel stopped in her tracks. Now she was crazy mad. She turned on the redhead and stepped so close to her that her face was inches from the young woman's. The girl went wide-eyed, as if expecting Mel to hit her.

"You're right," Mel said. "She isn't one of you. She has a beauty and grace that shines from within, not bought from a box or a bottle. You'd be lucky to be half the person she is."

The redhead glowered and gave Mel a contemptuous look. "That may be enough where you come from, but this is the big leagues. That little leaguer isn't up to the game and neither are you."

The girl's disdain was like a slap in the face. Mel refused to take it.

"Funny you should talk about the big leagues," Mel said. "Your nose is a major leaguer on a T-ball face. Probably, you should have that looked at." She then slapped the card Brandon Richards had forced on her into the girl's hand.

She heard the redhead gasp as she and Lupe strode away. It was unquestionably mean and immature of her, Mel knew. But for these girls, everything was about their looks, and Mel knew she could only dent the girl if she slammed her appearance. Had she gone after the girl's mean personality, the redhead would have shrugged it off like an acrylic sweater.

Mel knew her behavior had been revolting and she felt her insides twist in self-disgust for sinking to Sarah's level, but when Mel glanced at Lupe out of the corner of her eye, the young woman gave her a small smile of gratitude and Mel felt a little part of herself heal.

Growing up, she had been the one who was derided and picked on and she had never stood up to the bullies because deep down she was ashamed of her weight and afraid that the people who made fun of her were right. Somehow, standing up for Lupe made all those years of misery fade. For the first time ever, she didn't feel the need to stuff her face with comfort food after being insulted. It felt pretty good.

"Stan, you can't be serious," Joyce was chiding him as they joined them. "You know Lupe. You know she didn't do it."

Stan pinched the bridge of his nose between his thumb and forefinger. He looked as if he was trying to ward off a headache.

"It's just a formality," he said. "But we have to take her in for questioning."

"Fine, then I'm calling Steve and he'll meet us at the station," she said. Joyce began fishing her phone out of her purse.

"I figured you would," Uncle Stan said. Mel thought she heard a note of approval in his voice. She knew he had to hate this as much as any of them. His next words confirmed it. He looked at Lupe and said, "I want to be very clear, this is just protocol, do you understand?"

Lupe gave him a shaky nod and Mel squeezed her shoulder in reassurance.

"Can I at least let her get dressed and then take her in my car?" Joyce asked. Her voice was clipped and Uncle Stan looked pained.

"Sure," he said. "That would be fine."

"Watch her things," Joyce said to Mel. "I don't trust that viper pit not to tamper with her clothes and makeup."

Mel thought about her exchange with Sarah. If they did, it would be her fault.

Uncle Stan and Mel watched Joyce lead Lupe into the dressing room. Mel fell into step beside him as he headed down the hall to the lobby and asked, "Scale of one to ten, how serious is this?"

His face was grim. "New evidence has come to light from the medical examiner that makes it a nine point nine. That's all I can say."

Mel knew by his tone that she would get no further information. Still, she was mad at him. "So, you lied to her when you said it was just protocol?"

Uncle Stan gave her a flat stare. She was aware that she might have just made him mad, but damn it they were talking about a young girl's life. She didn't give a rip what anyone else thought. She knew Lupe was innocent.

"No, I didn't," he said. "Between you and me, and I mean that, I don't think she did it, but the evidence—"

He cut himself off from saying more as Oz came hurrying over.

"What's going on? I heard someone say that you're taking Lupe in," he said.

"I'll let you explain," Stan said to Mel. "I gotta go."

Mel nodded. She suspected Stan didn't want to face the teen boy's ire. Chicken.

Oz looked at her expectantly.

"Who's watching the cupcakes?" she asked.

"I called Marty in," he said. "Now what's going on?"

"Uncle Stan is having Lupe visit the police station for formal questioning."

"What?" Oz snapped. "He can't be serious. That's stupid!"

"Agreed," Mel said. "And if it helps, Stan told me he doesn't believe she did it, either. But I'm not supposed to tell you that."

Mel did not mention the new evidence part. She fully intended to grill Uncle Stan about it later, but she didn't think it would help Oz's frazzled state of mind right now.

"We should call Lupe's mother," she said.

"She's at work," Oz said. "She's a secretary at the high school and even though we're on break, she still has to be there. She'll get in trouble if she has to leave. Lupe's aunt is watching her sisters. I know Lupe will want to keep this from them so they don't worry. Her mother wanted to pull her out of the pageant after Mariel's murder because she was afraid it was too dangerous, like, the killer might go after Lupe or something."

"So, she has no idea that Lupe is a suspect?" Mel asked.

Oz shook his head.

"Do you think that's wise?" Mel asked.

"Lupe made me promise," he said. "She thinks her mom has enough to worry about just keeping a roof over their heads."

Mel looked at Oz's face. His features were pinched with anxiety and he was tapping his fingers against his thigh as if it was the only outlet he could find for his nervous energy.

"Go to the station with Mom and Lupe," Mel said. "She'll appreciate the support. You can probably catch them in the parking lot."

"Thanks." Oz looked so relieved that Mel knew that's what he'd been hoping she would say. "Are you sure?"

"Yes, Marty and I can handle this," she said.

"Cool." To her surprise, Oz reached forward and wrapped her in a hug that lifted her off of her feet. "Thanks, Mel."

Then he was gone, racing off down the hall toward the exit.

Mel hurried down the hall back to the dressing room. She glanced at Lupe's dressing table and saw Sarah reaching out to touch Lupe's gown, which was still hanging in its plastic cover. Oh, hell, no.

She hustled into the room and charged across the floor. Her expression must have reflected her rage because Sarah backed up quickly and found a mirror, where she started fixing her hair. Mel wasn't fooled, not even a little. She decided to pack up Lupe's things until she returned.

Her mind went right to Stan's words about new evidence. What could he have found? How could it be so damning that they needed to bring Lupe in for questioning? Mel carefully lifted Lupe's dress from the rack. She glanced around the room and noted that Lupe's gown was simple when compared to the others. It was a figure-hugging ivory sheath and while it was going to look amazing on her, Mel had to acknowledge that Sarah Hendrick's was right. It was going to appear rather plain compared to the low-cut, ruffled, and sparkly dresses of the others.

She hoped Alma could give them a quick fix just to kick it up a notch. Then again, if Stan arrested Lupe for Mariel's murder, she would hardly be needing the gown.

The murmur of voices in the room took on a frenzied sound, and Mel glanced behind her to see what the buzz was about. She hoped it was Stan or Manny hauling someone, anyone, in for questioning but no. When she turned around she saw an Asian woman enter the room, looking like she owned it.

The woman worked her way from station to station. She glanced at the contestants. Some she stopped to critique, others she gave a brusque nod to, and still others she paused in front of to adjust their blush or eye shadow. No one managed to get a smile out of her and Mel found herself clutching Lupe's gown to her middle as if nervous for what the woman would say to her, which was ridiculous given that Mel wasn't a contestant.

The woman wore little to no makeup, or at least if she did, it was impossible to discern. Although her features were not pretty or glamorous, she was handsome, with a flawless complexion that glowed against the backdrop of her long dark hair, which she wore in a side part. Mel stared at the woman in rapt fascination.

In complete contrast, roaring right up on the woman's heels was Brittany Richards. She led Destiny by the hand, giving the teen no option but to follow.

"Ji!" Brittany called. She was waving at the smaller

woman as if they were longtime friends. "You remember my daughter, Destiny, don't you?"

The woman turned and Mel saw her lips tighten just the tiniest bit before she forced them into a miniscule smile.

"Of course," the woman inclined her head. "Nice to see you again."

Brittany puffed up like a proud mama hen. She then proceeded to dangle Destiny in front of the woman, pointing out her ski slope nose and high cheekbones. It was quite clear that Brittany was making a pitch of sorts.

"Oh, that woman is the world's biggest suck-up," a woman standing near Mel griped. "Just because she's married to Brandon Richards she thinks she owns every pageant they enter."

The woman started to vigorously brush her daughter's hair. "Ow, Mom."

"Sorry, honey." The woman immediately calmed down her brushing.

Another mother nearby said, "I heard Brittany bribes the judges with trips to the Caribbean."

"Wouldn't surprise me," the first woman said. "Don't they have a private jet?"

"Four houses and domestic staff in every one of them, too," the other woman added. "All paid for by boob jobs and nose jobs."

"Why did we enter this pageant again? We don't stand a chance. That tiara is bought and paid for." The other mother sighed and put down the hairbrush.

"Well, Ji Lily owns her own cosmetics company," the second mother said. "Maybe one of our girls will get lucky and get a modeling contract with her."

Mel glanced over at the Asian woman. She remembered

Cici telling her that Ji Lily was their makeup consultant. She also remembered that Cici said that Mariel was in partnership with Ji Lily in a nail polish venture. She wondered how that had been going. Surely, Uncle Stan and Manny knew about it, too.

If Ji Lily was here, they must not have found anything suspicious about her business with Mariel. Still, Tate had loads of contacts in the business world. It couldn't hurt for him to ask around and see what he could find out. If the partnership had soured, that would be one more name to give Uncle Stan and Manny.

As if sensing her stare, Ji Lily turned away from Brittany, who did not look pleased to be abandoned in the middle of her monologue, and began to walk toward Mel. She had a sharp look in her dark eyes that Mel couldn't read, but she got the feeling that the woman was intent on chatting with her. Yikes.

Twenty-two

Ji Lily stopped in front of Mel. "You're the one who found Mariel?"

Mel just stared at her. She was unsure of what to say and found the woman's blunt manner more than a little off-putting. The woman seemed to grasp that the verbal offensive strike wasn't working for Mel.

"Excuse me. I'm Ji Lily, the cosmetic consultant for the pageant," she said. "And I believe you are Melanie Cooper, the baker providing the wonderful cupcakes I have seen in the lobby?"

Mel had to give the woman credit. With very little effort, she transformed into someone completely charming. Ji extended her hand and Mel clasped it in hers. The woman had a solid handshake.

"I am," Mel said. "But I'm not the person who found

Mariel. That was my partner, Angie DeLaura, who is not here today."

"Oh." Ji sounded disappointed.

"Was there something I can help you with?" Mel asked. "I was there right after she was discovered—" Mel noted that the mothers surrounding them were listening and she decided it would be prudent to move away. She tipped her head in the direction of the nearest door and led Ji out into the hallway. "I was there right after my partner discovered Mariel."

"Did you get a good look at her?" Ji asked.

"At Mariel?" Mel clarified. It seemed a grisly line of questioning and she couldn't fathom why Ji would want to know.

At Ji's nod, she answered. "Yes, I guess so."

"Was it true that she was strangled?" Ji asked. "The detectives would neither confirm nor deny."

"Oh," Mel said. She wondered at that and whether she should give out information if Manny and Uncle Stan were withholding it. Then again, there had been so many people in the lobby when she was discovered it wasn't as if people didn't know. "From what I saw, I would assume that was the cause of death. Why do you ask?"

Ji gave her a dark look that clearly meant she had no intention of sharing why she was asking. Mel frowned. That wasn't playing fair.

"I answered your question," Mel said. "Pony it up."

Ji gave her a small smile. "All right. Launching your own nail polish line is not cheap, and Mariel was stalling on paying me the second half of her investment money, you know, the money needed to actually launch the line. I think the police believe I might have tried to choke it out of her, literally."

"Did you?" Mel asked.

"Well, I was questioned and they released me, so I guess my alibi checked out. Hard to choke someone when you're up to your elbows in new nail polish colors. Speaking of which, I am launching Mariel's line in memory of her. My web designer thinks the ad campaign stands a good chance of going viral. We could make a killing."

"Figuratively speaking?" Mel asked.

"Of course." Ji's glee at the possibility of banking on Mariel's death caught Mel off guard. She would think if Ji had killed Mariel she would keep her enthusiasm on the down low. Perhaps that was why she was okay with showing her opportunistic side. She hadn't done it. Or she was the scariest sociopath *ever*.

"Since you were in business with her and worked closely with her on the nail polish, do you know of anyone else who might have wanted to do her harm?"

"Do her harm?" Ji asked. "That's the polite phrase for 'murder her,' is it?"

"Oh, please," Mel scoffed. "Don't nitpick when I'm surrounded by people who use the term 'facially gifted,' as if being pretty is comparable to being mathematically gifted or artistically gifted."

Ji grinned and Mel was momentarily stunned by how her handsome face transformed into one of real beauty. "Touché. Let me put it this way, to know Mariel was to want to kill her. Look around you. You can take your pick of would-be killers."

With that Ji turned and walked away, leaving Mel more worried about Lupe than ever. If the rest of the people in the pageant circle were anything like Ji or Brandon and Brittany, Mel had no doubt that the real killer would do everything he or she could to make Lupe take the fall for

Mariel's murder. Given that Brittany had already caused Lupe to fall, literally, Mel's fear seemed spot-on.

Mel took all of Lupe's things and walked them out to her car. She was not going to let anyone mess with Lupe's stuff on her watch. Back inside, she wondered how things were going at the police station. She took out her phone and sent Oz a quick text. There was no reply from Alma about the dress.

Mel could hear the cheers coming from poolside as the contestants finished up the bathing suit competition. She wondered if anyone else had fallen. Then she shook her head, refusing to think about it.

Mel wondered who outside this crazy pageant circus would know about Ji Lily. Even if Uncle Stan and Manny had let Ji go because her alibi was solid, it didn't change the fact that she was in business with Mariel, and with Mariel gone, who had the most to gain? Ji. She even admitted she hoped to make a killing.

Mel took her phone out of her pocket and scrolled through her contacts until she found the name she wanted. She pressed the little phone icon and waited.

"Christine's Salon, this is Juliet, may I help you?" a young woman answered.

"Hi, Juliet, this is Melanie Cooper. I'd like to speak with Christine," Mel said.

"I'm sorry, she's with a client. Can I have her call you back?"

"Tell her there's a dozen Hi-Hat Cupcakes in it for her," Mel said.

"One moment."

Mel waited. She supposed she could have offered up two

dozen, but Christine was a tough negotiator so it was better to start low.

"She wants to know if they'll be dipped in chocolate with a cherry on top," Juliet said.

Mel let out a put-upon sigh, mostly for effect. "Fine."

"One moment, please," Juliet said.

Mel waited again. She could hear the sound of blow-dryers and pop music in the background. Christine's Salon was right down the street from her bakery and Christine was the one responsible for Lupe's transformation. There was no one Christine didn't know in the local beauty scene.

"Cooper, those had better be super Hi-Hat Cupcakes," Christine said. "I just left a client under the dryer for you."

"They'll be amazing," Mel assured her. "So, what do you know about Ji Lily?"

"The cosmetic upstart?" Christine asked. She sounded intrigued. "She makes a good formaldehyde-free nail product that lasts. I haven't tried her lipsticks but I hear they're good, too. Why?"

"She's the beauty consultant at the pageant," Mel said. "And she was in business with Mariel Mars to launch a new nail polish line."

"I heard about that," Christine said. "I remember at the time thinking it was weird."

"Why?" Mel asked.

"Because Mariel is an old, dried-up prune."

"Harsh," Mel said.

"I know," Christine said. "But I'm not going to lie and say she was more than she was just because she's dead. The truth is, Ji had nothing to gain by having Mariel be the face of her nail polish line unless—"

"Yes?" Mel prodded her.

"Hang on, dryer check," Christine said.

Mel heard the phone being put down and she studied her own shriveled cuticles while she waited.

"Unless Mariel was staking Ji with a serious infusion of cash," Christine said. "Otherwise there really was no purpose in Ji helping Mariel out. I believe Mariel was the one with all the gain here."

"Ji told me that Mariel owed her a lot of money," Mel said. "In fact, she said she thought the police questioned her because Mariel owed her so much money that they might think she tried to choke it out of her."

"Huh," Christine grunted. Mel could tell she was back to fussing over her client's hair. "You're a businesswoman, would you work for free waiting for a big payoff from an almost celebrity? Mariel wasn't even a has-been, she was an almost-was. Did Ji strike you as being that stupid? Because the few times I've met her, *dumb* was not the word that leapt to mind."

"No, she seems pretty sharp," Mel said.

"My advice?" Christine asked. "Follow the money. When do I get my cupcakes?"

"Tomorrow," Mel said. "Baker's honor."

"Cool," Christine said and hung up.

Mel put away her phone as she pondered what Christine had said. She saw a crowd had gathered around the cupcake tower and she hurried over, assuming that Marty needed backup. When she arrived, she was surprised to find Marty surrounded by a bevy of beauties who all looked as if they'd be at home in a senior version of the Sweet Tiara.

"Oh, Martin, you are incorrigible," one of the ladies said as she swatted his arm playfully.

Another woman wiggled her way in between Marty and the woman who was laughing and said, "I think he was talking about me, Adele."

"Oh, Evie, you think everyone is talking about you," Adele snapped. "Just because a drunk once said you had eyes like Elizabeth Taylor's doesn't mean it's true."

Evie gasped. "It is so true. Look, they're violet; not blue, violet. Don't you think, Martin?" Evie batted her eyes at Marty.

"Oh, don't get all full of yourself, that's just your cataracts." Adele sniffed.

Mel opened her eyes wide at Marty to indicate he needed to smooth things over before there was a geriatric catfight on their hands.

Marty shrugged. It was obvious he was the typical male, useless in the face of female ire.

"Ladies, if you don't mind," Mel said. "Marty needs to start working the room."

Mel loaded cupcakes onto an empty tray. Perhaps if he was in motion, the ladies would disperse without launching into smashing each other with their canes or getting into a blue-hair-pulling fight.

"Who are you?" Adele glowered at Mel as if she were a rival.

"Yeah, who do you think you are bossing around the owner of Fairy Tale Cupcakes?" Evie asked.

Mel swiveled her head slowly in Marty's direction. He patted his bald head with one hand while hugging his middle with the other. The ladies were having none of that. They each flanked him, putting their arms through his as if they were about to pose for a group photo.

"Now, I never said that—" he began.

Marty didn't get to finish his protest, as he was interrupted by a voice that Mel was pretty sure could shatter glass if it was required.

"Someone please explain to me why these two old biddies have their hands on *my* boyfriend!"

Mel turned to see Olivia Puckett standing behind her with her hands on her hips, her eyes blazing. For once her crazy face was not directed at Mel, for which Mel was extremely grateful.

"Boyfriend?" Adele and Evie said together.

Mel extended the half-loaded tray to Marty as if she were opening an escape hatch for him.

"Back to work," he chirped under Olivia's hot gaze. "Nice to meet you, ladies."

With a spryness that belied his eighty-something years and was probably due to an ingrained survival instinct, Marty shot across the room as if he'd sat on a tack. Too bad for him, Olivia was hot on his trail. Mel had a feeling he wasn't going to get out of this one until he fully explained himself. Good luck with that.

"Men," Adele huffed. She then grabbed two cupcakes off of the tower and said, "Come on, Evie, I think I saw some hotties out by the pool."

"Cabana boys?" Evie perked up and followed her friend, their rivalry already forgotten. "Do you think they might be too young?"

"Huh. I'll be their Mrs. Robinson," Adele joked as she nudged Evie in the side with her elbow.

Mel watched them go and wondered if she'd just gotten a glimpse of her and Angie in the future. It was a sobering thought.

While prepping another tray for Marty, Mel watched as

the last of the bathing beauties came in from the pool area. She wondered how the judging had gone and if Lupe's spill was going to cause her to be bounced from the final round.

Cici was leading two well-dressed women and a man in black through the lobby. Mel recognized Jay Driscoll and Lexi Armstrong as the judges she'd already met. Mel assumed the buxom blonde with them must be Mariel's replacement, Anka Holland.

As Mel studied the woman, she couldn't help but try to find one part of her that hadn't had work done. Her hair was bottle blond, her lips were artificially puffy, her skin had the smooth sheen of someone who had injected entirely too many chemicals into her dermis. Her eyes were big and wide, as if they'd been lifted one too many times. Mel wondered if Brandon Richards had done her work. If so, Mel figured she was due a refund.

"This is Melanie Cooper." Cici paused by the cupcake tower. "She will be baking the cupcakes that the girls design. Obviously in the interests of fairness, we are keeping the decorative portion of the cupcakes to a minimum. It will be mostly about taste, with lesser points given for presentation."

"Ahem." Someone cleared their throat loudly from behind the group. Mel was not surprised to see Olivia standing there.

"Oh, yes, and this is our other baker, Olivia Puckett," Cici said.

Mel glanced around for Marty, but he was obviously dragging his feet as he made his way back to the cupcake tower.

"I own Confections," Olivia announced. "Three-time winner of the Best of Phoenix award."

"For your brownies," Mel added. "We've won twice for our cupcakes."

"And for my cookies," Olivia growled.

Cici glanced between them with a warning look. "I'm sure our *professional* bakers will do their best with each recipe submitted by the girls."

Mel and Olivia exchanged a glance. There was no mistaking the emphasis Cici put on the word *professional*. Mel took it as the warning it was and changed the subject.

"It's very nice to meet you all." Mel turned to Anka and said, "How very fortunate for the pageant that you happened to be in town and could be an emergency replacement."

Cici gave her a dark look, but Mel kept her expression innocent. Olivia began to prattle on at the creative director about how a spread in *SWS* featuring her bakery would be a boost to the magazine's sales, while also trying to get the photographer to agree to photograph some of her creations.

Anka's lips twitched in what Mel assumed was a smile before Anka lost all muscle control, leaving her expression blank.

"I'm just happy to be of help," Anka said. Her voice was a low purr and Mel had to lean in close to hear her over the noise of the crowded lobby.

"I heard that you and Mariel competed often over the years," Mel said. "You must have been quite devastated to hear of her demise."

Mel was pretty sure Anka's eyes would have narrowed at her if they could have. Instead, her full lips moved into a half moue and she said, "Yes, I was quite overcome."

As Cici ushered the judges away, Mel couldn't help but wonder if Anka meant she had been overcome with regret, sorrow, or something else, like joy.

Twenty-three

"Get this!" Tate was grinning as he read the next recipe. "They want us to use Red Bull instead of milk in the cupcake batter."

Mel lowered her head into her hands. She'd known it was going to be bad, but honestly, her gag reflex was in overdrive.

"I thought beauty queens were all about healthy living and eating. You know, so they have that natural glow," Angie said. "Shouldn't they be making cupcakes out of agave nectar and kale?"

"Apparently not," Mel said. She had been scribbling down a shopping list that Tate was taking to the grocery store to get their "special" ingredients.

It was early evening and Mel knew she had a long night of baking ahead of her in order to get ready for the next two days at the pageant. On the upside, Oz had popped in earlier to tell them that Lupe had made the final round, the top twenty contestants to move forward, despite her fall by the pool. He said he was going to help her with her talent and then he disappeared for the afternoon.

Alma Rodriguez, the designer, had texted Mel back and said she could give Lupe's dress some pizzazz but she was going to need some cupcakes as motivation. Cupcake blackmail, you had to respect it. Mel packed up an assorted two dozen and sent Joyce with the cupcakes and the dress to Alma's studio.

Tomorrow was the big talent day and the day after that was cupcake tasting and evening gowns. Marty was manning the front of the shop, while Mel and Angie began the baking for the shop and for tomorrow's cupcake tower. Mel had been given ten anonymous cupcake recipes, as had Olivia, and she would have to start those tomorrow.

Mel read the last recipe and scribbled *SpaghettiOs* and *Velveeta* on the list before she ripped it off the pad and handed it to Tate.

"Good luck with that," she said.

"Thanks," he said. He kissed Angie's head before heading out the door.

"So, the police didn't keep Lupe for very long," Angie said.

"No, and they didn't arrest her," Mel said. "So I'm taking that as a good sign."

"Still no word as to what the evidence was that made them bring her in to begin with?" Angie asked.

"No. Neither Uncle Stan nor Manny is talking," Mel said. "Lupe did say that they fingerprinted her, so I'm wondering if prints were found that they are trying to match."

"Prints on what?" Angie asked. "The sash used to strangle her? Can fabric hold a fingerprint?"

"Good question," Mel said. "Maybe I'll try to work that into conversation with Uncle Stan."

"You'd probably have better luck if you tried Manny and batted your eyelashes at him," Angie said.

Mel wasn't sure how to take that. Surely, Angie wasn't encouraging her to flirt with the cop.

"Just a thought," Angie said with a shrug. "I mean he obviously likes you and it couldn't hurt to find out what he's thinking."

"What who is thinking?" Paulie DeLaura asked as he entered the kitchen from the bakery with his little brother Al right behind him.

"Hey, guys!" Angie hopped off of her stool and hurried around the table to give her brothers hugs.

Mel gave them a little wave from her side of the table, but Paulie shook his head at her. "Aw, come here, Mel."

"Yeah," Al said. "Come in for the real thing."

Relieved that she wasn't still in trouble with the brothers for her relationship fallout with Joe, Mel hurried around the table for hugs, too.

There had been a tense couple of weeks when all six of the DeLaura brothers were mad at her. They'd let her know with the silent treatment and some fierce stink eye until Mrs. DeLaura told them to knock it off. She said that Mel would always be family, whether she married Joe or not. Then she took Mel aside and said that of course she fully expected that Mel would make the right choice. Yep, no pressure.

"How are my two favorite ladies doing?" Paulie asked.

Angie rolled her eyes. "You say that to all the girls."

"Yeah, but with you two I mean it," he said.

Mel laughed. Al shook his head as if he was embarrassed to be with his brother.

"We're looking for Oz," Al said. "He texted us that he needs some of our expertise."

"Last I knew, he and Lupe were going to work on her talent for the pageant," Mel said.

Paulie and Al exchanged a look. Mel took that to mean that they knew what Lupe's talent was.

"So, what is she doing?" she asked.

"We can't say," Paulie said with a shrug. "Oz told us to keep it hush-hush."

"Even from your sister?" Angie asked. She sounded outraged.

"Sorry, Sis," Al said, spreading his hands in a gesture of helplessness. "We promised."

Paulie was walking into the walk-in cooler to help himself to a cupcake, but Angie hurried across the room and slammed the door in his face.

"Oh, no, if you don't talk, you get no cupcakes," she said.

"Harsh!" Paulie said.

"Al," Mel used her most cajoling tone. "You know you can trust us not to say anything. Just give us a hint."

Al studied her. Then he nodded and said, "No."

Mel let out an exasperated huff.

"Just please tell me. We're not going to have one of those 'What is your daughter doing? She's kickin' ass . . . that's what she's doing,' moments," Mel said.

"Hey, that's from *Little Miss Sunshine*," Angie said. "I can't believe we haven't worked one of those quotes in before now."

"We've been busy," Mel said. She turned back to Al and Paulie. "So, really, not even a hint?"

"Yeah," Angie said. "Why does Oz need you two?"

"Not just us," Paulie said. "All of the brothers—"

Al cut him off with an elbow to the ribs.

"So, Joe is in on it, too?" Mel asked.

"Don't even try," Al said. "Joe is on strict orders to stay away from you, so you can't charm any information out of him."

"As if I could," Mel scoffed.

"Oh, you could," Paulie said. "Even though you crushed him, he's still crazy in love with you."

As soon as the words left Paulie's mouth, all four of them looked away from each other.

"Awkward," Al said. "And on that charming note, we'll just go look for Oz at our alternate meeting place."

"See ya," Paulie yelped as the younger and bigger Al hauled him out the door by the back of his collar.

"What do you suppose they're up to?" Mel asked.

"No idea," Angie said. "And if we can't get it out of Paulie, we won't know until they want us to know. I mean, we all know he's the weakest link in the DeLaura chain."

"You don't think they're teaching her stripper moves, do you?" Mel asked.

Angie laughed. "My mother would kill them."

"You're right," Mel said. "No need to worry then, right?"

"I didn't say that," Angie said.

Mel shuffled the recipes in front of her. "So, probably, I should focus on what we *can* do."

"Like bake cupcakes." Angie hefted the industrial-sized cupcake baking trays that they used out from under the table.

"Yeah, but I was thinking more along the lines of figuring out who murdered Mariel and why."

Angie glanced up. "Silly me, of course you were. So, what are you thinking?"

"I'm thinking that there are a whole lot of people who wanted Mariel dead," she said.

"Who is your favorite suspect so far?" Angie asked.

"If it comes down to money, I'm thinking Ji Lily has a solid motive," Mel said. "She told me that Mariel was deeply in debt to her because of their nail polish line, but I did a consult with Christine and she seems to think Ji is too smart to go into business with Mariel unless Mariel had solid backing, which Mariel proved by paying half up front. According to Ji, Mariel was stalling on the rest of the money. Now Ji is planning to sell Mariel's nail polish as a tribute item."

"Ew," Angie said. "What about that replacement judge, the one who looks like a walking mannequin?"

"Anka Holland?" Mel asked. "What would be her motive?"

"Well, she's never going to be second to Mariel again, now is she?"

"True, and I still find it convenient that she just happened to be in town during the pageant," Mel said. "If she's the murderer, in her mind this could have been long overdue. What do you think about Cici?"

"Hastings?" Angie asked. "But she's so petite, and despite looking amazing, Cici has to be somewhere in her eighties. Do you really think she could have strangled Mariel?"

"She's pretty spry," Mel said. "Also, do we know if Mariel was marking any other contestants low on their scores? There's a pretty nasty redhead named Sarah Hendricks who looks like she'd have no problem removing any-one who stood in her way of winning."

"Yeah, I saw her," Angie said. "She scared me."

"And there must be others," Mel said. "Maybe if we cozy up to Anka, we can check her out and see if anyone else seems a likely candidate."

The door to the bakery swung open. Marty stood half-way in it, as if he wasn't sure if he was coming or going.

"I don't think this is a good idea," Marty said over his shoulder to someone in the bakery.

"You said that about last night, too," a voice, a female voice, said from behind him. "Do you regret that?"

Mel saw the tips of Marty's ears go red with embarrass-ment and he turned away from the doorway to face them.

"Uh . . . I . . . the thing is . . ." he stammered.

"Oh, for Pete's sake just tell them I'm here." The wom-an's voice was strident and bossy.

Mel and Angie exchanged an alarmed look. Mel knew that voice. No, it couldn't be. Not in her kitchen. This was her sanctuary. Her oasis. Her insides clutched. Marty could not seriously be considering letting that plague enter it.

The door swung open, knocking Marty forward, and into the room strode Olivia Puckett.

Twenty-four

"What are you doing here?" Angie asked.

At least that's what Mel thought she said. It was hard to tell given that her voice was more feral growl than anything else.

"Relax, bite size," Olivia said. "I'm just here to talk shop."

"Livy, remember when we talked about not insulting them?" Marty asked. "Well, you just did."

Olivia shrugged. "Sorry. I'm working on it."

Mel eyed the woman who had been the irritating equivalent of a scorch mark on her countertop for the past few years.

"What do you want, Puckett?" she asked. Just because Olivia and Marty had some sort of weird relationship going did not mean Mel wanted to be drawn into her crazy.

"I came to commiserate," Olivia said. "Is that so wrong?"

Mel eyed her suspiciously. "Not wrong so much as completely out of character."

Marty glanced between the three of them as if he were trying to anticipate who would throw the first punch.

"You've got me there," Olivia said.

She sat down without being invited and Mel felt a pinch of annoyance. Sadly, her mother had raised her to be gracious and no matter how hard she tried she couldn't quite shake it off.

"Are these your recipes?" Olivia asked, pointing to the sheets of paper on the steel table. "I just read through mine and they made me want to stab myself in the eye with a cake tester."

Mel snorted. She had felt the same. Angie gave her an incredulous look and Mel shrugged.

"It's true," she said. "There were a few that are promising, but most of them are completely out there and totally uninspired."

"It's like these girls have never even heard of cooking from scratch," Olivia said. "And then I have one that I know the girl ripped off from Martha Stewart. I mean, come on, what seventeen-year-old girl knows about reducing?"

"At least that one will taste good," Mel said. "I have one that wants me to use cheese food."

"Oh, gag." Olivia made a face. "We should be getting hazard pay."

They glanced at each other across the table and they both began to chuckle. Angie gave Mel a disgruntled look, and Mel tried to stifle it but she just laughed harder.

Marty glanced between them and then slowly took a seat beside Olivia.

"See? No bloodshed." Olivia smiled at him and Mel saw a definite sparkle in Marty's eye. She sucked in a surprised breath. It wasn't just some strange matchup; Marty was truly smitten with Olivia Puckett.

Mel glanced quickly at Angie, but she was too busy scowling at Olivia to notice Marty. Mel looked back, wondering if she was wrong. No, the sparkle was there and what's more, Olivia sparkled right back at him. Oh, wow.

"I like your kitchen," Olivia said. "It's cozy."

"Is that an insult?" Angie half rose out of her seat. "Just because your kitchen is bigger doesn't make you a better baker."

Olivia blew out a breath. "That's not what I meant."

"Yeah, she was being polite," Marty said. "Maybe you should try it sometime."

"Ah," Angie gasped. "What's that supposed to mean?"

"Now, Martin," Olivia said as she patted his knee. "This is new for all of us and it's going to take some getting used to."

"What's to get used to?" Marty asked. He circled his finger at the three of them. "You all had a crazy thing, now she and I have a different crazy thing. NBD."

"Did you just 'No Big Deal' me?" Angie asked. She looked as if the hold she was keeping on her temper was tenuous at best. She frowned at Olivia. "The man is talking in acronyms now. Did you teach him that?"

"No, but it's just darling, isn't it?" Olivia asked. She wrinkled her snub nose and made kissy noises at him.

"I'm dry heaving on the inside if anyone cares," Angie said.

Mel glanced between Marty and Olivia. They were a thing. This wasn't just temporary insanity on his part. Not

to go all acronym, but in her head she was shouting "OMG!" She forced herself to remain calm.

"No, Marty's right," Mel said. "This is what it is."

"What?" Angie asked. Then she gestured across the table. "Do not encourage this! This needs to be ending—and soon."

"Why?" Olivia asked. She looked unhappy, like she was ready to roll up her sleeves and wade into a brawl, which Mel really didn't want in her kitchen.

"Because you're whacko," Angie said. "Have you forgotten how you've stalked us, tackled us, sabotaged our cupcake van, and tried to horn in on our photo shoot? Because I can assure you, I have not."

"I've changed," Olivia said.

Mel glanced at Marty. He nodded. "She really has."

"How?" Angie asked. "How have you changed?"

"I'm happy now," she said. She cast a shy glance at Marty. "I have more in my life than just the bakery. I'm not lonely anymore. It's made me see things differently."

Marty reached over and took her hand in his and gave it a gentle squeeze. Mel knew that if Angie pushed this and told Marty it was them or Olivia, they stood a really good chance of losing Marty. That was not an option.

"I'm sorry, but this is completely unacceptable," Angie said. "We've been patient but enough is enough—"

"Hey, when you hooked up with Roach, we didn't abandon you," Marty said.

"That was different," Angie protested.

"Uh, yeah, he was a rock star with a murder rap following him around like a bad smell and we still didn't make you choose," Marty said.

"He has a point," Mel said.

Angie rolled her eyes, then leaned across the table and glared at Olivia. "Fine, but if you hurt him, I will *reduce* you, if you get my drift."

Olivia nodded while Marty gave Angie a lopsided grin. "Aw, I love you, too, Ange."

Angie glowered at him and grunted, but her meaning was clear. Marty was her friend and she would protect him until the end.

"Well, on that peculiar note, I'd better get back to my bakery," Olivia said. "Sadly, and I do mean that, these concoctions are not going to bake themselves."

"Olivia, I know you came into the pageant late," Mel said, "but have you seen anything—"

"No," Olivia answered as Mel let the question dangle. "Marty and I have talked about it, but I haven't seen anything related to the murder."

"Well, thanks anyway," Mel said.

"Sure," Olivia said. She walked to the kitchen door with Marty by her side.

"Well, I'm not sure how I feel about this," Angie said as the door shut behind them. "I mean I know I don't like it, but it's nice to see Marty with a spring in his step."

"If Marty's happy, we're happy for him," Mel said.

"Even if we're not," Angie said.

"Exactly," Mel said.

Twenty-five

The next morning passed by in a blur of buttercream and sprinkles as they prepped the cupcake tower that would be on display during the talent competition and began baking the cupcakes for the contestant's recipe event the next day.

Mel was moving so fast she almost slammed into the back door when it was abruptly thrown open and Joyce charged into the room.

"You have to see this!" Joyce cried. She was holding a garment bag up in the air by the hanger and was actually jumping up and down.

Mel, Angie, and Tate all stopped packing the cupcakes to look at her.

"Your friend Alma did it," Joyce cried. "Lupe is going to kill."

"Probably not the best metaphor to use at this juncture, Mom," Mel said.

Jenn McKinlay

Joyce blanched. "Sorry. See what happens when I try to be hip? It just goes horribly awry."

Tate grinned. "We love you anyway."

Joyce smiled at him and said, "Here, let me just show you the dress and I'll get out of your hair."

She crossed the room and hung the hanger on the door-frame. She unzipped the bag and carefully moved it back around behind the dress.

Mel was a diehard jeans and T-shirt sort of girl; skirts were too hard to move around in, silky blouses never fit right, and high heels hurt. But even Mel knew a knock-you-to-your-knees gorgeous dress when she saw one and this was it.

Alma had taken the plain ivory sheath Lupe was going to wear and transformed it. A trail of black velvet roses were embroidered down the left side of the gown, branching at the waist to fan out across the hem in a thick garden of roses.

"Wow," Mel said. "She must have worked all night on that."

"No, I think it was one of her minions," Joyce said. "At least, there was a young woman asleep on a sofa in the corner of the studio who looked like she'd had a rough night, so I assumed it was her."

"We're going to have to send her more cupcakes," Angie said.

"Agreed," Mel said. "Where is Lupe? Don't you have to be at the resort for the talent portion?"

"She's going with Oz," Joyce said. "I promised to meet her mother and sisters there. How Lupe has managed to keep them out of the loop on all of the trouble, I don't know, but so far so good, so don't say anything that might clue her mother in, got it? Apparently, Lupe's family is very eager to see her performance."

"Any idea what she'll be doing?" Tate asked.

"No." Joyce bit her lip and Mel could tell she was nervous. "The only positive about it is that Lupe hasn't had time to worry about the murder investigation."

"They haven't called her back for more questioning, have they?" Mel asked.

"No, Stan said they were waiting for some test results from forensics before they make their next move," she said. "I keep telling myself we just have to get through tonight and be ranked in the top five and then she can pull it out for the win. I tried everything with her—singing, dancing, you name it. I can't imagine what Oz has come up with that I couldn't, but I'm hoping it can measure up to the years of ballet and such that the other girls have had."

"Don't worry, Joyce, I've heard a lot of contestants do dramatic readings," Angie said. "You know, if they can't sing 'Over the Rainbow' or show their jazz hands."

"I'm sure they came up with something solid," Mel said. "It can't be any worse than someone busting out a tired old cheerleader routine."

"Or a sad, baggy-pantsed hip-hop routine," Tate said. "Oh, even worse, how about a beat-boxer? That would be just embarrassing."

Joyce gazed at them with a look of wide-eyed horror. "I don't even know what beat-boxing is."

"Don't worry, Mom," Mel said. "Oz is pretty invested in Lupe's success. I'm sure they came up with something perfectly suitable."

"You're right," Joyce said. "I trust Oz. I do, really. So, I'll see you all at the show?"

"Wouldn't miss it," Tate answered for all of them.

Mel watched her mother go and wondered not for the first time if this was what Joyce had wanted from Mel in her younger days. Had she longed for a beauty queen or at least a daughter who would wear skirts and talk about makeup and boys? Mel had been neither of those things.

As they boxed up the cupcakes and loaded them into the van to take to the pageant, Mel couldn't help feeling as if she'd let her mother down. She knew it was ridiculous and that her mother loved her exactly as she was—well, maybe more if she were still engaged to Joe—but there was a little part of Mel that wondered if Joyce was living out her fantasies of having the beautiful daughter while helping Lupe with the pageant.

The thought was not pleasant. She wondered if maybe part of the reason Joyce was so into Mel getting married was so that she could plan the wedding with Mel in the big meringue dress and have the beautiful daughter she'd always been denied during Mel's robust younger years.

"Hey, Mel, you in there?" Angie waved a hand in front of her face. "Time to go."

Mel shook off her stupor and glanced around the kitchen. They were packed up and ready to ride. "Okay, let's roll out."

"Marty, we're off to the pageant," Angie called as she popped her head through the kitchen door to the front of the bakery.

Mel heard him grumble something in return. She smiled. At least they hadn't lost him completely to Olivia. She wondered if there would come a day when he would go and work at Confections. She rejected the thought immediately. No, Marty was loyal. He wouldn't leave them.

"You okay?" Angie asked her as they headed out the back door.

"Yeah, fine, why?" Mel asked.

"You have a worried look on your face," Angie said. "What's wrong?"

"I feel like change is coming," Mel said.

They paused while Tate locked the back door behind them. He threw an arm over each of their shoulders as he walked them to the van.

"Change is a good thing," he said. "Look at all of us. We're doing great, taking the business to all new levels."

Mel blanched.

"Probably not the best example," Angie said.

As they took their seats with Tate driving, Angie in the passenger seat and Mel in the fold-out jump seat in the back, Tate met Mel's gaze in the rearview mirror.

"Breathe," he said. "Turn your worry over to the universe and then ten minutes later, do it again."

Mel smiled at him and nodded. Tate knew her so well. The worry always circled back on her but he was right, she just had to keep turning it over to the universe until she let it go completely.

It didn't take them long to set up the cupcake tower outside of the auditorium where the girls would perform. Mel had been keeping an eye out for Oz and Lupe, but there had been no sign of them. Much to her surprise, Angie's brothers Al and Paulie were there, dressed in matching black jeans and T-shirts.

"You two are helping?" Angie frowned at her brothers.

"Yep, we're the crew," Al said.

"What is she doing that she needs a crew?" Tate asked.

Paulie looked him up and down. He was undecided yet as to whether he approved of Tate's new status as Angie's boyfriend. Tate stood straighter and looked him right in the eyes as if daring him to say anything. Paulie glanced at his sister and then back at Tate. Then he shrugged.

"We're not allowed to tell you," Al said around a mouthful of cupcake.

Mel had gone with variety for tonight's cupcake tower. It was fully loaded with everything from her signature Tinkerbells, a lemon cupcake with raspberry icing, to her Blonde Bombshells, almond cupcake with vanilla buttercream and toasted almonds, to her decadent Death by Chocolates.

"Mel, hurry," Joyce called from the doorway to the auditorium. "They're about to start."

"Coming," Mel said. "Are you sure you two are okay out here?"

Tate and Angie had agreed to man the cupcake tower so that Mel could sit with Joyce for moral support. Joyce was so nervous she had actually started biting her nails, a nervous habit she had broken years ago.

"Yep, we're good," Tate said. "We can see from here. Joyce needs you. Go."

Mel hurried into the auditorium. She had to scoot past several pairs of knees until she got to the seat Joyce was holding for her. There was another empty seat, which she assumed was for Ginny.

Sitting on the other side of Joyce was a lovely woman who appeared to be only a few years older than Mel. She was wearing a pretty skirt and blouse and had three younger girls sitting on the other side of her. It had to be Lupe's mom, Gloria Guzman, and Lupe's little sisters.

"Melanie, this is Gloria," Joyce said, confirming Mel's guess. "Gloria, my daughter, Mel."

"How do you do?" Mel asked as she shook the woman's hand.

"Terrified," Gloria said. She gave Mel a comically worried look and Mel laughed.

Looking at Gloria, it was easy to see where Lupe got her good looks from. Gloria had the same lovely features and glossy black hair. Mel realized she must have had Lupe when she was very young. Mel couldn't imagine being widowed with four daughters to raise. Suddenly, her own life and problems seemed ridiculously easy in comparison.

"I'm nervous, too," Mel said. "But Lupe is amazing and whatever she does, she is going to be terrific."

Gloria smiled at her in thanks. Mel blinked. Like Lupe, Gloria's smile was a stunner.

"Am I late? I didn't miss it, did I?" a voice asked from behind her.

Mel spun around to find Joe sliding into the empty seat beside her.

"Joe!" she cried. "What are you doing here?"

"I asked your mom to save me a seat," he said. "I couldn't miss this."

Impulsively, Mel reached forward and hugged him close. It meant more than words could say that he was here.

"Thank you," she said when she pulled back.

He studied her face a second. His voice was gruff when he said, "My pleasure."

A sigh from Mel's other side let her know that her mother

had heard the exchange. Thankfully, the lights abruptly dimmed, a rousing bit of music was pumped into the room, and Cici Hastings took the stage.

She was wearing a sparkly red gown that hugged her curves and had a daring slit up one side that showed off a righteous pair of gams for a lady of her years. She glided across the floor in her heels, and her hair was done up in its usual mass of curls, making her appear taller than she was.

"Welcome to the seventy-fifth annual Sweet Tiara Beauty Pageant," she addressed the crowd. "Tonight's portion of the pageant is devoted to our twenty finalists who will be displaying for you their many talents."

While Cici droned on, Mel felt Joe's hand on her upper back, gently gliding up and down as if he knew she was a nervous wreck and he was trying to calm her down.

Mel turned to smile at him, but instead she saw Manny and Uncle Stan at the far end of the room, working their way through the crowd. She frowned.

"Sorry," Joe said. He removed his hand.

"No, it's not you," she said. She nodded in Uncle Stan's direction. "I have a feeling something is about to go down."

Joe followed the direction of her gaze and blew out a breath. "I think you're right. Shall we?"

Mel nodded. While Cici introduced the judges, Mel and Joe climbed over the laps of the people surrounding them and hurried to the side of the auditorium. The room lights went all the way down as the stage lights went up. Mel could barely see a few steps in front of her face. Joe's hand at her back guided her to the wall.

A rousing march blasted through the speakers as a baton twirler burst out onto the stage. Mel stopped to stare as the woman's sparkly bodysuit dazzled while she marched and spun and tossed her baton high into the air.

"Focus, Mel," Joe said. "Where are we going?"

"Backstage," Mel said. "I got the feeling they were headed backstage."

They hurried out a side door and down the short hall that would give them access to the backstage area. Mel and Joe opened the door and climbed the dark stairs to the back. The booming march was still playing and Mel noticed many girls in costume clustered in the wings, watching their competition with nervous gazes.

"You can't take her now!" a voice, a deep male voice, shouted from the back corner.

Oz! Mel knew it was him immediately.

"This way," she said to Joe. They worked their way through the crowd until they reached a small cluster of people in the back.

Oz was standing in front of Lupe, going nose to nose with Manny. Paulie and Al flanked her while Uncle Stan stood next to Manny, looking very unhappy. Lupe for her part looked amazing in a black bodysuit with glittery purple flames shooting up the sides.

"The evidence from the lab just came in," Uncle Stan said. "We have to take her in."

"Not right now," Oz fumed.

Mel didn't hesitate. She strode forward. "What's going on here?"

"This doesn't concern you, Mel," Manny said. It was the wrong thing to say.

"Sorry, you're talking to my people, it very much concerns me," she said.

"Mel, we have a fingerprint match for Lupe," Stan said.

"On what?" Mel asked.

"The sash," Manny said. He was clearly unhappy about it.

"How can you get a fingerprint off of fabric?" Oz asked. "Is that even possible?"

"It's a new technology called VMD, vacuum metal deposition, where they heat up gold to evaporate it and spread a fine film over the fabric. Then they heat up zinc, which attaches to the gold where there are no fingerprint residues. The end result is like a negative of a photograph, only it's a fingerprint," Uncle Stan explained. "It revealed Lupe's fingerprints on the sash used to strangle Mariel. We have no choice, we have to take her in."

"Was it Mariel's sash?" Lupe asked. "Because she told me to put it on."

"What?" Manny asked.

"It was the day of the interviews," Lupe said. Her voice was low and it was hard to hear her over the applause of the crowd for the baton twirler. "Mariel told me to put on the sash and the tiara, so I did, then she taunted me saying that it would never be mine, because I didn't have what it takes."

Uncle Stan frowned. Manny looked annoyed.

"Do you know if anyone witnessed this?" Manny asked. "Did anyone see you touch that sash?"

"No, I was—well, she got to me and I was crying," Lupe said.

"Why didn't you tell me?" Oz asked. "I would have—"

"I don't think you want to go there, Oz," Joe said.

He moved in behind Mel and she took comfort in his presence at her back.

Manny squinted at him. "DeLaura."

"Martinez."

"I heard you had a big case to prep for," Manny said. "Should you really be here?"

"They're all big," Joe said. "Don't worry. I'll do what needs to be done."

Uncle Stan glanced between the two of them and then looked at Mel. She shrugged.

"Without a witness, we'll have to take you in for more questioning," Uncle Stan said.

"I'm a witness," a voice said from behind Paulie and Al.

Everyone turned. Destiny Richards stood there in a pale diaphanous gown that made her look like she had stepped right out of a book of fairy tales.

"I was there when Mariel had her try on the sash and the tiara," Destiny said. "Lupe is telling the truth. Mariel was very cruel to her. And if it's fingerprints you're looking for, you should check mine. I touched both the sash and the tiara when I helped her take them off."

Stan and Manny exchanged a glance. Mel didn't think she was imagining that they looked relieved.

"I'm sorry I didn't say anything at the time. I should have," Destiny said.

Lupe's eyes went wide in surprise. "No, I . . . it's all right. Thank you."

"Destiny! What are you doing back here?" Brittany Richards came across the backstage area like a steamroller. "Move it. You'll miss your cue. Go. Go. Go!"

Destiny darted away.

"So, you got your witness, are we good here now?" Oz asked.

Manny and Uncle Stan exchanged an uneasy look. Mel knew that they still felt the need to take Lupe in but they couldn't, not now, and not just because Lupe was about to perform. She remembered joining Angie by Mariel's body. In fact, the dead woman's image was emblazoned on her brain. And what they were saying was wrong.

"You can't take her in," Mel said.

"Mel—" Manny sounded exasperated.

"No, hear me out, you can't take her in, because I am quite sure that the sash wrapped around Mariel's neck wasn't her Miss Sweet Tiara sash."

Twenty-six

"You can check with Angie, but I am sure, very sure, that the sash used to strangle Mariel wasn't the sash that the winner wears," Mel said. "We saw that one and it was different. I remember it was a much deeper pink than the one used to strangle Mariel."

"Have you touched any other sashes?" Uncle Stan asked Lupe.

"Yes, we all have," she said. "They've had us wearing them for photo shoots and stuff. I'm sure they have all of our fingerprints on them."

Uncle Stan and Manny exchanged a look. Manny turned to Lupe. "Go ahead and perform but don't leave the premises without telling one of us." He turned to leave but then turned back. "And good luck."

Uncle Stan gave Lupe a thumbs-up. "Is Angie still by the cupcake tower?" he asked Mel.

"Yes, she should be," Mel said.

The two detectives left. Oz looked at Lupe and asked, "You okay?"

"Fine," she said. It was an obvious lie but Mel admired her for trying to pull it off.

"All right, the rest of you clear out!" Oz ordered. "My girl needs to focus."

Lupe's head whipped in his direction at the "my girl," but being intent on shooing the rest of them toward the stairs, Oz didn't notice.

"Got it," Joe said. He and Oz bumped knuckles and Joe took Mel's hand and led her through the dark toward the hall.

Mel could hear Destiny singing in the background and she noted that the girl had a very pretty voice. Nothing that would get her an *American Idol* win, but still, it was more pleasant than the booming march of the baton twirler.

"Let's not crawl over the crowd to get back to our seats," Mel whispered.

"Agreed," Joe said. "I don't want to give someone an inadvertent lap dance."

Mel smiled as they moved to stand at the side of the auditorium. Joe still had her hand in his and she found that it felt right. They felt right.

Joe released her fingers and Mel felt bereft. But then, what had she expected? She had been playing with Joe like he was a yo-yo for months. Pulling him close and pushing him away. It wasn't fair to him. She knew what he wanted— marriage, kids, the whole 'til-death-do-us-part package. If she couldn't woman up and agree to it then she had to let him go.

She glanced at him out of the corner of her eye. He

looked at her with a smile that was full of affection. Had she not worn him out yet? How could that be? If the situation were reversed, she'd have cut him loose weeks ago.

Rising up on her tiptoes, Mel went to kiss his cheek as a thank-you for being the incredibly patient, kind, and loving man that he was. As if anticipating her move, Joe moved and her lips landed on his. She felt him smile beneath her lips as he deepened the kiss.

When they parted, Mel was breathing hard and she was pretty sure she saw stars shooting in her peripheral vision.

Joe leaned close. "What was that for?"

"It was supposed to be a 'thank you for being so great' kiss," Mel whispered. "But it rapidly turned into a 'what are you doing later' kiss."

Joe chuckled and the sound seemed to echo low and deep inside of her. Mel glanced up to see if anyone in the auditorium had noticed them, but she figured she would have heard her mother cry "dear Joe" if she had.

As Cici took the stage to introduce the next talent, Joe leaned down and whispered, "Marry me."

No almost flew out of Mel's mouth just out of habit. Instead, she put her hand in his and squeezed his fingers in hers. She could feel Joe studying the side of her face, but just then Cici read Lupe's name and they both turned to the stage.

There was a rumble of noise from behind the curtain and Mel thought she heard Paulie, or maybe it was Al, yelp. She felt Joe stiffen beside her. They could hear movement, the scrape and scuffle of what sounded like heavy equipment, and then there was silence.

Mel felt her innards get taut with nerves. She let go of Joe's hand as her palm began to sweat and put her arm around his waist, holding on to him for support. He put his arm over her shoulder and pulled her close. She could tell he was nervous, too.

The grinding noise from behind the curtain started again, and Mel could see the crowd getting restless, and then it stopped. The audience was murmuring and shifting in their seats. Still, the curtain didn't move.

Softly, a guitar began to play. Mel recognized it immediately as the beginning of Oasis's "Love Like a Bomb." The stage curtain was yanked open. Two enormous glittery ramps were revealed and Lupe, in full skateboard gear and with her black hair flying beneath a purple sparkly helmet, shot down one of the ramps as the music swelled and blasted through the auditorium.

The speed with which she moved took Mel's breath away. Lupe hit the top of the opposite ramp and flipped her board under her feet before sailing back down and across the stage to the other ramp. The height she hit made Mel gasp and grasp Joe tight. They both stood frozen as Lupe executed a spin in the air before dropping back down.

Lupe dazzled the audience, weaving a spell over them as she worked the two curved ramps back and forth in a dizzying choreography of flips, spins, and twists, always keeping her board under her feet and moving at a breakneck speed.

She finished with the music, grinding the middle of the board across a rail that had been set across the front of the stage. She ended the routine by flipping the board with her feet, up into her arms.

The crowd went crazy. Mel could see Joyce standing on her chair and giving a piercing two-fingered whistle. She and Joe broke away from each other to applaud and cheer with all of the rest. Lupe beamed as she bowed. She went to leave the stage but the crowd was still cheering and chanting her name. Paulie caught her and turned her around and gave her a shove back out to the stage.

Lupe unstrapped her helmet and lifted it off her head. She then gave a deep curtsy that charmed the crowd all over again. Mel watched as she hurried off the stage.

From her view at the side, Mel could see where Lupe was headed. She dropped her helmet and her skateboard and ran full on straight into Oz's waiting arms. He lifted her up and spun her around and then he kissed her.

The curtain on the stage closed and Mel felt as if her heart was full to bursting. Their girl had done it. There was no way anyone could beat a performance like that, not even if they were a lion tamer who taught the big cats to bake cupcakes.

She glanced around the room and saw Angie and Tate standing just a few paces down the wall from her and Joe. Angie's brown gaze met hers and Angie wiggled her eyebrows up and down, letting Mel know she'd seen the teen's embrace as well. Mel grinned. She couldn't help but be happy for Lupe and Oz.

Cici took the stage and announced that there would be a brief intermission.

"I bet no one wants to go onstage after that," Joe said.

"I can't blame them," Mel said. She glanced across the room. "Do me a favor?"

"Name it," he said.

"Could you corral my mother?" She pointed to where Joyce was still standing on her chair along with Lupe's mother and sisters. "She'll listen to you. If there's going to be an intermission, I should really help at the cupcake tower."

"On it," Joe said and he pushed off the wall and waded into the crowd.

Mel turned and hurried out to the lobby, where Tate and Angie had already resumed their positions.

"Let's work the room and keep the mob to a minimum," Angie said as she handed Mel a fully loaded tray.

"Good plan," Mel said and she hoisted the tray up onto her shoulder and set out to work the far end of the room.

"That was *not* a talent," a voice hissed to her left. She recognized the high-pitched whine as belonging to Brittany Richards.

Mel decided to eavesdrop while she handed out cupcakes with a smile.

The Richardses were seated in plush chairs at the far end of the lobby. Mel worked the people around them while she listened.

"Did you hear me, Brandon? I want her disqualified," Brittany said. "There is no way *that* performance should be considered a talent. What will they do next? Let someone perform jump shots with a basketball?"

"Calm down, Brittany," Brandon said in a weary voice.

"Don't patronize me," Brittany snapped. "You're not the one who has invested all of their time and energy in Destiny winning. I am."

"Not invested?" Brandon snapped. "Do you have any idea how much our darling daughter's pageants have cost me? Between the professional pictures, the voice lessons, the coaches, the tailor-made gowns, the entrance fees, the travel fees, the hair and makeup artists, not to mention the deals brokered with certain people of influence, I can assure you, my dear, I am very much invested in her winning."

His voice was a low growl and Mel felt the hair on the back of her neck stand on end. His annoyance had morphed into rage in mere seconds. Of course, she imagined Brittany could do that to anyone. Still, she thought maybe a cupcake would help.

"Excuse me," she said as she approached with her tray out. "Can I interest you in a cupcake?"

Brittany gave Mel a hostile look, but eagerly helped herself to two cupcakes. Brandon waved at her dismissively, not bothering to say a word.

"Really, Brittany, two-fisting?" he asked. "Don't look at me when your thighs look like watermelons."

Mel cringed at the hostility in his voice. She sidled to the group to the right of the squabbling couple where she could still observe them.

Brittany's face crumpled and her lower lip began to tremble. She gave a tiny sniffle and Mel found herself scanning the area for a tissue for the poor thing.

"Don't you dare," Brandon hissed. "Don't try to manipulate me with your tears. It won't work."

Abruptly, Brittany's face became a cold, hard mask.

"Fine," she said and she took a huge bite of one of the cupcakes. Frosting smeared her upper lip and she licked it off, staring at her husband through her blond bangs as she did so.

Brandon swallowed as he watched her, and it was obvious that if tears weren't going to work, Brittany had other weapons in her arsenal.

"You make me sick," he said.

"But you still want me and you'll do anything for me, won't you?" she purred. "Anything."

Brandon hung his head in defeat.

Mel forced her gaze away. She couldn't help but feel there was something obscene about the interaction between the husband and wife. The power that Brittany had over her husband made Mel distinctly uncomfortable and she almost felt sorry for Brandon Richards.

What caused her even more concern, however, was his comment about deals brokered with people of influence. What people? What deals? Was Brandon Richards buying off judges or contestants?

"Mel, over here!" Steve Wolfmeier called to her from a nearby group. "Did you see Lupe? Wasn't my client amazing?"

"Have you been retained in an official capacity?" Mel asked.

"Who do you think sprang her from questioning yesterday?" he asked.

"That was you?"

"Well, no," he said. "They released her, but I was on the phone with your uncle when it happened, so I like to take the credit."

"Ah." Mel nodded.

"So, have you seen her?" he asked. "I wanted to congratulate her. If she doesn't win for that performance then I am declaring this pageant rigged."

"Agreed," Mel said. "But no, I haven't seen her since she finished and ran straight into—"

"Oz's arms?" Steve asked. "Yeah, I saw that—among other things."

Mel met his gaze and felt her face grow warm. Had he seen her and Joe? She was at once mortified and relieved.

"So does number two know that you're still in love with number one?" he asked.

Twenty-seven

Mel took a cupcake off of the tray and shoved it at him.

"There is no number one, two, or three," she said. She used her most discouraging tone.

"Excellent, so the field is wide open then?" he asked. His eyes twinkled with mischief and Mel shook her head.

"You're impossible," she said.

"I could have told you that," Manny said. "'Sup, weasel?"

"Now is that nice?" Steve asked as he unwrapped his cupcake. "Here I am minding my own business and—Oh, wow, this is amazing."

Mel smiled at him, handed a cupcake to Manny, and said, "Play nice."

"Huh," Manny grunted and took the cupcake. "Does this constitute a bribe?"

"Would it help?"

"No," he said. "Different sash, huh?"

"That was confirmed?" Mel asked.

Manny took a bite of his cupcake. "Yep."

"Meaning you don't have to haul anyone in for questioning?" she asked.

"For the moment," Manny said.

"Well, looks like my work here is done," Steve said. "Or not." He glanced behind Mel and she turned to find Joe crossing the room to join them.

"Joyce is down?" she asked.

"Yes, her feet are planted firmly on the ground," he said.

"This was fun until number one showed up," Steve said to Manny.

"Agreed," Manny said.

They both gave Joe a dark look.

"Number one?" Joe asked. He grinned as he helped himself to a chocolate cupcake with pomegranate icing.

"Don't listen to them," Mel said.

"Number two here," Manny said.

"I'm number three, but I think it's lucky," Steve said.

"Seriously, what are they talking about?" Joe asked Mel.

"Nonsense," she said. "Trust me."

"It's the order of dating Mel," Manny said. "Hey, that almost sounds like the name of a fraternal organization."

"Yeah, we've done the fraternity thing before." Joe gestured between him and Steve. "It didn't really work out for me."

"That's history," Steve said. "You need to let it go. I sort of dig belonging to the Fraternal Order of Mel."

"Oh. My. God," Mel said. She glanced at the three of them as if trying to decide which one she was going to smack first.

"You could be our supreme pooh-bah," Manny said to Joe.

"I think I'd rather be king," he said.

"That would make us princes or knights?" Steve asked.

"Knights, definitely knights," Manny said.

"Hey, I'm standing right here," Mel said. She stared at the three of them in disbelief. "And let me be clear on how there is no king, pooh-bah, princes, or knights."

All three of them looked at her and then turned back to each other.

"Maybe I can be a prince and you can be a knight," Steve said to Manny. "You're more macho than me."

"No," Manny said. "Princes are ranked higher than knights and I'm number two."

"I thought you were number three," Joe said.

"I think I'm getting a migraine," Mel said. None of them looked at her. She glanced down at her tray and made her way over to the tower.

Tate was manning what was left of the cupcakes. There was no sign of Angie.

"What's going on with the Mel Squad over there?" Tate asked as he gestured to Joe, Manny, and Steve, who were still deep in discussion.

"You mean other than the fact that they're morons?" she asked.

"Still working out a pecking order?" he asked.

"Don't go there," Mel growled. "I am so over the 'pair and a spare' thing."

"Well, you know how to solve that dilemma," Tate said. "Pick one."

"It's not that easy," Mel said.

"Yes, it is," Tate said. "You simply look at the one you want and say, 'I choose you.'"

"But—"

Sugar and Iced

"No, there's no buts about this, Mel," he said. He turned away from the tray he was loading for her. "You know when I was too chicken to man up and make a play for Angie, you were the one who called me on it."

"It's not the same," Mel said, even though she feared it was.

"Oh, yeah, it totally is," Tate said. He rested his hand on her shoulder. "Now, I know you have self-esteem issues. Remember I was there for all of the icky years, but they are long over and you need to get comfortable with the you that you've become, which is a knockout by the way."

"I am—"

"Let me finish," he said. "I know, too, how losing your dad crushed you. I was there for that also. I loved your dad, Mel, he was a hell of a guy. And I know you're afraid to let someone in because you may have to go through loss of one kind or another again. Here's the thing. That's life and you need to get over it."

"Harsh," Mel said.

"Takes one to know one," he retorted. Then his gaze softened and he pulled her into a half hug. "Mel, what would your dad think if he saw you were afraid to get involved because of him?"

"Knife to the chest—Ow!" she said. Tate didn't say anything, just gave her another squeeze. Mel sighed. "He'd be sad and probably a little disappointed."

"Yeah, he would," Tate agreed. "So, you know what you need to do."

Mel stepped away and met his gaze. "Yes, I do. I need to serve more cupcakes."

"No, that's not what I—"

But Mel had already hoisted her tray up and was moving through the crowd. She knew Tate was right. She knew her

195

dad would be unhappy that she was stuck in a holding pattern, afraid to move forward. She needed to make a decision about what she wanted. And she would, any day now.

When the scores were tallied for the talent show, Lupe was far and away the clear winner. While Destiny seemed okay with this outcome, Mel saw her mother approach the judges, looking furious.

Before Brittany could make contact, Brandon appeared and grabbed her by the arm, stopping her. She looked like she was going to forge on ahead, but he leaned in close and whispered something in her ear. Brittany tried to jerk her arm out of his hold, but he didn't let go, and finally she allowed him to lead her away.

As they broke down the cupcake tower, Paulie and Al showed up looking for leftovers. There were none.

"Meet us back at the bakery and we'll celebrate," Mel said.

Oz and Lupe joined the group and Mel noted that they were holding hands. She glanced at Oz and he gave her a sheepish shrug.

When Lupe let go of him to go and hug her mother and sisters, Mel gave Oz a squeeze.

"That was genius," she said. "You really made Lupe a contender in this competition."

"Nah," he said. "She did that just by being herself. She really is amazing."

As he watched her with her family, Mel could see the affection in his gaze.

"So, has there been a status change in the relationship?" Mel asked.

"Yeah, from what we saw you two aren't just pals anymore," Angie said as she joined them.

"Aw, what? You *saw* us?" Oz asked.

"Next time, save the smooches for when you're farther backstage," Angie said.

"Can we please not talk about this?" Oz's face turned a deep shade of red, and Mel felt for him, really she did, but not enough to not want some specifics.

"Oz, the pickup truck is loaded," Tate called as he entered the lobby. "You ready to roll out?"

"You have no idea," Oz said. He punched Tate on the shoulder as he passed. "Your timing is epic."

Tate rubbed his shoulder as he watched Oz hurry from the building.

"Was that a love tap or is he miffed at me?" he asked.

"No, that was love," Angie said. "You saved him from the inquisition.

Tate glanced between them and then understanding lit his eyes. "Ah, so no word on his new status with Lupe yet?"

"No, darn it," Angie said.

"Well, maybe he's unclear as to what the status is," Mel said. "I suppose we'll have to wait and see."

"Poor Oz," Tate said with a shake of his head.

"What do you mean?" Angie asked.

"Waiting is not your gift," Tate said as he dropped an arm over each of their shoulders and led them to the door.

Back at the bakery, Marty fired up the jukebox when he heard about how well Lupe had done, Oz raided the walk-in cooler for cupcakes and they all celebrated with Lupe and her family, Joyce, and Ginny.

Steve and Joe popped in, as well as Paulie and Al. Lupe's younger sisters would not take no for an answer when it came to dancing and so the men were put to work twirling the younger girls around until they giggled themselves into a case of hiccups. It was festive and fun and for the first time in days, Mel felt optimistic about Lupe's chances at winning the pageant.

Mel was in the front of the bakery, clearing cupcake wrappers from a booth by the window, when she saw a shadow loom over the glass.

"What the—?"

"Mel, look out!" Joe yelled as he grabbed her around the middle and dragged her down to the floor.

Twenty-eight

Boom! A brick landed on the floor next to Mel. She couldn't move, as Joe had her wrapped in his arms, covering her back with his front while glass rained down on top of them.

Shrieks sounded as Lupe and her sisters were dragged back against the display case and shielded by the men.

Joe stood, pulling Mel to her feet. He spun her around and looked her over. "Are you all right?"

Mel nodded, since her power of speech seemed to have momentarily fled.

"Is anyone hurt?" Gloria cried as she checked over her children.

"We'll catch him!" Paulie yelled as he and Al ran for the door. The door had just shut behind them when the sound of a car engine revving and tearing off down the street sounded.

Mel gaped at her window. Then she glanced around the

bakery. No one moved until Marty had the presence of mind to shut off the jukebox. Then Lupe's littlest sister began to cry.

"Stan, I need you *now*," Joyce said into her cell phone. "Someone threw a brick through the bakery's front window."

Mel glanced around the room. Glass shards were everywhere. The floor looked like a land mine. Gloria had Lupe's littlest sister in her arms and was trying to shush her cries.

"Take the girls up to my apartment. They can play with Captain Jack. My key is in the office," Mel said to Oz.

"I'll get them settled and be right back," he said. Together he and Lupe led her sisters and mother into the kitchen.

Paulie and Al came banging back in through the front door.

"We gave chase," Al wheezed.

"But they lost us," Paulie finished.

"But we did see the car," Al added. "No license plate, though."

"Thanks for trying, guys," Joe said.

Marty had gone into the kitchen and come back with two brooms and a dustpan. He handed one to Steve, who for the first time since Mel had known him seemed at a loss for words.

"Mel!" Angie cried. "You're bleeding!"

Mel glanced down at her body. She didn't see anything. Then she noticed the small pool of blood by her foot. That was when she felt the stabbing pain in her leg. She swayed on her feet and Joe caught her by the elbow.

"Come on," he said. "Let's get you in back where we can look at it."

Joe scooped Mel up into his arms just as the front door

was yanked open. In strode Stan and Manny. Manny took one look at Mel in Joe's arms and he rushed forward.

"What happened?" he asked.

"Brick through the window. I saw it just before it hit, but I didn't see the thrower," Joe said. He gestured toward Paulie and Al. "My brothers got a look at the car. You might want to talk to them while I take care of her."

Manny frowned. He looked at Mel. "You all right?"

"Yeah, I'm sure it's just a scrape," she said.

"I think I should take you to the hospital," Steve shoved his broom at Tate and strode over to where they stood.

"What?" Joe snapped. "I'll take her."

"I have a siren, I'll get her there faster," Manny said.

"I'm fine, really," Mel said. She pushed against Joe in an effort to get down, but his hold was unyielding.

"Scottsdale Osborn hospital is like three minutes away," Joe scoffed. "Your siren won't even get warmed up."

"Are you mocking my siren?" Manny asked. He looked irritated.

"Somebody has to," Steve said.

"Oh, for Pete's sake, the girl is going to bleed out while you three idiots squabble over her like she's the prize in a cereal box," Marty snapped.

"That's the problem with dating a pair and a spare," Tate said. He winked at her, but Mel was not amused.

"I am not—" Mel began to protest but Marty interrupted her.

"Joyce, Angie, you two take Mel to the ER," Marty said. "The rest of you, start cleaning and we need someone to board up the window."

"Ouch!" Mel cried.

"Sorry," Joyce said. She had rolled up Mel's pant leg and found the shard of glass that was stuck in the fleshy part of Mel's lower leg.

"Dear Joe, will you carry her to my car?" Joyce said. "I'm afraid to pull the glass out in case I miss a piece."

"Sure," Joe said.

"I'll get our purses and meet you at the car," Angie said. She hurried to the office to grab their belongings.

"I'll check on you later," Manny said.

"Me, too," Steve promised.

Joyce's car was parked in front of the bakery. Joe carefully placed Mel in the backseat, using a rolled-up blanket to elevate her foot.

"Do you want me to come with you?" he asked.

Mel glanced at Joyce and Angie in the front seat.

"I think I'm good, but thanks," she said.

Joe kissed her forehead and ducked out of the car.

"Take care of my girl, Joyce," he said.

Mel's mother sighed as she backed out of her parking spot.

"Don't say it, Mom," Mel said. "Or I'll let myself bleed all over your upholstery."

"Say what?" Joyce asked. Her voice was entirely too innocent.

"Whatever you're thinking," Mel said. "Don't say it."

"Fine," Joyce sighed, which of course meant that it wasn't.

Angie turned halfway in her seat, monitoring Mel as they made their way to the emergency room.

"You okay?" Angie asked.

"Someone just threw a brick through our bakery window," Mel said. "I'm hell and gone away from okay."

A very nice doctor in the emergency room removed the glass from Mel's leg and four stitches later she was free to go. When they arrived back at the bakery, it was to find Tate and Marty holding down the fort, while the rest of the crowd had cleared out.

"How are you doing, kid?" Marty asked as Mel hobbled into the bakery, flanked by Joyce and Angie.

"I'm fine," Mel said. She tried to keep her voice steady as she took in the large piece of plywood that had been nailed over the broken window.

"Where is everyone?" Angie asked as she cozied up to Tate, who put his arm around her shoulders and drew her close.

"Marty banished the men to the kitchen," Tate said. "We were tripping over Mel's boyfriends, so he made them wait it out in back."

"They are not my boyfriends," Mel protested.

"Whatever," Marty groused. "Just pick one soon before someone gets hurt."

"But—" Mel began to protest but Marty waved her off.

"Not my business," he said. Then he gave Angie a bug-eyed look. "See what I did there? Minded my own business— mostly."

"The operative word being *mostly.*" Angie returned his big-eyed glance with one of her own.

"Pardon me," Marty said. "I have a hot date."

Angie huffed a breath of annoyance when the door shut after him. Despite the truce with Olivia, she clearly thought an intervention was still in order.

"What did Uncle Stan say about the window?" Mel asked.

"We filed a police report," Tate said. "Stan and Manny canvassed the neighborhood but no one reported seeing anyone or anything suspicious."

"So it's a dead end," Mel said. Tate nodded.

"What about Lupe?" Joyce asked. "Are she and the girls okay?"

"Yes, they were shaken up but otherwise just fine. Oz took them home," Tate said. "Paulie and Al went home, too, as soon as we got the plywood up."

Mel turned and gazed at the big brown board that covered the hole but also kept her from seeing out. She desperately wished that she could blame it on a random act of violence, but she knew better. Someone was sending the bakery a message. The only problem was, she didn't know if it was directed at her or Lupe.

Were they trying to scare Lupe from competing or were they trying to keep Mel from baking the contestant's cupcakes? A few weeks ago, she would have blamed Marty's squeeze, Olivia, but now it just didn't seem likely.

"What do you want to do now?" Angie asked.

"I need to finish the cupcakes for tomorrow," Mel said.

"No, you need to go to bed," Joyce said. "I'll come over in the morning and help you with the cupcakes."

"Me, too," Angie said. "We'll get it done."

"All right, it looks like all I need to do is clean out the kitchen, then," Mel said. "Thanks for everything. I'll see you all in the morning."

"Do you want me to spend the night?" Joyce offered.

"Thanks, Mom." Mel leaned forward and kissed her mom's cheek. "But I'm good."

"Come on, Joyce, we'll walk you to your car," Tate said.

Angie made a "call me if you need me" gesture by holding her hand with thumb and pinky extended up to her ear. Mel nodded to let her know she would. She shut the door behind them and made her way to the kitchen.

She could hear voices on the other side of the door, and she knew it was horribly wrong to eavesdrop, but she did it anyway. "Stupid is as stupid does," as Forrest Gump's mother would say. She wished Tate or Angie were there to appreciate her movie reference, although it was an uber-easy one.

She leaned in close to the door.

"I wonder if this is how the girls in the pageant feel," Steve said.

"What do you mean?" Manny asked.

"Well, look at the three of us, all competing for the same girl as if she's a crown we get to wear on our heads," Steve said.

There was a beat of silence and then Manny said, "She's worth it."

Aw. Mel smiled.

"No question there," Joe said. "A guy spends his whole life looking for a girl like Mel."

Mel felt her heart trip over that one. Maybe this eavesdropping thing was underrated.

"Well, then you should really be out of the running, you had your shot and you blew it," Steve said. "Besides, with the high-profile case you've got going on at the DA's office, are you really in a position to be dating anyone?"

"You're just jealous because she picked me," Joe said. "And don't you worry, I can take care of my cases."

"You two really do have a history, don't you?" Manny asked.

"A very boring one," Joe said.

Mel was pleased to hear that he didn't sound the least bit irritated by Steve. She knew they had been friends who had become bitter rivals for grades and girls in law school.

"I wouldn't say it was boring," Steve said. "Oh, yeah, that's because I always won."

"Seriously, *number three*, do you really think you stand a chance with Mel?" Joe asked. "She's too good for you."

"Agreed," Manny said. "I'll happily let Joe have her if it means she doesn't end up with you."

"What? Are you making an alliance like we're on some lame reality show?" Steve asked.

There was a pause and then both Joe and Manny said, "Yes."

"How is that fair?" Steve asked.

"All's fair in love and war," Manny said.

"If that's the case, then I'll just have to turn up my game," Steve said.

"Really? You don't know Mel at all if you think you can buy her with fancy dinners and sparkly jewelry," Manny said.

"No, but trips to Paris might sway her," Steve said. "Face it, I can give her more than you two can. I can give her a mountainside mansion, a Rolls-Royce, dinner in Paris, a beach house in Malibu, in short, the life she deserves."

Mel felt her jaw drop. She couldn't even imagine a life like that.

"What she deserves doesn't come with a price tag," Joe said. "It's a partner who loves her for exactly who she is, someone she can count on to be there, even when she's pushing him away."

Mel felt her heart constrict. Joe had just described them perfectly and she couldn't help but feel that she had been treating him terribly.

"Spoken like a true public servant," Steve scoffed. "It sounds like you just don't want to face reality, Joe. Mel's not pushing you away, she's simply done with you. And by the way, everyone has a price tag."

"Would it be police brutality if I punched him in the mouth?" Manny asked.

"Only if there's a witness," Joe said. "I could leave."

"Hey, now," Steve said.

Mel doubted that Joe would leave or that Manny would throw a punch. Still, she pushed through the door, interrupting whatever might have happened next.

"Mel!" All three of them rose from the steel table where they'd been sitting. She noted a pile of empty cupcake wrappers and she frowned.

"Out!" she demanded and pointed to the door.

"Are you all right?"

"Did you get stitches?"

"Are you in pain?"

They fired questions at her as she held the door open and gestured them through.

"Yes, four, and not much," she said as they shuffled past her into the bakery. She crossed the room and opened the front door. Again she held it open and gestured for them to leave.

"Good night," she said.

The three of them stood staring at her through the door

as if they couldn't figure out what had just happened, while she shut and locked it.

Mel debated doing some baking, but her leg throbbed and she wanted to go snuggle her cat, Captain Jack, and go to sleep. She checked the bakery as she made her way through it. She hobbled up the back stairs to her apartment. When she opened the door, a ball of white fur with a black spot charged her and she realized that as far as she was concerned, Captain Jack was the only man she needed in her life at the moment. Period.

Mel played a fierce game of attack the paper bag with Captain Jack. It consisted of him climbing into a paper grocery sack while it lay on its side. She would then tickle the side of the bag with her fingers and he would go all kitty karate on the paper bag, trying to get to her fingers. So far the score was Mel ten and Jack zero.

While Jack attacked, retreated, and attacked again, Mel pondered her broken window, Lupe's chance of winning the pageant, and Mariel's murder. She refused to think about the three idiots in her kitchen.

When Jack had exhausted himself and climbed up onto the futon to knead his pillow into the perfect position for sleep, Mel switched off the lamp and tried to sleep. Like a movie reel loop, however, the events of the past few days kept repeating until she finally gave up. She kissed Jack on the head and he purred.

Slipping into a pair of jeans and a sweatshirt, Mel slipped out of her apartment to head down to the bakery. If she wasn't going to sleep, than she might as well work on tomorrow's cupcakes.

She got halfway down the steps when she noticed there

was a person sitting at the bottom. They had their back to her and were using a cell phone. The glow from the display outlined their body, which was big and masculine. Uh-oh. Had the person who tossed the brick returned?

Twenty-nine

Mel felt her heart clench hard like a fist in her chest. She had no weapon but her keys and she doubted she could get back into her apartment before the person caught her. She stood undecided for a second and then realized that the person hadn't heard her yet. Quite possibly, she could either hit them hard from behind and run away or slip back into her apartment and call the police.

She waffled. Fear had her immobilized, plus her leg really smarted and she wasn't sure if she could run on it. What if it went out from under her and she fell? Aside from being embarrassing, it could get her killed.

She decided to see if she could ease her way back up the stairs. She placed her foot on the step behind her and slowly moved backwards. One step, two steps, she started to move faster. *Squeak!*

Mel froze and held her breath. The person below her didn't

move. How could they not have heard what had sounded as loud as a gunshot to her? She waited, poised with one foot on the step behind her. When the person below didn't move, she let out her breath in a tiny sigh.

At that, the man below whipped his head around and jumped to his feet. "Mel?"

Joe DeLaura looked up at her and Mel felt every bit of resistance inside of her shatter and fall away. She walked down the steps, never taking her gaze from his.

"What are you doing here?" she asked.

Joe gave her a lopsided smile. "I knew you wouldn't be able to sleep. And I didn't want you to be alone when you came down here to do your baking, not until we know who threw that brick and why."

Mel leaned into him and Joe wrapped her in a hug. It was the first time her world felt right all night, and she hugged him tight, grateful that she had this man who knew her better than any other in her life.

It was Joe, always Joe. He was the one she wanted to bake cupcakes with in the middle of the night and raise Captain Jack with and spend the rest of her life with. Why had she been so afraid of saying yes to him, to them?

She leaned back and studied his face in the faint over-head light that illuminated the back door to the bakery. She couldn't read the expression on his face and she wondered what he was thinking. She waited for him to ask her to marry him again, as he had every time they were alone over the past few months, but to her surprise, he planted a kiss on her head and stepped away.

"So, what are we baking tonight?" he asked.

"A variety of things," she said. She kept her tone light. "You will not believe some of these concoctions."

She led the way to the back door and unlocked it. As she pushed it open and turned on the lights, she tried to tell herself it was okay if Joe had given up on marrying her. She certainly hadn't given him any reason not to. Still, it was bittersweet to realize that she had finally succeeded in pushing him away. Then again, he was here.

He stood by the table, reading the recipes she had left laid out on the surface. A small smile lifted his lips as he read the ingredients while his dark brown hair flopped over his forehead. Mel moved to stand beside him. She leaned into his side and slipped her arm around his waist.

Automatically, Joe put his arm around her shoulders and pulled her close while he read. His hand ran up and down her arm as if reassuring himself that she was here. It was the smallest of gestures, but like the beat of a butterfly's wings causing a tsunami across the globe, Mel felt its impact. The fear that she would never again hear Joe tell her that he loved her suddenly seemed much larger than the fear that he might one day leave her either by choice or by circumstance.

It hit Mel hard, the realization of how much she truly loved this man. If two people could be two halves of a whole, than Joe was her other half. And now, she just needed to be brave enough to commit to him, to them, to a life together full of all the stomach-dropping downs and heart-lifting highs. Surely she could do that, right?

"Oh, that is just disgusting!" Joe wrinkled his nose and puckered his lips.

"What?" Mel asked, worried that he'd somehow been in her head, reading her thoughts and was appalled.

"These girls may ruin cupcakes for me forever," he said.

Mel glanced at the recipe he pointed to, which used a highly caffeinated lemon-lime soda as its main ingredient.

"Oh, yeah," she sighed with relief. "You may want to steer clear of taste-testing these.

"Hey, are you all right?" he asked. He studied her face with a frown.

"Yeah, I'm fine," she said. She forced a smile to reassure him.

"All right then, let's get to work," he said.

He went over to the sink to scrub up and Mel sighed. The opportunity to tell him about her epiphany slipped through her fingers like melted butter and she didn't know how to snatch it back.

She crossed to the pantry and started to gather ingredients. Probably confessions of undying love were better saved for the morning. She caught a glimpse of her reflection in the glass containers where she stored some of her dry ingredients. Good grief, she had a case of bed head going that made her look as if she had been electrocuted.

Yes, definitely, confessions of undying love could wait until she had combed her hair, and brushing her teeth might be advisable as well.

Mel and Joe spent the next two hours baking. They talked about nothing of substance but instead made each other laugh as they discussed their families, their friends, and the crazy people at the pageant. As if by mutual agreement, they didn't discuss Mariel's murder, Lupe's shot at winning the pageant, or who might have smashed in the bakery window.

When the only task left was frosting the cupcakes, they decided to call it a night. Joe walked her to her door and kissed her forehead. Mel thought about dragging him into her apartment by his shirtfront, but then she yawned. Big romance was just going to have to wait until she had a comb and a nap.

Joe was at the bottom of the stairs and headed for the narrow alley that would take him to his parked car when Mel leaned over the railing of her small balcony and shouted his name.

"Hey, Joe!" she cried.

He stopped and turned to look up at her. "What is it, Cupcake?"

Mel smiled at the nickname. "You know I love you, right?"

He returned her smile, but in the dim light, his smile looked a little sad. "Yeah, I know."

He waved and Mel watched him disappear around the corner of the building. This felt like one of the stomach-dropping lows she'd been so afraid of. She didn't like it. In fact, if this was what life was going to feel like without Joe in it, she was firmly opposed to it.

Mel climbed back into her futon. Captain Jack opened one eye, looked at her, and then turned his back on her. Probably he was miffed that Joe wasn't here, too.

"I'm working on it," she said. Jack ignored her and she supposed it was no more than she deserved.

✦ ✦ ✦

A coffee cup being plunked down on the table beside Mel's head awoke her the next morning. Joyce was sitting in the chair beside her futon with Captain Jack in her lap. He was purring as loud as a V-8 engine while Joyce scratched under his chin.

"What time is it?" Mel asked as she wrestled her way out from under the covers to sit up.

"Well, I thought it was time to bake cupcakes," Joyce said. "But it looks as if someone had a busy night."

"Yeah, I couldn't sleep," Mel said.

"You should have called me," Joyce said. "I'd have come over to help."

Mel leaned back, cradling her cup of coffee. "I had help. Joe was here."

Joyce clasped her hands together and bit her lip but said nothing. Mel knew it was because she was afraid of getting her hopes up.

"He didn't spend the night," Mel said.

"Oh," Joyce said. She unclasped her hands and went back to petting Captain Jack.

"I've been afraid," Mel said.

Joyce didn't look up and meet Mel's gaze; instead she kept petting Captain Jack. Mel thought she heard her mother make a suspicious sniffing sound.

"When your father died, I wasn't sure I could go on," Joyce said. She paused and blew out a breath. "You and your brother were grown, and I didn't think you needed me anymore."

"I'll always need you, Mom," Mel said. Her throat felt tight and her voice came out high and squeaky.

Joyce glanced up and smiled at her. She reached over and smoothed back Mel's hair.

"Thank you," she said. "That's not true, but thank you. I know the loss you felt when your dad died. I felt it, too. At first, I couldn't imagine that I would ever laugh again, or be filled with joy, or look forward to what the next day might bring."

Mel nodded. She had felt the same.

"But then, my grandsons came along, and I could see your dad in them," she said.

Mel laughed. "Yeah, especially when they were bald, chunky babies."

"The similarity was alarming." Joyce laughed, too. "Was it tragic when your father died? Yes. But would my life have been a much bigger tragedy had I not had him in it, even if it wasn't for as long as I wanted? Yes."

Mel met her mother's gaze. Joyce's blue-green hazel eyes, so like her own, were full of warmth and love. Mel reached out and squeezed her mother's hand.

"Thanks, Mom," she said.

"You're welcome," she said. Joyce squeezed her fingers in return. "You and Joe will figure it out. I know you will."

Joyce let go of Mel's hand, then lifted Captain Jack off of her lap and said, "Now get changed and get downstairs. We have cupcakes to decorate and this is Lupe's big day, and I'm trying really hard not to freak out."

"Hey, Mom," Mel called to her mother before she turned away. "Were you disappointed?"

"About you and Joe?" she asked. "Devastated would be more accurate."

"No." Mel shook her head and plucked at the covers in her lap. "About me when I was Lupe's age?"

Joyce frowned and crouched beside the futon. "What are you talking about?"

"I just wondered if maybe you were disappointed that I wasn't, well, thin, pretty, talented, outgoing, you know, basically all of the things mothers are supposed to want in their daughters."

Sugar and Iced

"Oh, heavens, no," Joyce said. Her gaze was so surprised that Mel knew she meant it.

Joyce reached out and took Mel's hand. "The day you were born I fell in love with you. It was such a surprise. I mean I knew I'd love you and your brother, but I didn't know I'd fall *in* love with you. And that has never changed, ever. I've always thought that my children were the most beautiful, most talented, most amusing people to ever grace the planet, and I felt so lucky every day that I got to be your mom. Except for when you dumped Joe, then I thought you were an idiot."

"Mom," Mel turned it into a three-syllable whine and they both laughed.

Joyce leaned over and kissed Mel's head. "I wouldn't change a thing, not one thing, about you. Not then, not now, and not ever. I love you."

"I love you, too, Mom."

Mel smiled as she watched her mother leave and then rolled to her feet. At least the pageant was over today. Mel was ready to stick a fork in it, she was so over the Sweet Tiara Beauty Pageant. That being said, she really hoped Lupe won. The girl had too much to offer the world not to get a full ride to the university of her choice.

\'\,\'\

Angie, Mel, and Joyce did the best they could with the cupcake recipes they had been given. As Oz and Tate loaded up the van to take them to the pageant, Mel fretted that she had tried to make the presentation portion of the cupcakes as equal as possible. She didn't want to give anyone an advantage given that there was really nothing to be done about the taste portion. Some of those cupcakes were just going to be toxic no matter how hard she had tried to make them palatable.

"Are we ready?" Angie asked.

"As we'll ever be," Mel said.

They left Marty in charge of the bakery since Oz demanded to be at the pageant. Tate would do drop-off and then circle back to help Marty, since the window-repair workmen were supposed to be there in the afternoon to fix the front window. Needless to say, one of the DeLaura brothers "knew a guy" and so the repair was progressing much faster than Mel had anticipated.

Joyce had left early to help Lupe get waxed and polished for the evening gown competition later in the day. Ginny had offered up her own personal stylist and Joyce had taken her up on it. Mel did not envy Lupe the morning of primping she was about to endure.

⌇⌇⌇

When Mel and Angie arrived at the resort, it was abuzz with contestants and stage mothers. Olivia had arrived before them and the cupcakes she had baked for the contestants were already front and center in the lobby cupcake tower. Mel and Angie set to work unpacking the ones they had baked and arranging them in the spaces Olivia had left open for them.

"Really, Cooper?" Olivia snickered as she stood nearby in her blue chef's coat with her gray corkscrew curls twisted up on her head in a bun. "Is that the best you could do?"

Mel slowly turned to face her. "Are you seriously trash-talking me?"

Olivia nodded and grinned. "I can't help it. It's like old times."

"Intervention," Angie muttered. "I'm just saying."

Mel glanced at the tower and took in the sight of some of Olivia's cupcakes.

"Red Hots?" she asked. "And I thought Pixy Stix were bad."

"Yeah, I had to taste test some of these on my dog," Olivia said in an undertone. "Everyone else refused and even the dog turned his nose up at that one."

Angie opened her mouth to say something that Mel was quite certain should not be said, so she stepped on her foot.

"Ouch!" Angie yelped.

"Oh, so sorry," Mel said. She turned to Olivia, who was watching them with one eyebrow raised. "I'm such a klutz."

"That's okay." Olivia clapped her on the back with enough force that Mel almost went headfirst into the cupcake tower, only the edge of the table stopping her. "Not all of us are talented enough to make something yummy out of something yucky, so no hard feelings when my cupcakes kick your cupcakes right out of the competition."

Mel stepped in front of Angie, whose hands had come together in a strangling motion.

"Agreed, no hard feelings," Mel said. She would maintain the truce they had worked out even if it cost her a bout of indigestion. "You sound pretty sure of yourself."

"I should," Olivia said. "I have a lot riding on this."

"What do you mean?" Mel asked. "We get paid no matter who wins."

Mel watched as Olivia reached up and fiddled with a gray curl that had escaped her topknot.

"Well, since I have Destiny's cupcakes in my portion of the competition, her father has offered me a free eye tuck if they win," she said.

"What?" Mel asked.

"I know, so I really pulled out all the stops on my cupcakes," Olivia said. "Sadly, I don't know which ones are hers, but I glammed the heck out of all of them, so as long as they taste okay, I have a shot at some free nip and tuck."

"He's bribing you with plastic surgery?" Mel asked. "That has to be against the rules."

"Are you going to tell on me?" Olivia asked.

"I should," Mel said.

"No, you shouldn't. Technically, it's not a bribe," Olivia argued. She plunked her hands on her hips and looked Mel up and down. "It's a bonus if my cupcakes win. You're just sore that you didn't get the offer."

"I am not," Mel argued.

"Yes, you—" Olivia began to argue but Mel interrupted.

"Hey, there's a photographer from the *Arizona Republic*. Probably, they'll want your picture with the cupcakes."

Olivia's face lit up. Mel didn't move until Olivia walked away to greet the media. Then she spun around and saw Angie, holding her hands out, looking like she wanted to choke Olivia.

"Are you crazy? That's Marty's—well, I was going to say 'squeeze,' but that seems bad form. She's his something or other—you can't strangle her."

"But it would feel so good," Angie protested. She grabbed Mel's upper arms and shook her. Her voice took on a pleading tone. "Just one tight squeeze until her head turns bright red and she panics a little and then I swear I'll let go."

"Angie, get a grip. Okay, let me rephrase that," Mel said. "No, absolutely no strangling."

"Do you plan these menace-filled sentences just for my arrival?" a voice asked.

Mel turned to find Manny standing behind her with his arms crossed over his chest. He did not look happy.

Thirty

"Awkward," Angie said from behind Mel.

"And by strangling, I was referring to a frosting technique where we strangle the pastry bag," Mel said. She mimed piping frosting with an invisible bag and elbowed Angie to do the same.

"See? All perfectly reasonable."

Manny blew out a breath. He looked dubious at best, but he didn't push it.

He looked her over and asked, "How are you feeling?"

"Never better," she said. "Well, aside from the exhaustion and throbbing leg."

"Still no idea why anyone would lob a brick through your window?" he asked.

"Nope," she said. "I mean it could be someone's way of complaining about our cake-to-frosting ratio, but I take that very seriously and I really don't think my ratio is brick-throwing worthy."

A small smile played on Manny's lips. "If you think of anything—"

"I'll let you know," she promised.

"Hey." He cupped her chin in his hand and his eyes were serious when they met hers. "Be careful. Stan and I discovered that the sash used to kill Mariel had Lupe's prints on it because she wore that one to a group photo shoot. The sashes were kept in the green room, so anyone had access to them. Whoever strangled Mariel is still at large and we have no idea what their agenda is."

"Noted," she said.

Mel watched him leave and turned back to help Angie unload the last of the cupcakes.

"So, that was nice," Angie said. She gave Mel a sidelong glance and Mel knew she was trying to determine what the status of Mel and Manny's relationship might be without actually asking.

"Yeah, he's a good guy," Mel said. "He'll make someone a fine husband someday." Angie's eyebrows rose up and Mel grinned. "And by 'someone' I do not mean me."

Angie opened her mouth to fire questions at Mel, but Mel held up her hand.

"I need to go talk to Ji, the cosmetic consultant," Mel said. "Olivia gave me an idea and I think Ji might have the answer. I promise I'll be right back."

She left before Angie could respond, but she heard Angie shout, "Fine!" Which, of course, meant it wasn't.

Mel searched the first floor of the resort, looking for the petite Asian woman. There was no sign of her. She was making her third lap when Lydia the hotel manager stopped her.

"Can I help you find something?" she asked.

Mel paused. "I'm looking for Ji Lily."

"The pageant's beauty consultant," Lydia said with a nod. "I just saw her going over someone's foundation."

"Remember where?" Mel asked.

"Follow me," Lydia said. "I think they were in one of the break rooms."

Mel fell into step beside the dark-haired beauty. She wondered how much Lydia knew about the investigation into Mariel's murder.

"Pretty stressful event, huh?" Mel said.

Lydia shrugged. "You wouldn't believe some of the stuff that goes on in hotels. I thought the two o'clock in the morning drunken skinny-dippers were bad, but I'd take them over a murder any day."

"So, have the police said anything about who they think might be involved?" Mel asked, hoping she sounded casual.

"Not to me," she said. "But I know they were looking pretty hard at one of the contestants after she had a tiff with the judge over her score."

"She's innocent," Mel said. Then she realized she sounded a bit strident and added, "Or so I heard."

Lydia gave her a long look, and Mel smiled.

"Your cupcake boy has a relationship with that girl," Lydia said.

"They're friends," Mel said. "Although they're possibly more than that now that he's noticed she's a girl. How did you know?"

"It's my job to watch people and anticipate what they

Sugar and Iced

need," Lydia said. "They seem like good kids. If you tell anyone I said this, I'll deny it, as the resort can't be perceived as being partial, but I'm hoping she wins."

"Me, too," Mel said.

Lydia led the way down a short hallway. She knocked gently and when a voice answered, she pushed open the door. Inside Ji was consulting with Sarah Hendricks, the unpleasant redheaded young woman Mel had tangled with before, and her mother.

"Lipstick for redheads—" Ji began but the girl interrupted her.

"Auburn, my hair is auburn. Surely, you should know the difference," the girl snapped. Her nostrils were flaring.

Ji studied her for a moment. She reached into her cosmetic case and handed the girl a tube of lipstick. "I'd try this if I were you."

The girl snatched the lipstick out of Ji's hand and hurried over to a nearby mirror. She applied the bright red lipstick, pouting at herself in the mirror.

"Well, you finally got it right," she said. She fluffed her hair and turned to face them.

"You like it?" Ji asked.

"It's fabulous!" the girl declared. "So much better than that horrible nude color you were suggesting. Come, Mother, the cupcake testing is going to start soon."

The girl sauntered past them without acknowledgment or even a thank-you for Ji. Her mother hurried behind her, sending them an apologetic smile.

Mel watched the door shut behind them, turned to Lydia and Ji, and said, "She is a horror."

Ji and Lydia exchanged a glance, and Ji said, "You have no idea."

"If you two will excuse me," Lydia said. "I'd better get back."

Mel waited until after Lydia had left before she spoke.

"Ji, I was wondering if I could ask you some questions," Mel said.

Ji glanced at the slim watch on her wrist. "Only if you can walk and talk. I have two more contestants to consult with. My *redheaded* princess refused to meet in the green room with the others, so I'm on my way back there now."

"I can do that," Mel said.

Ji closed up her cosmetic suitcase and put it on the ground. A handle came out of the top of it and she dragged it behind her like a small carry-on.

They made their way out into the hallway and Ji asked, "Is this about Lupe? Is she worried about her makeup? She shouldn't be. She's nailed it with the more natural look. It really suits her."

"No, it's something else," Mel said.

"Oh?" Ji glanced at her as they rounded the corner and entered another room.

"The other cupcake baker mentioned to me that Dr. Richards has offered her a free eye tuck if Destiny's cupcakes win this afternoon's competition."

Ji stopped walking. "Really?"

Mel nodded. "And it got me to thinking that maybe he had made similar offers elsewhere."

"You mean to me?" Ji asked. She frowned and Mel knew she had offended her.

"Actually, I was wondering if he had made the offer to Mariel," Mel said.

"Because that would explain why Lupe's score was so

much lower than Destiny's," Ji said. She tapped her index finger against her lips as she pondered the possibility.

"Who would know for certain?" Mel asked.

"I would," Anka said as she joined them. "When Mariel was chosen to be the head judge and I was not invited, she called me to gloat about how this was just the beginning. She was launching a nail polish line with Ji and she was going to get nipped and tucked into being a contender in the pageant circuit again."

"Do you suppose that was her deal then?" Mel asked. "If she made sure Destiny won, then the good doctor would youthanize her?"

Ji and Anka both gave her startled looks.

"Sorry, I meant y-o-u-t-h-anize her, not the other, although—"

"Somebody did exactly that," Anka said.

Mel studied the two women before her. There was no question that they both had a motive to want Mariel gone. Ji because if Mariel did owe her a large sum of money, then their business venture was in jeopardy of not being launched, and Anka because she was always second to Mariel, and if there was no Mariel . . .

"Stop looking at us like that," Ji said.

"Like what?" Mel asked.

"Like we murdered Mariel," Anka said. "We didn't."

"Really? Because it seems to me like you both had solid motives. Didn't she owe you a lot of money for the nail polish line you two were working on?" Mel asked Ji.

Ji looked angry. "I don't have to answer that, but since I've already told the police all of this I will. Yes, she paid half up front and she owed me the rest upon completion of the line. When I was almost done, I asked her for it and she said she was talking to her investor."

"She had an investor?" Mel asked.

"Yes, which was why I went into business with her in the first place," Ji said. "I figured with an investor and her connections in the pageant world, we were guaranteed at least a modest success, which would give me a stepping-off place to bigger and better things. Didn't that gamble bite me on the butt?"

"Who was the investor?" Mel asked.

"I have no idea," Ji said. "She never gave me a name and no one has come forward since she died."

"How are you going to launch the line now?" Mel asked. "Won't that be a huge hit for your company?"

"I have been fortunate enough to find a new investor," Ji said.

There was something about the way they didn't look at each other that made Mel get it immediately. She looked at Anka and said, "You're the new investor."

"So?" Anka asked. She put her hands on her hips and tossed her hair in a defiant gesture.

"So you don't think it looks the least bit suspicious that Mariel's longtime rival is taking over her business venture upon her death?" Mel asked.

"It was just good business," Anka said. "Why should all of Ji's hard work go to waste? Besides, we're marketing some of the polishes as memorial items for Mariel."

Mel stared at them.

"We didn't kill her," Anka said.

"We would have been arrested by now," Ji said. "I was at work in my lab that night and have my assistant as a witness to put me there."

"And I was at a party for the Barrett Jackson car auction with my husband, who can testify that I was with him the whole time," Anka said. "We're no more to blame for Mariel's death than your little friend Lupe."

"Fine," Mel said. "Then who killed her? Another contestant who didn't like their low score?"

"Maybe. Or perhaps it was another pageant insider? Do you think Richards made the same surgery offer to Cici?" Ji asked.

"No!" Anka shook her blond head. "Like me, she's had about all the surgery her face can tolerate. Besides, it couldn't have been her. She's too tiny."

"What about your thuggish cupcake boy?" Ji asked. "He looks like he could snap a person's neck with his fingers."

"Oz?" Mel asked. "No! He could never—"

"It could have been a crime of passion to defend his girlfriend," Anka said.

Both Ji and Anka were staring at her and Mel could tell they were thinking that she was deluded.

"I'm telling you it wasn't him," Mel said.

The other two exchanged a look that said louder than words that they thought Oz was the most likely candidate to have killed Mariel. Mel felt a hot surge of temper erupt through her core like hot lava.

"If you slander him in any way . . ." Mel growled. She took a step toward Anka, who scuttled behind Ji. "I will make it my mission to bring down this pageant with my bare hands if I have to."

"Mel, uh, Mel?" A voice called her name and Mel turned around to find Angie standing there, looking alarmed. "They're going to start judging the cupcakes. We're needed out front. And they're looking for you, too, Anka."

Mel glanced down at where her hands were clenched into fists. She shook her fingers loose and glanced at Ji and Anka.

"Okay, I think I made my point," she said and turned on her heel and strode away from the room, with Angie hurrying to keep up with her.

Once in the hallway, Angie grabbed her arm, "Were you channeling me in there? What the hell was that?"

Thirty-one

"Walk and talk," Mel said. She wanted to put distance between them and the others. When they turned a corner, she paused and lowered her voice. "Anka and Ji think Oz is the one who killed Mariel."

"What?" Angie cried. "That's mental."

"Agreed, but they think because Oz and Lupe are obviously involved—"

"But that just happened," Angie protested.

"Yeah, *we* know that, but from outside looking in, and with Oz staking Lupe in the competition, not to mention arranging her talent act, he seems a likely suspect," Mel said. "It doesn't help that he looks like he eats small kittens for breakfast."

"What can we do?" Angie asked.

"As soon as the cupcake tasting thing is over, I'm going to find Uncle Stan and see if Oz is on his radar," Mel said.

Jenn McKinlay

"Can I help?" Angie asked.

"No, I've got it."

Angie frowned and Mel wondered if she was feeling left out.

"Don't worry," Mel said. "As soon as I know what's going on, I'll clue you in."

"Promise?" Angie asked. "Cause your track record for full disclosure sucks."

Mel turned so that she and Angie were facing each other. "Look, I'm sorry that I kept what was going on with me and Joe a secret. I really am. I just wasn't ready for a lot of the emotional stuff that came with it. Can you forgive me?"

Angie met her gaze, and then she slowly nodded. "Forgiven and forgotten."

Mel hugged her pal close. "Thanks. Now come on, I do not want to miss the judges' faces when they have to eat that Red Hot monstrosity of Olivia's."

Mel hooked her arm through Angie's and pulled her into the lobby at the front of the resort. The contestants who were participating in the cupcake recipe event were all there.

A twenty-something male reporter was interviewing Lupe, and Mel noted that Oz was standing nearby. It was good that he was looking out for Lupe, but she couldn't discount what Ji and Anka had said about him looking a bit mean and scary, and that was without his usual piercings. She knew he probably didn't mean to be looming over the reporter, but still she noticed the reporter glancing nervously at him before asking his next question.

"I'll be right back," Mel said to Angie. She jerked her head in Oz's direction and Angie nodded in understanding.

"I'll keep an eye on the cupcakes," Angie said and she

pointed at the display tower where Olivia was watching the goings-on.

Mel nodded, circled the crowd that was gathering, and squeezed in beside Oz.

"Hi, guys," she said with a chirpiness usually reserved for cheerleaders and soccer moms. "Isn't this exciting?"

Oz looked at her suspiciously while Lupe gave her a distracted smile and the reporter looked relieved.

"A word, Oz?" Mel asked and then she yanked him away as if he'd said yes.

"Where were you when Mariel was killed?" she asked.

"What?" Oz asked. He was looking over her head at Lupe and the reporter as if he were getting ready to do battle if the reporter said anything he didn't like.

Mel snapped her fingers in front of his face. "Focus, Oz, we have a situation."

Oz reluctantly pulled his gaze from Lupe and looked at Mel. "What situation? I don't want to leave her. What if that brick was meant to harm her? She needs protection."

Mel felt her heart soften as she looked at the anxiety on her young friend's face. "We're in a crowded room. She'll be okay. Listen, since your status with Lupe has changed, people have taken notice of you and some are speculating that you might have done Mariel in to give your girlfriend a clearer shot at winning the pageant."

"But we weren't even a couple until after the talent show when she kissed me, and I'm not even sure what that means," Oz said. His handsome face flushed with color.

"I know that and you know that, but given that you paid her entrance fee, it looks like your relationship was established before the pageant," Mel said. "So do you know where you were?"

Oz frowned. "You don't really think Stan and Manny will believe I had anything to do with it, do you?"

"They have to run down all leads," Mel said. "And if people are starting to point to you . . ."

She heard the crowd begin to murmur, and glanced over to see Anka taking her seat at the judging table. The reporter left Lupe, and Mel felt Oz shift his feet as if he wanted to race right back to her side. Fortunately, Joyce arrived and stood with Lupe.

"My mom is with her," Mel said. "Now, do you remember where you were?"

"I don't know. It was days ago," Oz said. He dug his hands into his slicked-back hair and Mel wondered if the large amount of product used would make his fingers adhere to his head. He blew out a breath and released his head. His hair fell down over his face, making him look even more fearsome. "I don't know, I think I was with Marty at the bakery."

"You think or you know?" Mel asked.

"I think," he said. "Maybe I was at school. I'm not sure."

"Well, you'd better get sure," Mel said.

"Hey, a lot of stuff has happened to me this week," Oz protested. "I can't even remember my life before Lupe kissed me. It was like a punch to the head or something and now I can't even remember my name."

"Aw," Mel gushed. "That's so sweet."

"Argh." Oz shook his head as if he could rattle the memory of where he'd been loose. He blinked at Mel. "I've got nothing."

"Text Marty," she said. "Maybe he remembers where you were. Now try to keep a low profile. I'll keep an eye on Lupe."

"No offense, Mel, but that is not as reassuring as you might think," Oz said while his thumbs zipped across the front of his cell phone, typing a message faster than Mel could say it. "Trouble finds you before you even get out of bed in the morning."

"I resemble that remark," Mel said. She was trying to make a joke out of it, but she had to admit she felt the sting of truth in his words. "Just text Marty and then go help Angie with the cupcake tower. She's keeping guard to make sure Olivia doesn't get up to her usual tricks."

"On it," Oz said. He cast one more moony look at Lupe before skirting the crowd to go stand by Angie.

Mel pushed through the throng to stand by Joyce and Lupe.

"How are you doing?" she asked Lupe.

"Nervous," Lupe said. She gave Mel a worried smile.

"You're going to be fine," Joyce said and patted Lupe's arm. "You are by far the favorite after your amazing performance last night."

"I know, but now it's all on the gown and the cupcake," Lupe said. She fretted her lip between her teeth.

"Which one was yours?" Mel asked. She was praying it wasn't the one with the Pixy Stix.

"The white chocolate macadamia nut one," Lupe said.

"Oh, I liked that one," Mel said. "It's right there, see?"

She pointed to a section of white cupcakes on the tower.

"It's my favorite cookie, so I figured it would make a good cupcake," Lupe said. "Then, of course, I panicked because not everyone likes white chocolate. I mean, what if the judges hate it?"

"They won't," Joyce said. "Look at it. Mel, you really outdid yourself."

Mel puffed up a bit at her mother's praise. Over the past three months she'd really missed Joyce's unwavering belief in her. It felt really good to have it back.

"Thanks, Mom," she said.

They watched as the judges were served the cupcakes. Tension mounted each time a contestant recognized her cupcake when the recipe was read out loud to the room.

"I don't know if I can stand this," Lupe said when her cupcakes were brought forward.

Each judge tasted the cupcakes and then wrote their scores on a sheet that was not shared with the crowd. Cici would tally the score sheets at the end and announce the winner then.

"Oh, look, the male judge is taking a second bite of yours," Joyce whispered to Lupe. "He hasn't done that with any of the others. I bet it's because he likes yours the most."

"Or he hates it, and he just wants to be sure how much," Lupe whispered back.

"No, Mom's right," Mel said. "No one takes a second bite of a cupcake they hate." Lupe gave her a hopeful look and Mel added, "Trust me. This, I know."

They watched and waited as the judges worked their way through the remaining cupcakes. Mel noted when Destiny's cupcake came up because her mother, who was standing at the other side of the gathered crowd, stood on her toes and craned her neck to study the reaction of the judges. Destiny stood beside her mother, looking bored and texting on her phone.

By the time all of the cupcakes had been evaluated, the judges looked a bit sickly. Mel noted that Anka was pale and sweaty. Mel figured either the energy drink or the lemon-lime soda cupcake had done her in. She felt her own throat contract at the thought of having to eat either.

Cici stood off to the side. Two of her assistants were tabulating the scores. There was some frantic whispering. Cici shook her head. They went back to the score sheets. There was more whispering and Cici shook her head again.

"Something's wrong," Joyce said. "It shouldn't be taking them this long."

"I bet there's a tie," Ginny Lobo said as she wiggled her way through the crowd to join them. "That always happens and then no one knows what to do."

"Why not just declare it a tie?" Mel asked.

"They like clear-cut winners," Ginny said. "No gray areas. Otherwise, people get upset."

Sure enough, while they watched, Cici called the judges over. She had them review their score sheets. The judges seemed satisfied with the way they had evaluated the cupcakes.

"What is taking so long?" Brittany Richards shouted.

Some of the other parents in the crowd grumbled as well. Cici spun around and gave Brittany a quelling glance. Brittany tipped up her chin in defiance. Mel was surprised. She had thought Brittany would be more of a suck-up on her daughter's behalf, but maybe that was just to people like Ji, who could get her daughter a modeling contract.

Cici crossed over to the microphone. "We're having one final review. Thank you for your patience."

The crowd all glanced in Brittany's direction, as it was quite obvious from Cici's laserlike stare that the last bit was for her. Brittany glowered at Cici, but if the other woman noticed, she didn't show it.

Finally, after Mel was pretty sure her nerves were stretched to the breaking point, Cici came back to the microphone.

She looked the epitome of a former beauty queen with her large blond hair perfectly coifed and dressed in a chic sea-foam green chemise with a matching jacket.

She leaned into the microphone and the room grew quiet. Mel could hear her heartbeat in her ears and her breath rasp in and out of her nose. She glanced at Lupe and noted that she was looking at Oz, who was giving her an encouraging nod in return.

"The third runner-up in our cupcake competition is Sarah Hendricks," Cici announced. "For her peanut-butter-and-banana-flavored cupcake."

Polite applause broke out and Mel glanced over her shoulder to see the mean-looking redhead, standing in the corner. She tipped her chin up and it looked as if she tried to smile, but then she spun and faced the wall, dissolving into silent sobs.

Mel had no doubt she had been hoping to win and raise her rank in the competition. Mel hadn't baked those cupcakes, so at least the mean girl couldn't come after her. She was pretty sure Olivia could take her.

"Our second runner-up is Kelly Lester, with her coconut cupcake with lime frosting," Cici said.

This time the applause was louder and a pretty brunette beamed at the crowd and waved. Mel glanced over at the cupcake tower and Angie gave her a thumbs-up. The coconut-lime had been one of theirs.

Cici waited for the noise to die down. She glanced across the crowd as if looking for someone. Mel felt as if a swarm of butterflies had been let loose in her belly. Oh, she wanted this so much for Lupe, and yeah, she wanted to be the one to have baked the winning cupcake just to shut Olivia up.

"And the winner of the cupcake portion of the Sweet Tiara Beauty Pageant is . . ." Cici paused and Mel suspected it wasn't solely for dramatic effect. "Ladies and gentlemen, we have a tie."

An outraged murmur rumbled through the crowd.

"I know it is unusual, but since this is the first time cupcakes have been a part of the competition and the judges went over their scores and could not find any reason to alter their votes, we will uphold the tie."

There was more muttering until Cici held up her hands for silence.

"Our winners are Destiny Richards for her chocolate cupcake with espresso frosting and Lupe Guzman for her macadamia nut cupcake with white chocolate icing."

Joyce and Ginny grabbed Lupe and hugged her close while Mel sagged a bit at the knees with relief. Joyce was crying and she reached out and pulled Mel into their group hug while Lupe's family swarmed forward and joined in the melee. Lupe looked happy and relieved and Mel noticed that her gaze strayed up to Oz, who looked as if he was about to burst with pride.

"Hug him later," Mel whispered to Lupe. The young woman met her gaze and nodded.

Mel glanced over at Destiny and saw that the young woman was smiling and waving at the crowd while her mother had cornered the reporter and was yammering his ear off. There was no sign of her father. Mel wondered if a tied score would make Olivia's free eye tuck null and void.

A glance over at the cupcake tower and Mel saw Olivia and Angie exchanging words. Angie's dark brown eyes looked like they were going to spit sparks. Mel pushed through the crowd to run interference. The last thing they needed was Angie to get into another cupcake-throwing debacle with Olivia.

Mel dashed up to the tower just in time to hear Angie say, "Congratulations to you, too."

She and Olivia shook hands, briefly. Okay, it was more a brushing of fingertips than a handshake, but Mel was impressed with both of them.

"Well done, Pr . . . er, Mel," Olivia said.

Mel smiled. "You were about to call me Princess, weren't you?"

Olivia heaved a big sigh. "Being nice is too stressful. I'm going back to my bakery now. I think I need to eat a Dutch chocolate brownie smothered in caramel sauce with whipped cream and pecans to get my sanity back."

"I hear you. I'm thinking of mainlining some frosting myself," Mel said.

Olivia's lips twitched, but she turned her face away before Mel saw her smile.

"Olivia, forgive me, I know it's none of my business," Mel said. "But do you think your deal with Brandon Richards will hold since we tied?"

Olivia looked chagrined. "Yeah, I was talking to that cub reporter from the *Arizona Republic* and you'll never guess what he told me about Richards."

Mel waited but Olivia didn't continue, so she waved her hands and said, "Yes?"

"What? You're not even going to guess?" Olivia looked disappointed. "Fine. I was pointing out notable people in the crowd to the reporter and when I pointed out the good doctor, the reporter's eyes lit up. Turns out *Dr. Richards* is under investigation."

"Oh, really?" Mel asked.

"Yes, come to find out he had to voluntarily suspend his practice, because he was found in the pharmacy of his medical building helping himself to some of the goods."

"When was this?" Mel asked.

"Several months ago," Olivia said. "He's got a trial coming up, he's under review by the Arizona Medical Board, and he's got a string of lawsuits from patients who say he took money for follow-up appointments that of course he couldn't keep since he's suspended. I'm telling you, I wouldn't let that man near me if my jowls could be used to store nuts for the winter."

"I think that's a wise decision," Mel said.

"Besides, Marty was not thrilled with the idea, he says he likes me just the way I am," she said. The smile she gave them at the mention of Marty's name took twenty years off of her and a little dimple appeared in her cheek.

"Marty's right," Angie said. "You're fine just the way you are."

Olivia and Mel looked at her in surprise.

"Thanks," Olivia said uncertainly. She left them with a small wave.

Mel turned to Angie. "That was uncharacteristically civil of you."

"I thought so," Angie said. She looked quite pleased with herself.

"Do you think Uncle Stan knows about Richards?" Angie asked.

"I'm sure he does," Mel said. "But I don't see how it's

relevant. Richards had nothing to gain by Mariel's death, especially if he was planning to swap nips and tucks for high scores."

"I suppose," Angie said.

"How are you holding up, Oz?" Mel asked as he joined them.

"I want to throw up," he said. "How can people stand this pressure cooker? I don't know how I'm going to get through the next couple of hours. I may stroke out before the gown portion even starts."

Mel smiled. "Just be there for Lupe and you'll be fine."

He nodded. "I'm going to keep an eye on her until this thing is over. I'm still worried that someone was trying to hit her with that brick."

"Good idea," Mel said. "Emotions are going to be running very high, I imagine."

Mel watched as Oz joined Lupe and her family. She and Angie were left to hand out the remaining cupcakes to the spectators. She tried not to be annoyed that Olivia had ducked out without helping. Truthfully, it was for the best, but Mel was feeling more than a little tired of this whole pageant situation. The brick through her window last night had finished her.

Mel's cell phone rang and she checked the window. It was a text from Tate. He and Marty had arrived with the cupcakes for the final event. They had all agreed to close the bakery early so that everyone could watch Lupe in her gown strut her stuff.

"Come on," Mel said to Angie. "Tate's here with our last batch of pageant cupcakes."

"Hallelujah," Angie said. She fell into step beside Mel as they left the lobby to meet Tate and Marty on the loading dock. The four of them carted cupcakes into the lobby for the final cupcake tower.

Mel had sent Uncle Stan a text that she wanted to talk to him, but she hadn't heard back yet. She knew he was busy with the case, but she really wanted to talk to him about Brandon Richards and his offers of free surgery to benefit his daughter and, yeah, to feel out whether he was looking at Oz or not.

Mel fussed over each cupcake on the tower. Of all the cupcakes she had made for the pageant, these were far and away her favorites. She hated to admit it, but in pastel hues with tiny tiaras perched in the frosting, they were so cute they made her teeth hurt even as she felt the need to say, "Aw."

As she arranged the sparkly cupcakes so that the tiny tiaras perched on top of them faced out and caught the overhead lights just right, she wondered how Lupe was doing.

Tonight was it. The finalists would walk the catwalk and answer a few questions from Cici, and then the judges would decide who was crowned Miss Sweet Tiara for the next year.

Mel was surprised to find that her palms were sweating. Gah! She was so nervous.

"Would you look at that?" Angie asked.

Mel glanced up and saw Lupe, walking toward them, with Oz at her side.

Lupe twirled in her ivory dress with the black velvet embroidery. Her long hair swept down her back and her makeup accentuated her beautiful eyes and lips.

"We found a small tear on the hem," Lupe said. "But your mom managed to fix it. She's a wonder."

"That she is," Mel agreed. "You look amazing."

"Hooee, 'amazing' isn't word enough!" Marty clapped his hands to his bald head as he goggled at the beautiful young woman before them. "And to think I thought you were a guy for the first six months of our acquaintanceship."

"Marty, I don't know how to tell you this," Lupe said in a low voice. "But I'm really a dude."

Marty stared at her for a second and then she winked at him.

"I love this girl," he said to Oz. "If you mess it up, I swear I'll take you out and whup you."

"I won't," Oz said. His face was red but he looked at Lupe, and Mel could see his heart in his eyes when he said, "Assuming there is an 'it' and by that I mean an 'us' to mess up?"

Lupe looked at him, mirroring his expression of love and affection, and said, "Why, Oscar Ruiz, are you officially asking me out?"

Oz toed the ground with the rubber bumper of his Converse sneaker then squeezed her hands, blew out a breath, and said, "Yes, I am. So, will you—go out with me?"

Lupe stepped closer to him and lightly kissed his lips before she stepped back. "Yes."

They stood grinning at each other and then Mel heard a big, snotty snuffle come from the direction of Angie and Tate. She glanced over and saw that Angie had her face buried in Tate's shirtfront and he was holding her close, his chin resting on her hair.

His eyes were suspiciously watery when he said, "Good for you, Oz. I wish I'd been that smart at your age."

Angie stepped back and they stared into each other's eyes for a moment before Tate kissed her.

"Oh, for Pete's sake," Marty said. "You're not as smart as him now."

Tate and Angie broke apart and looked at him. Tate looked like he was about to protest but Marty held up a hand.

"What?" Marty asked. "You know it's true. Quit trying to prove yourself, grab the girl, and be freaking happy. It's not brain surgery."

Tate stared at Marty as if he'd just been hit in the head with a two-by-four. "You're right."

He glanced around him as if looking for something and then he reached over and grabbed a tiny tiara off one of the cupcakes. Then he knelt in front of Angie.

Mel felt all of the blood rush to her head and she grabbed Marty's arm to steady herself. He put his hand over hers and squeezed her fingers back, letting Mel know he was as stunned as she was.

Angie stood frozen, as if afraid to move, while Lupe and Oz watched with huge, matching grins.

"Angie, I love that you punch first and ask questions later, I love that you enjoy pizza dipped in ranch dressing, I love that you think it's reasonable to have an intervention over a relationship. Angie, I love *you*."

Angie looked at him with wide eyes. Then he grinned as he glanced up at her and said, "'When you realize you want to spend the rest of your life with somebody, you want the rest of your life to start as soon as possible.' Angie, will you marry me?"

Thirty-two

Angie opened her mouth to answer but no words came out. Instead, she nodded while the tears coursed down her cheeks. Then she dropped into Tate's arms, almost knocking him over with the ferocity of her hug.

"*When Harry Met Sally*!" Angie cried. "I can't believe you quoted my favorite relationship movie ever!"

Their image was blurry and Mel realized she was sobbing. She glanced at Marty and saw that his cheeks were wet as well.

They watched while Tate slid the mini tiara onto Angie's ring finger.

"Someday this will be . . ." Tate began, but Angie interrupted him with a kiss.

"It's perfect, absolutely perfect," she said.

With a strength that surprised her, Marty turned and

scooped Mel up, swinging her up in the air before setting her back on her feet.

"Now that's what I'm talking about!" Marty said.

He hurried over to Tate and slapped him on the back and then hoisted Angie up and twirled her in the air as well.

Mel pulled Tate to his feet and kissed his cheek. "I'm so proud of you."

Then she turned and grabbed Angie. They squealed together and jumped up and down. Angie looked happier than Mel had ever seen her. and she felt her throat get tight again with emotion.

"You're getting married," Mel said.

Angie looked at her and beamed but then her face fell. "Oh, Mel, I'm sorry. This must be—"

"No," Mel interrupted. "This is the greatest event ever in the history of great events. I couldn't be happier. My two best friends getting married is just the best thing— *ever*!"

Angie hugged her close and Mel felt her throat close up again as the tears spilled down her cheeks.

"Lupe!" Joyce came hurrying out of the ballroom. "What's the holdup? Sweetie, you need to be inside. They're about to start."

"Oh, but—" Lupe began to explain but Angie cut her off.

"No, this is your night," she said. "Go and shine! We'll share the news later."

Lupe nodded and hurried away with Joyce.

"Shall we go grab seats?" Marty asked.

Tate and Angie were standing by the cupcake tower, looking at each other as if they had just met.

"Come on," Mel said. She used a napkin to wipe the

tears off her cheeks and blow her nose. "Something tells me those two want to be alone."

She put one hand on Marty's elbow and one on Oz's and led them into the ballroom. They saw Lupe's family and were making their way to the available seats beside them when Mel spotted Uncle Stan on the far side of the room. She knew that he and Manny probably already knew about Brandon Richards and his current difficulties, but it couldn't hurt to be sure.

"Will you two save me a seat?" she asked. "I need to talk to Uncle Stan."

"Sure, but hurry up," Marty said. "You don't want to miss this."

Mel cut across the room, moving as fast as she could, but the crowd was thick and she had to pause for little kids running through the aisle and for older folks easing their way into the hard seats. By the time she got to the place she'd seen Uncle Stan, he was gone.

She glanced around the room but didn't see him anywhere. Up ahead was a door and Mel wondered if Uncle Stan had gone out that way. The lights were still up, so she figured she had a few minutes. She hurried forward and slipped through the door. It led into a hallway that was empty.

She hoped he wasn't back with the contestants, badgering Lupe before she had to go on. Mel hurried in the direction of the dressing room. Before she could open the door, it slammed open and she had to jump out of the way to avoid getting hit.

"Hey!" she cried.

Brandon Richards stood there. He looked upset and when Mel went to move around him, he turned and sneered at her.

"You need an enhancement," he said.

"And you need to learn some manners!" she snapped.

He was staring at her meager chest and she had to resist the urge to kick him. Ugh! She didn't care if he was a doctor. It was rude. She crossed her arms over her chest and moved around him to enter the room. It was empty except for the costumes and clutter that littered every available surface.

No Uncle Stan. No Manny. Just Brandon Richards the creep who offered surgery for favors. Except he was really in no position to be offering anyone plastic surgery, now was he? She wondered if Mariel knew and, if so, had she called him out on it?

Mel turned to leave but Richards stopped her by grabbing her arm.

"You're with that Lupe girl, aren't you?" he asked. His eyes narrowed as if he were doing calculations in his head.

"I'm not with her, but she is a friend, yes," Mel said.

"She has to lose," he said. "Make her lose tonight. Have her trip or offend the crowd with her answers in the interview."

"Why would I do that?" Mel asked. "Or did you miss the part that she's my friend?"

"I'll give you a killer bust line," he said. He let go of her arm and cupped Mel's breasts. She was so shocked, she gasped. Then she punched him right in the side of the head.

"Go to hell!" Mel snapped. Her temper got the better of her and everything she'd been thinking flew out of her mouth in verbal vomit that was practically projectile. "You are suspended pending a review by the medical board for raiding your pharmacy. You can't offer up any surgery, not legitimately. So what happened? Did Mariel figure out you couldn't uphold your end of the bargain for free surgery and refuse to keep throwing the pageant Destiny's way? Is that why you strangled her?"

Brandon went perfectly still. He looked stunned. Mel clapped a hand over her mouth in shock. It was true, she hadn't thought it out, but everything she had just said was true.

"No, that's not what happened," he said.

He didn't look at her when he spoke. Mel could tell he was lying.

"You don't understand," he said. "I'm broke. The way Brittany spends money, I can't keep up. If I don't give Brittany a pageant win, she'll leave me. Mariel knew what she had to do, but she found out about my legal issues and she balked."

"You killed her," Mel said.

"It wasn't my fault. It was an accident," he argued. "We were alone in the green room, and I just wanted to talk to her, but she was being such a diva. She was demanding the money I had promised her for her stupid nail polish line. I didn't have it, but she just kept badgering me. I . . . I snapped."

"You strangled her with a sash."

"I just wanted to scare her, but she put up such a fight and then she was dead. I tried to bring her back, I did." His look was pleading, as if begging Mel to understand. She didn't. She couldn't. To take a life over a beauty pageant win? It was too horrible.

"How did she get under my cupcake table?" Mel asked. She tried to keep her tone neutral and not cause Brandon Richards to freak out. Maybe if he thought she was sympathetic she could convince him that confessing all to Stan and Manny was the only way out,

"When I couldn't resuscitate her, I put Mariel's arm over my shoulders and carried her out of the dressing room. I figured I'd pretend she was drunk and I was helping her out. But then I realized they'd know I was the last one to see her alive, and if they tested her blood alcohol, the drunk story would prove to be a lie.

"I had used the sash near Lupe's changing station. I knew her prints were probably on it. So I rolled Mariel's body onto a luggage trolley I found in the green room. When the lounge was clear, I simply off-loaded her under the cupcake table, knowing the sash would lead back to Lupe."

The horror of it all washed over Mel in a deluge. He had murdered someone and thought nothing of framing an eighteen-year-old girl for it.

"You're insane," she said.

Brandon doubled over amidst the beauty pageant shrapnel as if trying to catch his breath. He was shaking, and Mel knew this was her chance to get out of there and get help.

"You have to help me," Brandon pleaded, glancing up at her. "I can't lose Brittany."

"Yeah, sure," Mel said. Her heart was thumping hard in her chest. The man in front of her was a monster and she needed to appease him any way she could, even if it meant agreeing with what he said. She needed to calm the crazy man. "In fact, I'll go get Lupe to ditch the pageant right now."

She began to back away. When he reached for her, Mel instinctively smacked his hand away.

Richards staggered back and Mel turned and ran toward the door. She was so rattled she was shaking, making the turning of a doorknob much more difficult than it should have been. Before Mel could push open the door, Brandon Richards dropped a satin sash around her neck and yanked her back into the room.

"I don't believe you," he hissed in her ear.

Mel struggled against his hold. Her voice was raspy when she wheezed, "Killing me is not going to save you. It will only make things worse."

"Shut up! With you dead and Lupe the outsider blamed for killing the baker because she only got her a tie in the cupcake competition, well, I win. There's no way they'll crown her Miss Sweet Tiara now."

"No one will believe it," Mel gasped. She clawed at the sash that was cutting off her airway.

"Sure they will," he said. "I had planned to shred Lupe's dress with a scalpel but someone came into the green room and interrupted me. But now, it's perfect. Clutched in your dead hand, those black roses should be all the evidence they need to charge her with your murder and Destiny wins."

"No!" Mel clawed at the sash that was tightening about her neck. Is this how Mariel had died? She couldn't catch her breath. Panic was making her scratch even harder at her own skin. She kicked behind her with her leg and heard him grunt when her foot connected with his shin. The sash loosened just enough for her to draw in some air.

She let go of the sash. Fighting his hold wasn't helping. She thrust her arms behind her, leading with her elbows, and aimed for his middle. She connected and he let out a whoosh of air. Again the sash loosened enough for her to get a breath.

She and Angie had taken self-defense classes, at Angie's brothers' insistence, and the one thing the instructor had said was that the best chance you have of fighting off an attacker in the very beginning was to put up a fight and be very difficult.

Mel took the words to heart and she kicked backwards and punched anything she could hit behind her. The sash fell from around her throat, as Brandon was so busy defending himself that he couldn't keep hold of it. Mel used his distraction to rip the sash away.

She stumbled away from him as she sucked air into her burning lungs. She looked for a weapon, but unless she was going to curl him to death with an electric wand, she was out of luck.

Brandon lunged for her, but Mel sidestepped. She saw Lupe's skateboard on the ground and she hopped over it, keeping it between them. He charged for her and Mel jumped back against the vanity. Brandon stomped onto the skateboard, which shot out from under him, sending him to the floor with a hard smack. Mel took the opportunity and ran.

She shoved through the door. Legs and arms pumping, heedless of her throbbing stitches or raw throat, she raced down the hallway toward the lobby. She could hear shouts and cheers coming from the ballroom. She dashed into the lobby to find her friends, but the cupcake tower stood alone, its mini-tiaras sparkling for no one.

Damn it! Tate and Angie must have gone in to see the crowning of Miss Sweet Tiara. Across the room, three men sat at the bar. Mel raced toward it. At the very least, the bartender could call the police.

She was halfway there when she heard Brandon enter

the lobby behind her. His nose was bleeding and he was limping but he looked deranged and he was definitely coming for her.

"Help!" Mel cried. Her voice was gruff from near strangulation and it couldn't compete with the noise from the basketball game on the television over the bar. She tried again, her voice still not much more than a whisper.

Brandon reached a hand out to grab her when one of the men from the bar spun around as if his ears had heard her small cry. It was Joe. Seeing Mel in trouble, he raced forward and caught Brandon in a tackle worthy of an NFL linebacker. As they skidded across the floor and slammed into a table and chairs, the other two men at the bar turned to see what the ruckus was.

Mel was surprised to see that it was Manny and Steve. She pointed at Brandon and said, "It's him. He killed Mariel and he just tried to kill me."

The words were faint, but Manny heard her. He jumped out of his seat, pulling a pair of handcuffs out of his pocket as he went. Steve stood staring as if he couldn't believe what was happening.

"Number three, a little help here!" Manny called.

Joe was sitting on Brandon and using the opportunity to punch him, repeatedly. Steve raced forward and helped Manny haul Joe off of Brandon.

Once Manny had Brandon cuffed, he dragged him to his feet. Joe slumped against the front of a chair and Mel glanced at him and winced. He had a cut on his head from where it had connected with a sharp corner of a table, and blood was pouring down his face.

Mel grabbed a rag off of the clean stack from the bar

and hurried to Joe's side. She knelt down and pressed the cloth to his head.

"You heard me?" she asked. She cringed, as her throat felt scraped raw.

Joe reached out and grabbed her hand. He laced his fingers with hers and then said, "Yeah, and then I saw some nut chasing my girl so I took him out."

"It was a good hit, too," Manny said. "I guess we know why you're number one."

Joe grinned and Mel rolled her eyes.

"You can't hold me," Brandon thrashed in his handcuffs. "You have no proof of anything."

"Except for the small detail that you admitted to me that you killed Mariel and tried to kill me the same way," Mel said.

Steve joined them with another bar rag, but this one had ice in it. "For your neck."

Mel glanced down and realized she'd clawed her own skin bloody, just like Mariel. She shuddered. She had come so close to losing everything. She tightened her hold on Joe's hand. As if he understood, he squeezed her fingers back.

"Can you tell me what happened, Mel, from the beginning?" Manny asked.

She nodded. She began by telling them about her conversation with Olivia about the free eye tuck, and Anka's confirmation that Mariel had a deal with Brandon for surgery. She said she had wanted to tell Uncle Stan about the free plastic surgery, and had been looking for him, when she found Brandon instead. She disclosed their horrifying conversation.

When she got to the part about Lupe's black roses, Manny put on a glove and searched Brandon's pockets until he found the crushed black velvet. Mel ended the story with Joe's tackle. Brandon argued and objected and called her a liar but Mel ignored him. The roses were evidence enough.

"One thing I can't figure out," Mel said. "What about the brick?"

"What brick?" Brandon asked.

"The one that sailed through my bakery window," Mel said. "Were you trying to hit Lupe?"

Brandon gave a harsh laugh devoid of humor. "Someone else gets the credit for that. My money would be on the mean redhead in need of a nose job. She's crazy."

Mel thought of Sarah Hendricks and thought Brandon might be on to something. After all, it took one to know one.

"Mel, I'll want you down at the station to give a statement as soon as you have Joe's head looked at," Manny said.

She nodded. She would do whatever it took to put Brandon Richards behind bars.

As Manny led Brandon Richards away, Steve fell into step behind them.

"Where are you going?" Joe asked.

"I'm number three, remember?" Steve asked. "I'm pretty sure my presence isn't needed unless Mel wants to reconsider the arrangement of the Order of Mel?"

Joe looked at Mel to see if she was interested but she just shook her head. Steve heaved a sigh and followed Manny out of the building.

Joe looked her over. His finger brushed the scratches on her neck and gently fingered the bruises. "I should have punched him harder when I had the chance."

"How's your head?" she asked. She pulled his hand away and noted that the bleeding had slowed.

"It's fine," he said. Big fat lie.

"Let's get you to the ER," she said.

"No, they're about to announce the winner," Joe said. "Let's go see if our girl nailed it."

They ducked into the back of the ballroom. The lights were low but the stage sparkled with all of the glamorous contestants, not to mention the huge glittery tiara suspended from the ceiling.

Mel scanned the crowd until she spotted her mother with Lupe's family, Marty, Oz, Ginny, and Joe's brothers, Paulie and Al. Tate and Angie were with them, but they were still lost in each other's eyes.

Joyce, Ginny, and Gloria looked tense as did Marty, Paulie, and Al, but Oz… Strangely enough, Oz looked perfectly relaxed and composed. His eyes were fixed on Lupe and Mel noted that their gazes met several times and when they did, Oz gave her a small nod of encouragement and she beamed.

"I think Oz is convinced that she's won it," Joe said.

"I think no matter what happens, she's his Miss Sweet Tiara," Mel said.

Cici Hastings strolled across the stage. She looked as glamorous as an old Hollywood movie star with her pile of platinum curls and her rose-colored gown that was beaded from her neckline to the floor-length hem, and sparkled with every move she made. She clutched three envelopes in her hand and Mel tightened her grip on Joe's arm as she realized this was it.

Cici paused by the microphone, and in a breathy voice, she said, "And now the moment we've all been waiting for." She tore open the first envelope and said, "The second runner-up for Miss Sweet Tiara is Jordan Hooper."

There was applause, and a cute brunette strode forward with a big smile and got her flowers and sash.

Cici returned to the microphone. "Our first runner-up for Miss Sweet Tiara is Destiny Richards."

Destiny was standing next to Lupe, and Mel watched as she turned and squeezed Lupe's hand before striding forward with a big smile to accept her sash and flowers. Mel saw a commotion near the stage and she wasn't at all surprised when Brittany looked as if she was going to storm the stage.

Destiny smiled and waved to the crowd, then she stepped forward and hissed, "Sit down, Mother, you're making an ass of yourself."

Like a real beauty queen, she then turned and walked with her head held high and stood next to Jordan.

"I like that girl," Joe said to Mel. "Her parents are awful, but I like her."

"Me, too," she agreed.

Brittany sat down with a sob, but the crowd grew quiet. Cici looked at the third envelope and then she looked at the crowd. "Are you ready to greet your new Miss Sweet Tiara?"

The cheer was deafening.

Cici began to open the envelope. "Ladies and gentleman, our seventy-fifth Miss Sweet Tiara is Guadalupe Guzman."

"Yes!" Oz shouted and punched a fist in the air. Joyce and Ginny hugged each other while Gloria and her girls jumped up and down. Paulie and Al hugged each other, although they broke apart immediately and then knuckle-bumped each other.

On stage, the girls nearest Lupe hugged her and pushed

her forward. Mel watched Sarah Hendricks stalk off the stage. She was not at all surprised that the girl was a sore loser.

Cici greeted Lupe with a kiss on the cheek, draped her sash over her head, and handed her a big bouquet of pink roses while last year's Miss Sweet Tiara put her crown on Lupe's head. Lupe strode forward, walking the catwalk and waving to the crowd. She even blew a kiss to Oz. She looked as if she'd been born to wear a crown.

"She did it," Joe said.

A flash of white and black caught Mel's eye as Lupe strode forward. Mel grinned. Underneath her beautiful gown, Lupe was wearing her favorite black Converse high tops, and Mel knew that all the glitz and glam in the world wouldn't change their Lupe.

"She sure did," Mel said.

Thirty-three

Mel waited beside Joe in the emergency room. She had texted Angie to have everyone meet back at the bakery for a celebration. She mentioned that she and Joe would be late but she didn't explain why.

Joe got four stitches on his head. Mel joked that they matched the four stitches on her leg. The doc looked at them as if they were a troubled couple, and Joe used his position as an assistant district attorney to explain that they had been swept up in a police investigation and had helped apprehend the bad guy. They gave the doctor Manny's name if he felt the need to verify their story. From the set expression on the doc's face, Mel had a feeling Manny would be getting a call.

While they waited in their curtained room, Mel paced and Joe rested. She watched an older couple shuffle past them to the next curtained partition and she wondered if that would be her and Joe in forty years. Probably not, if he never asked her to marry him again.

When the doctor had examined Joe, he had told them that Joe was lucky he hadn't taken a harder hit to the temple, as it could have caused bleeding on the brain or severe brain damage.

Joe had blanched but Mel had been hit with the sudden clarity that even if her man did get injured she would do everything she could to take care of him just like he had risked everything without hesitation to take down the man who was chasing "his girl."

She thought about what her mother had said, that her life would have been infinitely more tragic if she had never had Mel's father in it. The fear of losing Joe, while still very real for Mel, had lost its power when she realized that by pushing him away, she was losing him anyway. There were no half steps in a relationship. Either you were in or you were out.

She thought about her dad and how Tate had said he would be disappointed in her for not going after what she wanted. Then she thought about Tate springing the question on Angie out of the blue and how right it had been. Then she thought about how it was always Joe that she measured every man against and how every man fell short, even the really good ones.

"You're going to pace a hole in the floor," Joe said. He was reclined on the hospital bed, watching her. He looked pale and it made Mel's fear kick up in her chest. She smacked it back down.

Mel took his hand in hers and brushed his hair back from his forehead with her free hand. "Sorry."

"No need," he said. "What's on your mind, Cupcake?"

Mel looked at him. What could she say? That she had finally come to her senses and wanted to marry him, but he had quit asking her? Yeah, that wouldn't be awkward, especially if he had changed his mind. And what if when he found out that Tate and Angie were engaged, he thought her sudden change of heart was because she didn't want to feel left out? It wasn't true, but she could see how he might see it that way.

"I was thinking—" Mel was about to confess all when a nurse pushed back the curtain and entered their area.

"Mr. DeLaura, your discharge papers are all set," she said. "You're free to go."

"Thanks," Joe said as he sat up.

Mel studied him to see if he was woozy at all, but he rolled off of the bed as if he was just fine.

The nurse was listing off the things he had to watch for and Mel listened with half an ear as she followed him out of the hospital.

She was parked in a visitor's space near the door. She helped Joe into the front of her car and hurried around to the driver's side.

"Do you want me to take you home?" she asked.

"No, I want to see our girl," he said. "To the bakery."

"All right," Mel said. "But if you look woozy, I'm taking you home."

Joe gave her a small smile. The hospital was minutes from the bakery and when Mel parked in front of her new glass window, she saw that the window shades were down and the closed sign was flipped, but the jukebox was playing and it was easy to see there was a crowd in the joint.

"I'm glad we didn't miss the party," Joe said. He climbed

out of the car and led the way to the door. Mel used her key to let them in.

And soon as they entered, Joyce pounced. "Dear Joe, are you all right?"

"I'm fine," he said. He reassured her with a hug.

"Stan called and told us everything," she said. "I can't believe Brandon Richards was the killer, and he went after Mel. Oh, if you hadn't been there, I shudder to think what would have happened."

"Mel would have been okay," Joe said. "She's very resourceful."

"Nice head, bro," Paulie said. "How many stitches?"

"Four," Joe said.

"Aw, that's nothing," Al said. "Remember when Sal was in that motorcycle accident and he left his scalp on the road?"

They all shuddered.

"I heard how you took down Brandon Richards," Marty said as he joined them. "Nicely done."

"Thanks," Joe said.

"Isn't it wonderful?" Joyce asked. "Lupe won, and Tate and Angie are engaged! I'm just so happy!"

"What?" Joe looked stunned.

"You didn't tell him?" Joyce asked Mel.

"No, I didn't get a chance," Mel said. She knew it sounded weak when Joe looked at her and frowned. There had certainly been plenty of time while they were cooling their heels in the ER.

"It's pretty big news," Al said. "The rest of the family is coming over to celebrate."

"That's great!" Joe said. Mel wondered if it was just her

who heard the bittersweet tone in his voice. He strode across the room and hugged his sister. When Tate held out his hand for a shake, Joe pushed it aside and gave him a manly hug instead. Mel smiled. It was good to see Tate being accepted into the DeLaura fold so easily.

"That could be you," Marty said.

She turned and glanced at him. "No, I don't think Angie is interested in marrying me."

"You know what I mean," he said. "That could be you and Joe."

"Assuming they didn't keep it a secret," Joyce said from her other side.

"Are you two ganging up on me?" Mel asked.

Marty and Joyce both leaned forward and looked at each other before they leaned back. "Yes," they said.

Mel glanced at the crowd in front of her. Oz and Lupe were standing with her family while Tate and Angie and Joe were just off to the side. Al and Paulie had drifted over to join the newly engaged couple. Everyone was smiling and happy.

"No, it can't be me," Mel said sadly. "Joe has stopped asking me to marry him. I think he's given up on me."

"Oh, no," Joyce said. Her face looked as sad as Mel felt.

"Well, so what?" Marty snapped.

"What do you mean 'so what'?" Mel asked. "He's given up. As in, I finally managed to push him away."

"And you're going to let that be the end?" Marty asked. "That's lame."

"Lame?"

"Totally lame," he said.

"Is this how you mind your own business?" Mel asked.

Their voices were rising in volume and she noticed that the rest of the gathering was beginning to look at them. She didn't care.

"Yes, it is," Marty snapped. "I've been watching you for the past few months messing up your life and I've said nothing, because I was sure that brain in your head would kick in and you'd figure it out. But you are slower than molasses on a cold day. So what if Joe stopped asking you? Is he the only one in your relationship?"

Mel felt her face get hot as she realized everyone in the room was staring at them. But then she glanced up and saw Joe, gazing at her with his warm chocolate brown eyes filled with concern, and everything clicked into place.

"Joe, will you marry me?" she asked.

The entire room froze. The only noise was coming from the jukebox, which, appropriately, was playing Elvis crooning "Love Me Tender."

"You don't have to do this, Mel," Joe said. "In fact, you really shouldn't."

"Oh, for Pete's sake," Marty muttered to Joyce. "Did he fall down the stupid tree and hit every branch?"

Joyce hushed him.

"I know I don't have to and I love you for that even more than I thought possible," Mel said. "The truth is I have been in love with you since I was twelve years old, Joe DeLaura. When you asked me to marry you, everything in my world was right, but then I got scared. I couldn't bear the thought that I might lose you someday and I got the wiggins. It was stupid and I'm sorry."

Joe crossed the room to stand beside her. His face was pinched as if he were in pain.

"I really think we should talk about this somewhere else," he said.

Mel studied his face. He looked like a man being torn in two. *Oh, no!* She had been right. He had changed his mind. She had thought it would be the humiliation of being publicly rejected that would kill her, but no. She clutched her chest. This was not angina that hurt so bad; rather, it was the feeling of her heart breaking and shattering into a million pieces.

"Oh, I see," she said.

"What the what?" Marty protested beside her.

Again, Joyce hushed him.

"Come on," Joe said. He took Mel's arm and led her out the door. "We need to talk."

The door closed behind them and Mel could still hear Elvis crooning, which was only slightly louder than the furious chorus of whispers that broke out as soon as the door shut.

"You don't have to explain," Mel said. "I was an idiot. I'm so sorry I kept pushing you away. I understand if your patience has run out."

Joe moved into her personal space and cupped her face in his hands.

"Listen, Cupcake," he paused and took a deep breath as if trying to figure out exactly what to say. "I meant it when I asked you to marry me. Every. Single. Time."

Mel gazed into his eyes and she knew he was telling the truth. She supposed it was some consolation that he looked as if he was in as much agony as she was.

"But?" she prodded.

He pushed back a lock of her hair that had fallen forward. His fingers moved slow as if savoring the feel of the blond curl. He leaned forward and placed a kiss on her forehead. Mel felt her throat get tight. She closed her eyes, trying to memorize the feel of his lips against her skin. She knew a kiss-off when she got one.

His voice was gravel-rough when he said, "But things change. I'm sorry, Mel."

She couldn't speak. She stepped back and nodded. Joe met her gaze for a heartbeat. It hurt too much and Mel glanced away. When she looked back up, he was gone.

She didn't think she could go back inside and face everyone just yet. She slumped against the wall and let the tears fall silently down her face. The irony that losing Joe hurt even worse than she had feared was not lost on her. And it didn't help, not even a little.

"Uh, Mel?" a voice called her name. "You all right?"

She hastily wiped her cheeks and cleared her throat.

"Yeah," she answered.

She turned to find Manny walking down the sidewalk toward her. The overhead light shone on his black hair. He looked rumpled and tired and in need of a big lemon cupcake. Funny, she could use a few dozen herself.

"I'm looking for Joe," he said.

Great, just hearing his name was a knife to the chest.

"You just missed him," Mel said. She tried not to blanch but she couldn't help it. Having Joe walk out of her life was going to take some getting used to.

Manny stopped beside her and studied her face. "Oh, hell. He did it, didn't he?"

"Did what?"

"Walked away," he said.

"Walked. Ran. Left skid marks," Mel said. "Take your pick. I suppose I had it coming since I rejected him so many times. What's that lovely expression? Payback's a bitch?"

Manny blew out a breath. "You know, I thought I would be happier about this, but I'm not. I hate to see you hurting."

"I'll be all right," Mel lied.

A noise sounded from the shop and Mel suspected that the party was breaking up. Probably, the jocularity was cut short by the awkward scene she and Joe had caused.

"We can't talk here," Manny said. He grabbed Mel's hand, giving her no choice but to go with him.

They circled the building until they were at the back stairs that led up to her apartment.

"Sit," Manny ordered.

"I'm really not up for a convo just now," she said. The thought of rolling up in her futon and not coming out for a week or two . . . Now that had appeal.

"This isn't a conversation," Manny said. "I'm going to talk and you're going to listen."

Mel straightened up. He had her attention now.

"What's going on?" she asked.

Manny began to pace. "You know if you could just fall for me this would all be so much easier." He sighed. "Your heart belongs to Joe, doesn't it?"

"Always," Mel choked.

Manny nodded. "This is ridiculous. I'm considered one of the toughest detectives on the force, but I can't do this."

"Do what?"

"Lie to you," he said. He stopped in front of her. "The brick that came through your window, it wasn't meant for Lupe."

"What?"

"It was meant for you," he said.

"Me?" Mel gaped. "But why?"

Manny started pacing again. He looked to be thinking through something. Mel didn't interrupt for fear that he wouldn't share. Finally, he stopped.

"If you were a very powerful criminal with an incredibly long reach, how would you try to stop the assistant district attorney who was gunning for you?" he asked.

Mel stared at Manny. What was he saying?

"I'd go after what he valued most," she said.

"The brick was just a warning," Manny said. "Joe's been getting death threats from a case he's working and it looks like they'll go even further to discourage him from pursuing it."

"Death threats?" Mel asked. Her voice was faint. "Oh my god, what case is this?"

"I'm not telling you that," Manny said. "In fact, I'm not telling you anything more about it. You have to stay away from him, Mel. They will hurt you to get to him."

"I don't care," Mel said. "That's not for him to decide."

"Actually, I think it is," Manny said. "Which is why he walked. If it's any consolation, I know it wasn't easy for him."

Mel half rose from her seated position and patted her pockets. She wanted her phone. She had a few choice words for Joe DeLaura, most of which included that if he thought he was shaking her off like a bad case of fleas, he had another think coming.

"Mel, don't do it," Manny said.

"Do what?" she asked.

"Contact Joe," he said. "If you do, you'll be putting

yourself in jeopardy. Mel, you could get him killed trying to protect you."

Mel sat back down. "It's that serious?"

Manny nodded. "If you love him, really love him, you have to let him go, Mel."

Recipes

Salted Caramel Cupcakes

A Buttery Brown Sugar Cupcake Topped
with Decadent Dulce de Leche Icing

½ cup butter, softened
½ cup packed dark brown sugar
½ cup granulated sugar
2 eggs
1 teaspoon vanilla extract
1¾ cups all-purpose flour
1¼ teaspoon baking powder
¼ teaspoon salt
¾ cup milk

Preheat oven to 350°. Line cupcake pan with paper liners. In a large bowl, cream butter and sugars until light and fluffy. Add eggs, one at a time, beating well after each addition. Beat in vanilla. In a medium bowl, sift together flour, baking powder, and salt. Add to creamed mixture alternately with milk, beating well after each addition. Fill paper-lined muffin cups two-thirds full. Bake 18–22 minutes or until a toothpick inserted in center comes out clean. Cool completely. Makes 12 cupcakes.

Dulce de Leche Icing

4 oz package cream cheese
½ cup unsalted butter, room temperature
3 cups powdered sugar
½ teaspoon salt
½ cup dulce de leche*
Sea salt
Turbinado sugar

In a medium-sized mixing bowl, beat cream cheese and butter on high speed for three minutes, until light and fluffy. Mix in powdered sugar and salt until fully combined. Lastly, mix in dulce de leche. Spread or pipe onto cupcakes. Makes three cups of icing. Sprinkle with sea salt and turbinado sugar (optional).

* Dulce de leche is caramelized condensed milk. You can usually find it in your grocery store, in the baking aisle next to the condensed milk.

Pretty in Pinks

A Strawberry Cupcake with a Dollop
of Vanilla Buttercream, Rolled Around
the Edges in Bright Pink Sprinkles

½ cup butter, softened
1 cup sugar
2 eggs
1 teaspoon vanilla extract
1¾ cups flour
1¼ teaspoons baking powder
¼ teaspoon salt
¾ cup milk
1 cup fresh strawberries, chopped

Preheat oven to 350°. Line cupcake pan with paper liners. In a large bowl, cream butter and sugar until light and fluffy. Add eggs, one at a time, beating well after each addition. Beat in vanilla. In a separate medium bowl, combine flour, baking powder, and salt. Add to creamed mixture alternately with milk, beating well after each addition. Lastly, fold in the chopped strawberries. Fill paper-lined muffin cups two-thirds full. Bake 18–22 minutes or until a toothpick inserted in center comes out clean. Cool completely. Makes 12 cupcakes.

Vanilla Buttercream Icing

1 stick (½ cup) salted butter, softened
1 stick (½ cup) unsalted butter, softened

1 teaspoon clear vanilla extract
4 cups confectioner's sugar
2 tablespoons milk
Pink sprinkles

In a large bowl, mix the butters and vanilla until smooth. Gradually add sugar, one cup at a time, beating on medium speed. Scrape sides of bowl often. Add milk and beat at medium speed until light and fluffy. Pipe or spread onto the cupcakes. Pour bright pink sprinkles onto a plate or a bowl and carefully roll the edges of the frosting in the sprinkles before the frosting sets. Makes 3 cups of icing.

Destiny's Winner

A Rich Chocolate Cupcake with Espresso Frosting

1⅓ cups flour
¼ teaspoon baking soda
2 teaspoons baking powder
¾ cup unsweetened cocoa powder
¼ teaspoon salt
3 tablespoons butter, softened
1½ cups sugar
2 eggs
1 teaspoon vanilla extract
1 cup milk

Preheat oven to 350°. Line cupcake pan with paper liners. In a medium bowl, sift together flour, baking soda, baking powder, cocoa, and salt and set aside. In a separate large bowl, use an electric mixer to cream the butter and sugar, adding eggs one at a time. Mix in the vanilla. Add in the flour mixture alternately with the milk until well blended. Fill paper-lined muffin cups two-thirds full. Bake 18–22 minutes or until a toothpick inserted in center comes out clean. Cool completely. Makes 12 cupcakes.

Espresso Buttercream Icing

1 stick (½ cup) salted butter, softened
1 stick (½ cup) unsalted butter, softened
1 teaspoon clear vanilla extract
2 teaspoons espresso powder
4 cups confectioner's sugar
2 tablespoons milk
Chocolate-covered espresso beans
Espresso beans (optional)

In a large bowl, mix the butters, vanilla, and espresso powder until smooth. Gradually add sugar, one cup at a time, beating on medium speed. Scrape sides of bowl often. Add milk and beat at medium speed until light and fluffy. Pipe or spread onto cupcakes. Top with a chocolate-covered espresso bean (optional). Makes 3 cups of icing.

Lupe's Winner

A Macadamia Nut Cupcake
with a Tasty White Chocolate Icing

1½ cups flour
1½ teaspoons baking powder
¼ teaspoon salt
1 cup sugar
½ cup butter, softened
1 teaspoon vanilla extract
2 eggs
½ cup milk
1 cup chopped macadamia nuts

Preheat oven to 350°. Line cupcake pan with paper liners. In a medium bowl, sift together flour, baking powder, and salt. Set aside. In a separate large bowl, use an electric mixer to cream together sugar, butter, and vanilla. Add eggs one at a time. Add in the flour mixture alternately with the milk until well blended. Lastly, fold in the macadamia nuts. Fill paper-lined muffin cups two-thirds full. Bake 18–22 minutes or until a toothpick inserted in center comes out clean. Cool completely. Makes 12 cupcakes.

White Chocolate Cream Cheese Frosting

4 oz cream cheese, softened
¼ cup butter, softened
1 oz white chocolate, melted and slightly cooled

Recipes

1 teaspoon vanilla extract
3 teaspoons milk or cream
3 cups confectioner's sugar
White chocolate curls (optional)

In a large mixing bowl, cream together cream cheese, butter, and melted chocolate. Beat in vanilla and milk, then slowly add confectioner's sugar until the frosting reaches your desired consistency. Pipe or spread onto cupcakes. Makes 3 cups of icing. Decorate with white chocolate curls (optional).

Dear Reader,

Well, the shenanigans certainly continue for our girls, Mel and Angie, in the bakery, don't they? They'll be back with more mayhem and murder in their next Cupcake Bakery Mystery coming soon.

In the meantime, I'd like to invite you to go on vacation with me in . . . wait for it . . . London! A charming hat shop in Notting Hill called Mim's Whims, with its irrepressible owners Scarlett Parker and Vivian Tremont, is the setting for my newest mystery series, appropriately called the Hat Shop Mysteries.

In *Cloche and Dagger*, the first Hat Shop Mystery, Scarlett Parker's life implodes in America and much to her horror her public meltdown goes viral on the Internet. At her cousin Viv's urging, Scarlett catches the first plane across the pond to join her cousin in the hat shop their grandmother bequeathed to them. Scarlett thinks she'll be able to regroup and get her life back under control in merry old England. Yeah, not so much.

In the second book in the Hat Shop Mysteries, *Death of a Mad Hatter*, the cousins take on the task of designing hats for an *Alice in Wonderland* themed charity tea. Little do they know that the cast of characters they are about to meet are as strange and bewildering as those from Lewis Carroll's original tale, but with one big difference: One of them will not survive the party. With the police looking at the milliners' hats for a clue about the murder, it is up to Scarlett and Vivian to find the real killer before the cousins are capped for good.

Turn the page for a preview of *Death of a Mad Hatter*, available May 2014 from Berkley Prime Crime. You can preorder it now from all major retailers at jennmckinlay.com.

Happy reading!
Jenn

"Take it off, Scarlett. You look like a corpse."

My cousin Vivian Tremont stared at me in horror as if I had in fact just risen from the grave.

"Don't hold back," I said. "Tell me how you really feel."

"Sorry, love, but pale redheads like you should avoid any color that has gray tones in it," Viv said. Then, because calling me a corpse wasn't clear enough, she shuddered.

I crossed the floor of our hat shop to the nearest free-standing mirror. Our grandmother, Mim, had passed away five years ago and left her shop, Mim's Whims in London, to the two of us. Viv was the creative genius behind the hats, having grown up in Notting Hill just down the street from the shop, while I was the people person—you know, the one who kept the clients from running away from Viv when she got that scary inspired look in her eye.

Being raised in the States, I had chosen to go into the

hospitality industry. Things had been going well until I discovered that my rat-bastard boyfriend, whose family happened to own the hotel of which I was assistant manager, was still married. At Viv's urging, I escaped that fiasco and came here to take up my share of the business. So far London had done quite a lot to take my mind off of my troubles. Viv in particular kept me on my toes, making sure I didn't lose my people skills.

In fact, just the other day she'd gotten swept up in an artistic episode and tried to convince the very timid Mrs. Barker that wearing a hat with two enormous cherries the size of beach balls connected by the stems and with a leaf the size of a dinner plate would be brilliant. It was—just not on Mrs. Barker's head.

It had taken me an afternoon of plying Mrs. Barker with tea and biscuits and yanking Viv into the back room and threatening to put her in a headlock to get them to an accord. Finally, Mrs. Barker had agreed to a black trilby with cherries the size of golf balls nestled on the side and Viv had been satisfied to work her magic on a smaller scale.

I ignored my dear cousin's opinion of my complexion and stood in front of the mirror and tipped the lavender sunhat jauntily to one side. It was mid-May and summer was coming. I'd been looking for a hat to shade my fair skin from the sun and being a girly-girl, I do love all things pink and purple.

"Oh, I can just see the headstone now," a chipper voice said from behind me. "Here lies Scarlett Parker, mistakenly buried alive when she wore an unfortunate color of sunhat."

I glared at the reflection of Fiona Felton, Viv's lovely young apprentice, glancing over my shoulder in the mirror.

Viv laughed and said, "I can dig it."

"In spades," Fee quipped back.

"Fine," I said. I snatched the hat off of my head. "Obviously, the hat is a grave mistake."

They stopped laughing.

"Oh, come on, that was a very good quip," I said. They shook their heads in denial.

"You need to bury that one and back away," Viv said. They both chortled.

"I still think you're being a bit harsh," I said. I replaced the pretty hat on its stand and shook out my long auburn hair.

"No, harsh was that hat on your head," Fee said. She smiled at me, her teeth very white against her cocoa colored skin. Her corkscrew bob was streaked with blue—she was always changing the color—and one curl fell over her right eye. She blew it out of her face with a puff of her lower lip.

"But I need a sunhat," I complained.

"Plain straw would look very nice," Viv said. "Perhaps with a nice emerald green ribbon around the crown."

"I'm tired of plain and I'm sick of green."

I knew I sounded a tad whiney, but I didn't care. I was jealous of Fee and Viv. Fee's dark coloring looked good with everything and so did Viv's long blonde curls and big blue eyes, both of which she had inherited directly from Mim. I only got the eyes. So unfair!

The front door opened and I glanced up with my greet-the-customer-smile firmly in place. It fell as soon as I recognized the man who walked into the shop.

"Oh, it's you, Harry," I said with a sigh.

Harrison Wentworth, our business manager, raised an eyebrow at my unenthusiastic greeting.

"Harrison," he corrected me. "Pleasure to see you, too, Ginger."

I felt my face get warm at the childhood nickname. Yes, Harry and I had a history, one in which I did not come out very well.

"Sorry. I didn't mean anything by it," I said. "I was just hoping you were a customer so everyone could stop telling me how gruesome I look in lavender."

"I didn't say you were gruesome," Viv corrected me as she rearranged the hats on one of the display shelves. "I said you looked like a corpse. Good morning, Harrison."

She stood on her tiptoes and kissed his cheek.

"Now that's a proper greeting," Harrison said, giving me a meaningful look.

"Hello, Harrison," Fee said. She also kissed his cheek and smiled at him. He returned the grin. I glanced between them. They seemed awfully happy to see each other.

Harrison was Viv's age, two years older than my modest twenty-seven years, but Fee was only twenty, entirely too young to be considering a man in his advanced years, in my opinion. And no, it had nothing to do with the fact that Harry and I had a history, if you consider me standing him up for an ice cream date when I was ten and he was twelve and breaking his adolescent heart a history. I did mention that I didn't come out very well in it, didn't I?

As Fee stepped back, Harrison looked at me expectantly. Before I could stop myself, I found myself looking at him from beneath my lashes and giving him my very practiced, secretive half smile. Sure enough, the man looked as riveted as if I had just propositioned him.

Ugh! Honestly, I am a dreadful flirt. It's like breathing to me and I don't discriminate. I flirt with everyone, kids, pets, old ladies, men, you name it. Probably that's why the hospitality industry was such a natural fit for me. I am very good at managing people.

I blame my mother. After thirty years of marriage, she still has my dad wrapped around her pinky and it's not just because of her charming British accent, either. My mother is an incorrigible flirt and my dad a complete sucker.

After my last relationship disaster, I made a promise to myself that I would go one whole year without a boyfriend. So far it had been two months. Prior to that, the longest I'd gone was two weeks. Shameful, I know.

I shook my head and forced myself to give Harrison my most bland expression. He looked confused. I really couldn't blame him. I was probably giving him emotional whiplash.

Mercifully, the front door opened again and this time two ladies entered. I charged forward, relieved to escape the awkward moment.

"Good afternoon, how may I help you?" I asked.

"You're not Ginny." The older of the two women frowned at me.

"No, I'm Scarlet and this is my cousin Vi—"

"Ginny!" The older lady shot forward with surprising speed and hugged my cousin close.

Viv looked startled, but she hugged the woman back, obviously not wanting to offend her.

I quickly examined the two ladies. The older one had gray hair and wore a conservative print dress that had Marks & Spencer all over it, while the younger woman, a pretty brunette who looked to be somewhere in her twenties, was much more fashion forward, wearing a tailored Alexander McQueen chemise.

"You haven't aged a day," the older woman exclaimed.

She cupped Vivian's face and examined her closely. "How have you managed that?"

Viv gave an awkward laugh, as if she was quite sure the woman was teasing her, but the woman frowned. "No, really, how have you managed it?"

"Um, my name is Vivian," she said. "I think you might be confusing me with my grandmother Eugenia, everyone called her Ginny."

The older woman stared at her for a moment and then she laughed and said, "Oh, Ginny, always such a joker. Didn't I tell you, Tina?"

"You did at that, Dotty," the other woman said as she stood watching.

"Oh, heavens, where are my manners?" Dotty said. "Ginny, this is my daughter-in-law, Tina Grisby. Tina, this is my friend, the owner of Mim's Whims, Gi—"

"Everyone calls me Viv," Vivian interrupted as she extended her hand to Tina. "This is my cousin Scarlett, our apprentice Fiona, and our man of business Harrison."

"You changed your name?" Dotty asked Viv. "How extraordinary."

Viv stared at her for a second and then clearly decided that it did no good to insist she wasn't Mim.

"Yes, I feel more like a Viv than a Ginny," she said.

"Huh." Dotty patted an errant gray curl by her temple. "Maybe I'll change my name. I always fancied myself a Catriona."

Tina gave her mother-in-law an alarmed look. "Dotty, we really should explain our purpose so that we don't keep these kind ladies from their business."

"Yes, you're right," Dotty said. "But I do love the idea of a new name."

"Are you in need of a hat for a specific occasion?" I asked, thinking to get the conversation on track. "Fee, would you bring us some tea?"

"Right away," she agreed.

"I'll just go and attend the books," Harrison said. "If you'll excuse me, ladies."

I watched as he and Fee shared a laugh as they left the room and wondered what they could be discussing that was so amusing. I suspected it was me in my lavender hat.

"Don't you agree, Scarlett?" Viv asked. She was seated in our cozy sitting area with the Grisbys and all three of them were watching me.

"Um," I stalled and when I glanced at my cousin, she had her lips pressed together as if she were trying not to smile. I sat down quickly.

"The Grisby family is hosting a tea in honor of Dotty's late husband and they are planning to have an *Alice in Wonderland* theme," Viv said.

"Oh, I like that idea," I said. "How can we help?"

"Well, it's to be a fund-raiser so that we can name a wing of the hospital after my late husband," Dotty said. "Each family member will host a table and we'd like them to wear a hat that can be tied to a character from the book."

I glanced at Viv. Being the creative quotient in the business, this was really her call.

"When would you need these by?" she asked.

"We're hoping to have the tea in late June," Tina said. She gave us an apologetic look. "I know it is short notice."

"Ginny doesn't mind, do you, dear?" Dotty asked. She patted Viv's hand as if they were old friends.

I tried to remember Mim mentioning Dotty Grisby, but I couldn't bring the name up in any of my memories. Of

Jenn McKinlay

course, given that I was only here on school holidays, I wouldn't have as broad a frame of reference as Viv would. However, judging by Viv's surprised expression when Dotty had hugged her, I was betting Viv didn't remember her, either.

Fee came out with a tray loaded with tea and biscuits, some cheese, and fruit. The Grisby ladies enjoyed a cup each and nibbled some of the food. It was agreed that Viv would work up some sketches and they would come in to see them next week.

Dotty took Viv's arm as we walked them to the door. The older lady looked so happy to see her dear friend that I was glad Viv had decided to go along with Dotty's faulty memory. I fell into step beside Tina.

"Your cousin is being very kind," Tina said. "Please tell her that I appreciate it."

"I will," I said. "It must be hard to watch Dotty struggle with her memory."

"Honestly, she's been like this since her husband left her thirty years ago. Her reality is different than everyone else's and as my husband explained it to me, it is just better if we go along with her."

"Thirty years ago?" I asked. "I'm sorry, but did I understand that she wants the wing of a hospital named after him?"

"Yes, well," Tina lowered her voice. "They never divorced. He lived in Tuscany with his mistress until he died a month ago. She always told everyone that he was away on business, and I think she managed to convince herself that was the truth. One does wonder though . . ."

"What?" I asked.

"If that's why she is slightly addled," Tina said. "She never got over him leaving her."

A driver was outside waiting for them, and Viv and I waved as they drove away.

Harrison came out from the back room. "The books are done for this week and I'm pleased to announce you're still in business. How did it go with the Mmes. Grisby?"

"They want a tea party a la *Alice in Wonderland*," Viv said. "It'll be tight, but I think I can get it done."

Harrison made a face.

"What? I think it will be great fun," I said.

"You would," he retorted. I was pretty sure this was an insult, but I didn't press it.

"What about you, Viv?" Harrison asked. "How do you feel about it?"

She was quiet for a moment, staring out the window as if contemplating something. When she turned around, she gave us a wicked smile.

"If it's a Mad Hatter that they want, then it's a Mad Hatter that they'll get," she declared.

I exchanged an alarmed glance with Harrison. Between Mrs. Grisby's dottiness and Viv's Cheshire Cat grin, I was beginning to feel as nonplussed as Alice when she fell down the rabbit hole. Oh, dear.

From *New York Times* Bestselling Author
Jenn McKinlay

CLOCHE AND DAGGER

THE FIRST IN THE BRAND-NEW HAT SHOP MYSTERIES

Not only is Scarlett Parker's love life in the loo—as her British cousin Vivian Tremont would say—it's also gone viral with an embarrassing video. So when Viv suggests Scarlett leave Florida to lay low in London, she hops on the next plane across the pond to work at Viv's ladies' hat shop, Mim's Whims, and forget her troubles.

But a few surprises await Scarlett in London. First, she is met at the airport not by Viv, but by her handsome business manager, Harrison Wentworth. Second, Viv seems to be missing. No one is too concerned about it until one of her posh clients is found dead wearing the cloche hat Viv made for her—and nothing else. Is Scarlett's cousin in trouble? Or is she in hiding?

"A delightful new heroine!"
—Deborah Crombie, *New York Times* bestselling author

jennmckinlay.com
facebook.com/TheCrimeSceneBooks
penguin.com

M1340T0613

"[McKinlay] continues to deliver well-crafted
mysteries full of fun and plot twists."
—*Booklist*

FROM *NEW YORK TIMES* BESTSELLING AUTHOR

Jenn McKinlay

Going, Going, Ganache

A Cupcake Bakery Mystery

After a cupcake-flinging fiasco at a photo shoot for a local
magazine, Melanie Cooper and Angie DeLaura agree to make
amends by hosting a weeklong corporate boot camp at Fairy
Tale Cupcakes. The idea is the brainchild of Ian Hannigan, new
owner of *Southwest Style,* a lifestyle magazine that chronicles the
lives of Scottsdale's rich and famous. He's assigned his staff to a
team-building week of making cupcakes for charity.

It's clear that the staff would rather be doing just about
anything other than frosting baked goods. But when the
magazine's features director is found murdered outside the
bakery, Mel and Angie have a new team-building exercise—find
the killer before their business goes AWOL.

INCLUDES SCRUMPTIOUS RECIPES

jennmckinlay.com
facebook.com/jennmckinlay
facebook.com/TheCrimeSceneBooks
penguin.com

M1287T0313